Stealing The Marbles

By

E. J. Knapp

We support Food and Trees for Africa

Our commitment to the Environment is through publishing eBooks and Print on Demand Books: Preserving the Environment One Book at a Time.

ISBN: 978-0-9869731-7-8
First published by Rebel e Publishers 2010
http://www.rebelepublishers.com/
Cover design by
http://www.stenvert.co.za/

For Maria and Gerasimos, may the Marbles come home one day.

Acknowledgments

First and foremost I'd like to thank the Ambatielou family of Athens Greece, especially Maria and Gerasimos, for their kind generosity and love of their country. Had it not been for them, I would never have seen Greece through other than a tourist's eyes and never would I have found the island of Kephalonia, my heart's second home.

I'd also like to thank Alix Davis for showing me the beauty of the South of France where a portion of STM takes place.

Many folks helped along STMs long and rocky road to completion, offering shoulders to cry on, sounding boards to rage at, steady hands when I faltered or fell and invaluable advice. I'm sure I'll forget some names, forgive me if I do.

There's Gail Henigman, my eternal San Francisco buddy, who always believed in me and Rebecca del Rio who helped me through some early plot problems.

Thanks go to Treacle and Pinkerton for sitting patiently as I furiously wrote and for being so attentive as I read them the early drafts, and to Smokey Jo for keeping my lap warm.

To all my friends at Backspace – the best damn writers' forum on this or any other planet – mainly the Jan 06ers (you know who you are) and many of those who came afterward. Special kudos goes to Karen Dionne and Chris Graham who started Backspace. With a thousand-plus writers milling about in the same virtual room, they must have a level of tolerance a god would envy.

Special thanks go to Backspacers Mike Coombes, Mark Bastable, Keith Cronin and A. S. King for always being there, and Marlys Pearson for kicking my ass with her honesty when I most needed it. I doubt STM would have seen the light of day without you all.

A special shout out to all the folks at Rebel e Publishers, especially my editor, Jayne Southern, who raked me over the adverbial coals. It's said a good editor can make an author shine and she has made me a bright star in the firmament. You're the greatest, Jayne.

STM has a glorious cover and I have Jacques Stenvert to thank for that. He really captured the spirit of the story with that art work.

And, to our small but growing band of rebel writers: Cat Connor, Joan De La Haye, Caroline Addenbrooke, William Freedman and Ian Barker. A guy couldn't ask for a better publisher or a better bunch of writers to be connected with. Check 'em out.

Finally, I want to thank James N. Frey for his friendship and early teachings and, especially, Cindy Ford, my mentor and friend all these years.

You must understand what the Parthenon Marbles mean to us. They are our pride. They are our sacrifices. They are a tribute to the democratic philosophy. They are our aspirations and our name. They are the essence of Greekness.

Melina Mercouri

Chapter 1

His eyes narrowed. His dark skin flushed darker. From under his breath came a Greek word having something to do with immorality, someone's mother and a donkey.

"Pasty-faced, uptight bastards," he said aloud. "Sheep! Passive sheep, he called us. The great Athenian general Pericles commissioned the architects Iktinus and Kallicrates and the sculptor Phidias to construct the Parthenon four hundred and forty-seven years before the birth of Christ. Where were the British at this time? I'll tell you. They were scurrying about in loincloths and animal skins, worshiping trees and howling like rabid dogs at the moon, that is where they were!"

I sipped my beer in silence as Gerasimos went off on the rant, as I knew he would. There had been a debate on the mainland, at the Zappeion in Athens earlier in the week, over whether the Marbles should be returned to Greece or remain in the British Museum. From what I'd heard, the debate hadn't gone well, ending in a riot that saw hundreds arrested, including Gerasimos himself, which delayed his return to Kefalonia.

Diplomatic salvos were now being fired across the European continent between England and Greece. All the newspapers were carrying the story, most staying neutral, others falling on one side of the controversy or another. Because the discussion had been televised, news clips of the *melée* were featured on every newscast for three days running.

"That bad, huh?" I said.

"Worse," he said, finishing the dregs of his beer and removing another from the bucket. "The Committee for the Return of the Marbles is in complete disarray. Those in England who seemed in favor of discussing

1

the issue will no longer talk to us. And the damn reporters … I live in fear of any stranger who approaches me."

He uncapped the bottle, lifted it to his mouth and drained half.

"So what happens now?" I asked.

"Now? Nothing happens now. A hundred and fifty years we've sought the return of our antiquities and this fiasco has set us back to square one. Not that I've ever believed the Brits would return what rightfully belongs to Greece in the first place."

I savored my beer, letting the comment hang in the air. We were sitting at an outside table of the small taverna where we often ate, the air redolent with the scent of grilled lamb and oregano. The faint strains of a Haris Alexiu tune drifted from the kitchen.

"Can't you just, you know, go over and take them back?" I asked.

The look on his face was one you would give a child who insisted that space aliens lived beneath its bed. "Take them back?" he asked.

"Yeah. You know, go up there and just tell them to give them back or else."

"You Americans" he said, shaking his head. "Force is the only thing you know. He who has the biggest gun wins, is that it? Well, it doesn't work that way. In case you hadn't noticed, Greece and Britain are on the same team. Even if we had the military strength to challenge Britain, we would not. Issues of this nature are handled diplomatically, not militarily."

"Well, your diplomacy doesn't seem to be getting you anywhere," I said. I tore a chunk of bread from the basket and dipped it into a bowl of *tzatziki*. The yogurt was tart, the garlic strong. Gerasimos uncapped another

2

beer. "Maybe you could just hire somebody to steal them or something," I continued.

"Steal them!" he shouted, nearly dropping the just opened bottle in his lap. Several people at other tables glanced over at us. "Steal them," he said again, leaning toward me, his voice lowered. "Are you taking drugs? Do you have any idea what the Parthenon Marbles comprise?"

I sighed. I'd heard an accounting of the Marbles so often over the last year I knew the inventory by heart. "The British Museum has fifteen metopes, fifty-six panels from the frieze, and seventeen pedimental statues," I recited. "They have one of the columns from the Erechtheion and one of the ladies from the Porch of the Maidens."

"The Caryatid," he whispered, staring past my shoulder into some distant place where the Maidens were once again united. His eyes refocused and he said, "And you think someone could just walk in there and haul all that away? You've been reading too much science fiction. Even if they could get past the security, how would they do it? Beam it aboard the Enterprise?"

"Okay, okay, I admit it would be almost impossible ..."

"Not almost, my friend. Totally!"

"Okay. But what if, just for the sake of argument, mind you ... what if they, you know ... just sort of showed up one day?"

"Showed up?" He took a sip of beer and set the bottle on the table.

"Yeah," I continued. "Like, someone goes to open up the Acropolis one morning and there are a couple of trucks out there and inside, are the Marbles. What do you think would happen? Would you just give them back?"

"The idea is preposterous," he said, waving his hand in the air as though brushing away a mosquito.

"Okay. Preposterous. But go with me here. I'm just curious. What would the government do? Would there be a fight? Or would the Greeks just capitulate and return them to the British?"

"Over my dead body," he roared and once again disturbed the patrons at the other tables.

"So you would fight to keep them?" I asked.

He leaned back in his chair and began to rub his lower lip with his finger.

"They, the Marbles, show up at the Acropolis," he mused.

"Or somewhere in Athens," I said. "Back in Greece, anyway."

He thought a moment longer; the tip of his finger moved to the dimple in his chin. "I suppose," he said at last, "there would be those who would want, or feel threatened enough, to give them back. The diplomatic pressure would be intense."

"Would there be those who would fight to keep them here?" I asked.

He took a deep breath and let it out slowly. "Yes. Yes there would be. I, for one. If the Marbles were to find their way home again … yes … I would fight to keep them here. To hell with the British, the Marbles belong to Greece!"

This was the moment. What would be the point of stealing the Marbles if it was a sure bet they'd be returned in the end? Gerasimos was the key to that question. I had learned early on in our friendship that he had a real hard-on for them. His great-great-grandfather had been conscripted by the Turks who had 'given' the Parthenon Marbles to Lord Elgin at the turn of the nineteenth century. Gerasimos had been weaned on the stories of the sacred shrine's desecration, passed down from one generation to the next. He had a passion for the Marbles that rivaled Melina Mercouri's and though not the Minister himself – as she had been – he did hold an elevated position in the Ministry of Culture. If the Marbles were to suddenly appear outside the Acropolis, the Ministry of Culture would surely be one of the government agencies involved in what to do with them. I was hoping Gerasimos had enough power and influence, that he would be able to persuade the powers that be to keep them in Greece.

I leaned forward, hesitant to voice the all-important question. "Do you have that kind of power, Gerasimos? To keep them here?"

"I don't know," Gerasimos said after a long silence. "There are many who think as I do: that the Marbles belong here. I believe I carry enough influence in the government to pull together a coalition: one at least as strong as any coalition in a position to send them back. It would be a fight, to be sure. The British would not be happy … and they are a powerful neighbor to provoke."

"So, you would fight to keep them," I said.

"Yes. I would do everything in my power to keep the Marbles in Greece. But," he said, reaching for his Spaten, "this is all quite hypothetical. A fascinating mind game, perhaps; surely a gratifying thought. But, nevertheless, impossible."

"Yeah," I said. "You're probably right. Still, it sure would be entertaining to watch."

"You are bored my friend," he said with a wry smile. He tipped his beer back and took a long drink. "I think you need a woman to share your bed."

Chapter 2

A woman to share my bed. Wasn't that, in the end, what this crazy scheme was all about? I opened the last Spaten and watched Gerasimos as he disappeared into a scattering of tourists meandering about Ballianos Square. One obstacle down anyway; an important ally in an important position, however ignorant of his part he may be at the moment. Would he remember this conversation, if I were successful in the end?

Throwing some euros down on the table, I left the square and headed up the Piccolo Gyro toward the Fanari lighthouse where I had parked my car. As the din of Argostoli began to recede, I considered the next obstacle to my plan; money. I had some funds put away but the job that had forced me to go to ground on this island, made the risk of tapping those accounts out of the question. The American authorities had yet to identify who stole the Gilbert Sullivan painting of Washington from the White House. The list of possible suspects was small and I was near the top of that list.

I had other contacts, other sources of funds; though none that might consider fronting the kind of money I had in mind, knowing upfront there would be no merchandise in return. But I did know one person who might have reasons other than greed for backing me. Making a quick call to ensure she was there, I headed for Pessada.

The front gate to Eleni's estate was open when I arrived. I hadn't seen her in about a year and I felt somewhat guilty coming to call with my hat in my hand. She and Dimitri – or Dino as he preferred to be called; 'like the singer' he would say, 'you know the drunken Italian one' – had been good to me. I took a deep breath, passed through the gate and angled up the long, marble pathway to the house.

Iriscs and calla lilies were in full bloom along the walkway. I could smell a mixture of honeysuckle and jasmine wafting on the gentle breeze coming off the Ionian Sea. Bordering the house, gigantic roses were just coming into bloom, bright petals of scarlet, gold and white slowly unfurling in the sun.

The maid was waiting at the door when I arrived. Without a word, she led me down a long hallway, past the living room, the immense dining room and up a short flight of stone stairs, to a part of the house few people ever saw.

Dimitri's office was a massive room: dim, cool and comfortable. Maroon velvet curtains blocked the sun, giving what light leaked about the edges a blood-red tint. The walls, the trim around the velvet cloth of the furniture and the immense desk, which sat before the curtains, were dark walnut. The rich wood gleamed in the soft light.

A floor-to-ceiling bookcase covered one wall, the books worn from many readings, their leather and cloth bindings creased. A huge stone fireplace, big enough to walk into, dominated the opposite wall. I knew that with the lowering of a hidden lever, the fire plate would slide aside and a door to the rear would open, revealing a staircase leading to a secret room below the house. There were paintings in that room that would make the harshest art critic weep.

Above the mantel, enclosed in a hermetically sealed case, hung a Rembrandt, the first painting I had stolen for Dimitri nearly twenty years ago. I was a cocky kid then, eager and proud of myself, about to hand over a painting, whose worth was beyond estimation, to a man I had never met.

The Rembrandt was considered one of his 'lost' works but, like so many pieces of art, it was 'lost' only in the sense that it was sitting in the private, climate-controlled gallery of some rich and influential personage. Though I didn't know it at the time, that is what I would come to specialize in; the rearranged ownership of the 'lost' old masters.

The maid brought me a brandy in a squat crystal glass and departed. I took a sip and looked about the room. The only thing missing was the smell of Dino's cigars and the Dean Martin music he so loved.

And him.

I walked over to the Rembrandt to study it closer. I'm not much of an art expert, know very little about it in fact. I had never understood the depth of Dino's feeling for this painting. Of all his possessions, it was the one he loved most.

"An ancestor of his posed for that painting. Did he ever tell you that?"

I turned. Eleni was standing in the doorway. She would turn seventy-five in a month, though she could pass as a much younger woman. Her hair was the same rich brown it had been when I first met her, like grated nutmeg. She was dressed in black, as was the custom for widows. The only hint of color was the red rose pinned to her blouse.

"No," I said. "He never mentioned that."

"His was a long line of sailors," she said, stepping into the room. "We tried to trace it back soon after we were married. He was just a first mate then." She smiled.

"It was difficult. Records were not well kept on the island and the great quake in '53 destroyed what little there was. But we kept at it and over the years managed to go back several centuries. It was during that time we discovered it was an ancestor of his who posed for that painting. He became obsessed with it, with owning it. Sometimes I think it was the desire for that painting that drove him to accumulate the wealth he did."

She sat down and I followed suit, across the coffee table from her.

"He was a driven man, Daniel. Devoted and kind, mind you; not like some of the rich I have known in my years, but driven nevertheless. But something settled in him the day you delivered that painting. It was as if he had found contentment, reached his goal. He stepped away from the race and began to enjoy the moments of his life."

"You must miss him a great deal," I said.

"Every moment of every day, Daniel. And all the moments of my dreams. But you didn't come here to speak of Dimitri or ... chit-chat, now did you?"

I took a sip of the brandy, trying to gather my thoughts. "No, Kyria, I didn't," I said, acknowledging her as the noble lady she was.

"You're planning a job, aren't you?"

I smiled. She had such an uncanny knack of reading my mind. "Yes," I said. "I am."

She rose and walked to the mantel, picked up a small silver-framed picture, stared at it a moment and then set it down. She turned to face me. "You realize, of course, that while I can protect you on the island and to an extent even on the mainland, beyond the borders of Hellas, my authority diminishes. The Americans want – what is that Red Indian expression? – your hair."

"Scalp," I corrected.

"Scalp, yes. So I have to wonder what is so important that you would risk them capturing you? What is it you plan to steal?"

I took a deep breath and let it out with measured deliberation. I stared up into the eyes of the sailor in the painting and decided that the only way to say it, was to just say it. "I plan to steal the Parthenon Marbles from the British Museum."

She stood there, unmoving, for so long that I thought she hadn't heard me. I was about to say it again when she spoke.

"Yes," she said, a hint of anger in her voice. "And, do you have a buyer for these ... these artifacts?"

"Well, no," I answered. "Actually, I plan to give them back."

"Back?" she asked, surprised. "To those you steal them from?"

"No," I answered. "Back to Greece."

"To Greece," she said, nodding her head as she embraced the idea. "I see."

She moved away from the hearth and over to Dino's desk. She ran her hand across its smooth, dust-free surface, turned and sat in his chair. I had to swivel all the way round in my seat, then stand to see her. I couldn't discern the look on her face.

"You are aware, I assume, that I have some ... interest in the Marbles?"

"I know that you've funded some studies, in addition to a group in Athens that is very vocal in their opinion that the Marbles be returned to Greece," I said. "I know you've contributed beyond generosity and patriotism to the new Acropolis museum and that it was you who agreed to pay for the original version of the plans, the one designed with the return of the Marbles in mind."

"The fools!" she said, spitting out the word. "They quibbled over space, failing to appreciate that building the smaller museum would proclaim to the world that we believed the Marbles would never see Hellas again.

Cowards! As much so as those who failed to lift a hand when the Marbles were stolen by Elgin!"

She was standing now, her jaw tight, fists clenched, the color high in her face. I didn't think it prudent to point out that the Greeks didn't have a lot of say in the matter, being under Turkey's oppressive thumb at the time. Slowly she relaxed and sat again, saying as she did, "Never mind. It's an old argument. An old anger."

Folding her hands in front of her, she stared at me, her gaze intense. "Do you honestly believe you can do this, Daniel?" she asked. "And of greater importance: why? You risk everything with this foolish idea."

It was my turn to move about the room. I walked over to the mantel, stared at the same picture she had gazed at. It was of her and Dino many years ago. He had that familiar, amused smile on his face. She was laughing, holding his hand. I decided to tell her the truth. "I'm dying here, Eleni. Don't get me wrong. I appreciate everything you've done for me, everything you've risked for me. But my work is all I've ever had."

I turned away from the mantel and faced her.

"I miss the planning, the preparation, the fear of it all. I feel trapped here. It's a beautiful prison but a prison all the same. And yes, I do think I can do it. I haven't covered all the angles yet, but yes, if it's doable, I can do it."

She leaned back in the chair, cocked her head to one side and examined me.

"In many ways you remind me of him," she said, her voice soft and far away. "We never had children. I used to watch the two of you together. Always planning, always scheming, always laughing. You were the son he never had. In many ways, his drive for wealth was much like your drive to steal. It wasn't the quest for riches that fueled the two of you: it was the pursuit, the game, the battle of wits and resources that drove you on."

She closed her eyes for a moment and I saw a tear form at the corner of her lids. I knew how she felt. My own father had died, or disappeared, long before I entered the world. To this day I've never been sure which.

I'd been in Paris when word of Dimitri's death arrived and it shook me far more than I ever expected any death would. It wasn't until he was gone that I realized how close we had been, how much I would miss him. If, as Eleni said, I was the son he never had, he was the father I had never known.

"This is not a job you can do alone, Daniel," she continued.

"No. I can't. Nor can I finance it myself. I need help, backing from someone I can trust, someone who won't expect merchandise in exchange for their money. I know you have a vested interest in seeing the Marbles returned to Greece. I'm working on a plan to steal them. It seems like a good quid pro quo."

She nodded her head. "Indeed," she said, glancing at the mantel, at the small picture that rested there. "If I were to be foolish enough to go along with this ludicrous idea, what would you estimate the cost to be?"

"I'm afraid I'm not that far along in my research," I said. "But it could go as high as five million euros."

"Five million euros," she said. "For your crew?"

"Yes. And expenses."

"Do you know who you will use?"

"I have some people in mind. I need to make some inquiries, check some things out, talk to a couple of people."

"Would some of this checking things out, as it were, have to do with matters of the heart?" she asked.

I blushed and turned away. I couldn't keep anything from Eleni. "That's a possibility," I said.

"Good. It's about time you tended to that, Daniel." She fondled the silver chain that hung about her neck, turning the locket over and over. I knew it contained a picture of Dino inside. The long moment dragged out before she spoke again. "What do you think Dimitri would say of your plan?"

I took a deep breath. It took little thought to answer her question. "I think he would tell me I was out of my mind," I said. "And then give me the money and his blessing."

"Yes," she said, inclining her head. "I think he would too."

She rose from the chair, came over to where I stood and kissed me lightly on the cheek.

"You will have your financing, Daniel. I will have Spiros set it up in the usual way. And, you will have my blessing as well."

And with that she walked from the room.

Chapter 3

A storm moved down from Mt. Ainos during the night, waking me to the sound of thunder and a sharp wind that rattled the shutters. Before I was fully awake the rain began, pecking at the tin roof like bird shot. I lay in bed, staring at the dark ceiling, dreading what I needed to do next.

I hadn't been to the United States since my last heist, the one that confined me to exile; I wasn't all that excited about having to return. But I needed floor plans, security layouts, phone and electrical systems diagrams and data on the museum, and there was only one place I knew, and trusted, to get those things. San Francisco.

But first, I had to get into the U. S. and that would not be easy.

There was a time when entering and leaving the States surreptitiously was about as difficult as walking to the store for cigarettes. And, considering the way the Greeks drive, probably less hazardous. Security at the airports and border crossings in America was so lax as to be non-existent. I have carried multi-million dollar paintings, rolled up in a set of architectural drawings, past airport security and customs with not so much as a break in my step. The attack on the twin towers of the World Trade Center changed all that. You can't get a pair of nail clippers past them now. The metal strip in the arch of your shoe is cause for a frisking. On top of that, my face was known to nearly every FBI and Customs agent working.

I spent the morning going through my collection of papers. It's an oddity of my life that I have never owned a passport of my own or, for that matter, a driver's license. I don't have a social security number or even a birth certificate. Indeed, I have no idea what state I was born in, much less what city, and it never occurred to me to ask my mother before she died.

Removing the rubber band from my current crop of passports I noted that the top one, British, had expired. I tossed it aside. The second one, American – the passport I had used the last time I was there – was equally of no value. It followed the British one. The remaining three were Swiss, Irish and a duplicate of the Greek one I kept in my possession. I settled on the Swiss and rewound the others.

I showered, dressed in black 501 jeans and a comfortable chambray shirt the color of moths' wings and made myself a quick breakfast. As I sat in the kitchen eating, the cats began gathering on the windowsill. There were eight or nine all told, though the only consistent one was the little calico that had come with the house. The others kept changing from week to week. Kefalonia is known for its feral cats and word must have gone out that there was an easy mark living on the island.

After watering the plants and filling two bowls of food for the cats, I went into the pantry, pried off one of the wooden slats on the back wall of a floor-to-ceiling cupboard and pulled out the strong-box I keep in there. I have similar strong-boxes stashed all over the island and in several places in the Plaka in Athens. Some with gold, some with jewelry, most with bundles of cash. Just in case. I counted out five thousand euros and slipped them into my money belt. By 10 a.m. I had my Dell laptop stuffed in a bag along with a change of clothes and I was on my way to Argostoli.

I parked my car at the bus station and walked into town. The Premier restaurant is an expensive place to eat but serves some of the finest pastries found outside of France. I ordered a *galaktoboureko* and a cappuccino and watched the square for half an hour. It was early in the game but I have found that a touch of paranoia is helpful right from the start. When I was sure nothing was amiss, I found a cab and took it to the airport. Three hours later I was in Frankfurt.

The man I had come to see was known as the Dutchman, even though he was not Dutch, nor even German. He was Austrian by birth, a reclusive man of indeterminate age who had to be pushing eighty at the very least. You wouldn't know it to look at him. Dieter Shultz was as trim and fit as any man of fifty, with the energy of a twenty-year-old.

In the waning months of World War II, he'd come into a sum of money, mostly in the form of gold and silver and precious stones. As the Russians moved in from the east and the Americans and Brits from the west, many high-ranking Nazi officials were seeking ways to make a clean exit, without having to abandon the loot they'd plundered. Though not a Nazi himself, Dieter found himself in a perfect bargaining position. It was so much easier to sneak out of the country with a suitcase full of gold or diamonds, than it was with rolled-up pieces of canvas. Rembrandts, Monets, Van Goghs, Bruegals: all manner of paintings found their way into Dieter's hands for a tenth of their actual worth.

Afterward, when the Israeli Nazi hunters were swarming over Europe, Dieter began to put together his own small army. Using the knowledge he'd gained from the fleeing Nazis, he tracked them down himself, taking back from them what gold or diamonds they still possessed. The Nazis he turned over to the Israelis, collecting what rewards there may have been for them. Currently, he ran one of the largest, most vicious, crime syndicates in Europe, easily a rival to the Sicilian or Russian mafia. He was a treacherous, cold man – not to be trusted – but I needed him, so here I was, preparing to walk into his lair. The only advantage I held was that, for some reason, the old man liked me. Not that I counted on that to protect me if his affection turned to scorn. Dieter would have his mother killed if she stood in his way.

A light rain was just ending and the sun was breaking through the clouds as I stepped out of the airport. The air smelled fresh with a hint of honeysuckle. Droplets of rain sparkled from every surface. I glanced toward the line of taxis and nodded my head. The first one in line started his engine but before he could move, another cab swept by him and screeched to a halt in front of me. I jumped in and the cab sped off into traffic.

"There's a big tip and double the fare if you drive me to Aschaffenburg," I said. The driver nodded and I gave him an address of a small hotel there. Once I arrived, a phone call would guarantee a ride to Dieter's. I sat back in the seat and tried to relax. I've never liked flying. It always leaves me tense and irritable. After several blocks I noticed the driver glancing, agitated, in his rear view mirror. I turned around and looked out the back window but couldn't discern anything amiss.

"Is there a problem?" I asked.

"Well, sir," he said with a faint British accent, "I believe we're being followed."

I turned around again. "Which car?"

"The black one, sir," he answered. "Three back, inside lane."

"How long?" I asked.

"Several blocks now," he answered. "I noticed him when he ran a red to stay with me."

I spotted the car. A Mercedes sedan with two men in the front seat and what looked to be a third in the back. The sun slanted in from their left, leaving two of the men in shadow. Only the driver was lit up. He was a sallow looking man with bushy eyebrows and a blue beret pulled low on his forehead.

"You're quite sure?" I asked.

"Oh yes, sir. I'm sure."

I considered it. Who would know? I'd told no one on the island I was coming to Germany. Dieter would know by now. I had called ahead, working my way through the phalanx of humans he keeps between himself and the outside world until I had spoken to Helga. Helga was as far as you could go. Dieter never spoke to anyone on the phone. But why would he have any reason to have me followed? No. That wasn't his style. Had he wanted to confront me it would have happened the moment I stepped from the airport.

"Five hundred euros if you lose them," I said.

"Very good, sir," he said. "May I suggest you fasten your seatbelt?"

I took his advice just as the little cab accelerated. The driver cut sharply in front of a heavily-laden lorry and then made a teeth-clenching, tire-screaming right turn that nearly spun the cab around. I caught a glimpse of the Mercedes as it dropped behind the lorry. In an attempt to follow us it cut across two lanes of traffic but couldn't make the third in time to make the same turn.

The driver hit the gas and the cab leapt down the street. Newspaper stands, kiosks and shops became a blur of color as we flew past them. I was thrown hard against the seat belt when the driver stood on the brakes and made a sharp left turn that slammed me against the door, followed by an immediate right that flung me in the opposite direction.

18

We were in a narrow alleyway now, traveling at high speed, trash cans toppling over in our wake. The alley opened up into a large, truck-filled lot. I spotted several exits but the driver didn't seem to be turning toward any of them. I looked out of the back window. There were no cars behind us. When I turned back it looked as though we were heading rapidly toward a brick wall. I was about to question the driver's sanity when he stood on the brake again and made a dazzling one-eighty-degree turn, slipping us behind a large eighteen-wheeler, skidding to a halt and killing the engine.

"My lord, sir," the driver said. "I haven't driven like that since my racing days."

We sat for several minutes, listening to the ticking of the cooling engine. Something nagged at me. A truck pulled out and then another but there was no sign of the Mercedes. After twenty minutes I pulled out five one hundred euro notes and extended them over the front seat. When the driver reached for them, I pulled them back.

"Who are you?" I said.

"Pardon me, sir?" he said.

"You're not a cab driver," I said. "You weren't in the taxi line. You swept in off the street. No German cab driver would do that at the airport. Not if he intends to continue to drive a cab."

"I'm sorry, sir," he said. "But I have no idea what you mean."

I stared at him for a moment. "Fine," I said. I dropped one of the hundred euro notes on the front seat. "That should cover the fare thus far." I slid across the seat and started to open the door.

"Wait," he said.

I turned to him. He had removed his hat and was running his hand through his sand-colored hair. "The Dutchman sent me," he said, his British accent more pronounced now. "He told me to fetch you at the airport. He said we'd be followed."

"By whom?" I asked.

" 'Fraid I'm not high enough up the food chain to be privy to that," he said.

"Who are you?"

"Name's Kellerman."

"So what now, Kellerman?" I asked.

"I suppose we should finish our ride. Unless you still want to get out?"

I paused a moment longer, considered, then slid back into the cab and closed the door. Kellerman started the engine and in moments we were out of the lot and back onto the city streets, moving more or less south. I tried to make sense of it all. Dieter wouldn't send anyone to the airport to collect me in this secretive way unless he had good reason. But what could the reason be?

Interpol? Technically, I wasn't wanted by Interpol despite how much the U. S. wanted me. One advantage of stealing stolen goods is that the authorities are rarely brought in and, though I have hit a few museums across Europe, there was no concrete connection between me and the thefts. I knew Interpol had been alerted about the heist in America but the American authorities were so embarrassed by it, they were keeping it close to the bone. There wasn't even a public warrant for me in America, much less in Europe.

As the cab accelerated onto the freeway, I looked out over Frankfurt. The sun was just about overhead and the wet streets shone bright and sharp. Who was looking for me and why? Who could know I was even here? As we sped southeastward, passing slower vehicles, I wondered what was going on. I didn't like being in the dark. I had a strong urge to turn back and retreat to my island, my sanctuary. But the thief in me was soaking up the fear, reveling in it. I could feel the buzz tingling across my skin; hear the blood singing in my ears. I lay back against the seat and dozed.

When I awoke, we were just leaving the town of Aschaffenburg. The Main River was to my right. The roadside sloped down to the water's edge. The tall grass was scorched at the top, dark nearer the ground, like a fake blonde whose roots were showing. I watched a small, pastel blue pleasure boat make its easy way up the river. A tall, dark haired woman was standing on the bow. As I watched, she removed her bikini top and dropped it on the deck. She stretched her arms out as though beckoning the afternoon sun. She reminded me of someone I didn't wish to be reminded of at that moment. A row of tall bushes cut her from my view.

A mile or two later, the cab began to slow. I knew what Kellerman was looking for. The turn off to Dieter's estate was obscure at best. I said nothing as we passed it by. I hadn't been here in over four years, the last time at night, and I had seen the turnoff. That he didn't meant he hadn't been working for Dieter for very long, leastwise not at the estate. He turned the cab around and just about missed the entrance again. Hitting the brakes, he reversed direction for several yards and then turned onto a heavily overgrown trail.

The surrounding area was deceptively pastoral. To our right was a wooded area, sparse, with oaks and some small, spindly pines. To the left lay a fallow field, with broken clumps of dull-colored earth circled by a broken-down wooden post and barbwire fence. I knew a sparrow couldn't land on that fence without someone inside the estate knowing. The tread of anything heavier than a chipmunk would be picked up by the hundreds of ground sensors.

After a mile of listening to branches scrape along the side of the cab, we broke out into a wide, sun-drenched field. The grass was as manicured as a putting green on a golf course. Two stocky men in green fatigues and armed with Uzis stood off to our left, watching our slow progress. Two more stood off to the right. Kellerman stuck his arm from the window and waved. Neither of the men waved back.

A long, rectangular building appeared, the corrugated metal sides shining dully in the sun. As we approached it, a wide door slid aside. Kellerman drove in, wove his way around a group of men working on a tractor and parked the cab next to a Cadillac limousine.

"Here we are," he said.

I said nothing, just opened the door and stepped out. Kellerman did likewise. The air smelled of dry grass and diesel fuel. There were several vehicles in the building; a white delivery van, another limo, several smaller cars and, over in the far corner, a small Bell helicopter. I spotted seven cameras mounted on the walls and guessed there were more. The entrance to Dieter's inner sanctum was familiar to me and I started to make my way toward it.

"Hey," Kellerman said and leaned over the top of the cab. I stopped and turned.

"Yeah," I said.

"You owe me four hundred euros," he said.

I stood there for a moment and sized him up. He was taller than I had thought, close to my height and several kilos heavier. His hair was damp with sweat. His pencil-thin mustache was the same sandy color as his hair. It was curled at the tips though the curls were

22

beginning to droop with the heat. His eyes were an intense shade of blue, cold and humorless. At the corner of his eyes a spider's web of veins seemed to flicker and pulse. I realized I disliked him, though I couldn't say why.

"You'll have to talk to the Dutchman about that," I said. "You're in his employ, not mine."

I turned and walked across the barn. Two men were polishing a Silver Cloud Rolls-Royce. I could feel Kellerman's eyes on me with every step I took. It wasn't a pleasant feeling.

Chapter 4

I recognized the woman waiting for me at the door to the tunnel that would lead me to Dieter. We'd had a few flirtatious moments the last time I was here, though I'd been in no mood to pursue it then and even less now. I tried to recall her name; it came to me just as I reached her.

"Alix," I said. "It's been a long time."

She blushed and said, "Yes, Herr Samsel. It has been."

She turned and led me down a long bank of stairs. Though I tried not to, I couldn't help but admire the way her flowing blonde hair swept across her bare back, the way her body moved beneath her loose silk dress. Stopping at the bottom of the stairs, she pushed a red button on the wall and turned.

"Gisela will meet you below," she said, as a section of the brushed chrome wall slid aside to expose a small, mirrored elevator car.

"Thank you, Alix," I said and stepped past the door.

The ride was quick, the smell of her perfume lingering in the small, enclosed space. I knew I was descending fifty feet or more below the surface. Dieter's fortress had started out as an underground fuel and munitions bunker during the war. He had enlarged it over the years, extending it both outwards and downwards.

Gisela was waiting when the doors slid open. I didn't recognize her. She was blonde – no surprise there – wearing a red leather, knee-length skirt, calf-high boots of the same dark color and a white leather vest with nothing beneath it but her. Dieter had something of a James Bond/Hugh Hefner delusion and liked having beautiful women around. But make no mistake, these were not cuddle bunnies. Any one of these ladies could kill you in a heartbeat and forget you existed before your body hit the floor. I smiled. She smiled back.

We walked in silence down another long corridor. There were paintings spaced every ten feet or so, bathed in soft light from overhead spots. Copies, all of them – but damn good copies. I knew this because I had turned Dieter onto their creator, a *kvetching* old Israeli I'd met early in my career. Gail Henigman spent half her time with her forehead pressed against the Wailing Wall and the other half turning out forgeries that would fool half the art historians of the world.

One story that still circulates involves the famous theft of a Bruegel from a museum in Rome back in the late seventies. The thieves had replaced the original with one of Gail's forgeries. Unfortunately, their van hit a gate post in their haste to get away and they were caught. No one knows for sure how it happened but the two paintings, *sans* their frames, became mixed up and the authorities couldn't tell the difference.

The elite of the art world were brought in to try and determine which was which. After six months they made their decision. Unbeknownst to them, they chose the forgery as the real Bruegel, whilst the real one was sold for a paltry sum of money to a real estate developer in Sicily.

It was several years before the mistake was discovered and several more after that for the case to wend its way through the Italian courts. In the end, the real Bruegel was returned to the museum but not before they had spent what it would have cost them to buy the thing in the first place.

I asked Gail once why, if she was so good, she painted forgeries but not work of her own. She laughed and told me she wanted to be rich in her own lifetime, not long after her bones had turned to dust.

Gisela and I came to another brushed chrome door. She smiled and placed her palm on a low pedestal that flanked the door. There was a hum, a click and the door swung out into the corridor half an inch. I was impressed. Dieter had changed a few things since the last time I'd been here. He had even taken some of my security advice; the palm print locks, the door opening onto the user rather than into the room. I wondered what other changes he'd made.

Gisela pulled the door open, stepped aside and ushered me in. We hadn't exchanged a word from the moment I arrived. She smiled as I started forward. I smiled back and at last stepped into a room I was familiar with.

Helga was sitting at an expansive chrome and glass desk large enough to use as a ping-pong table. There was nothing on the desk but air. She was murmuring into a slim cell phone. Giving me a hard glance, she turned away. That was to be expected. Helga didn't like me. She suspected that I was behind the disappearance of two Picassos from Dieter's all but impenetrable gallery. I could have confirmed her suspicion had I an insane wish to leave this vale of tears in as much pain as possible, spending my last hours with Helga and her gadgets.

The room was as stark as the desk, with all the charm and ambience of a fast-food restaurant dining area. The walls were painted a pale green; a matching curtain covered the thick glass window that looked into Dieter's gym. The floor had toning green tiles. They gleamed in the harsh, overhead fluorescent lights.

There were no paintings in this room, no art of any kind. The furniture was utilitarian, brutal in design.

Finally, Helga snapped the phone closed and turned in my direction. I smiled. She didn't smile back. She rose from her desk and stepped around it.

Helga is every cliché a good German girl should be, right down to her name, with thick blonde hair and arctic blue eyes. She stood close to two meters and had to tip the scales at eighty-six kilos or more. Every muscle she had was the epitome of taut. The woman was a piece of animated rock.

"Herr Samsel," she said, cutting across the room in five quick strides. "How good to see you again."

"Helga," I said. "Always a pleasure."

She took my hand and squeezed it so tight, I gasped. When she let go, it took me a second to breathe again.

"Your journey from the airport was uneventful, I hope?" she said.

I had the distinct feeling she knew every detail of my journey. I decided to take a risk and contradict her.

"Actually, Helga, it wasn't."

I gave her the cliff notes version but I could tell she didn't hear a word of it.

"Yes, I was afraid something like this might happen," she said when I finished my tale.

"So it was you who sent Kellerman?"

She hesitated, clearly surprised that I knew the driver's name. "Yes. There have been some ... problems of late. I thought it best you were protected on your journey, though of course, I saw no reason to alarm you as these ... problems don't concern you."

"Don't concern me?" I asked. "Dieter then?"

"Yes," she said, jumping on the thought too quickly for my liking. "As you well know, Dieter has many enemies. There has been some ... tension amongst the ranks. Nothing that involves you."

There it was again, the denial that I had any part of it. Why did I think Helga protested too much? I considered pushing it but decided not to. I wouldn't get anything from her that she wasn't willing to give.

"And, Herr Samsel," she continued, "I would ask you not to mention this to Dieter. He has not been well and I have the situation in hand. Come, he is anxious to see you."

She turned and made her way to the other side of the room, trailing a musky scent of sweat and what smelled like turpentine. I followed, more confused and apprehensive than I had been in the cab.

A device similar to the one that guarded this room was mounted on the wall, next to what looked like the door to a large safe. Gleaming chrome, bolt heads the size of silver dollars ringing the outside edge, no discernable handles on the door. Helga placed her palm on the flat glass screen on the wall. A light flashed and the door clicked open. She stood to one side as I stepped into an airlock chamber. The huge door whooshed closed behind me.

The small chamber was white and made of a seamless, glossy material. Four white lockers stood along one wall. There were sprinkler heads on the ceiling. A chrome device in the corner held a large white plastic bag, empty. I opened one of the lockers and took out a white smock, paper slippers, a cap and a surgical mask. I had undergone this procedure a few times before. Dieter had a thing about germs.

When I stepped through the opposite door, looking like I was on my way to major surgery, Dieter was huffing away on a Stairmaster on the opposite side of the room. He certainly didn't look sick.

I noticed that the painting I'd stolen for him, the one that had caused me so much trouble, was hanging in a case on the wall behind him. As I looked about the room, I could see its reflection in the mirrors that made up the walls.

"You know, Daniel," Dieter said, his words coming in short gasps. "I believe I have climbed halfway to the moon on this infernal contraption."

"Only halfway, Dieter?" I paused a short distance away.

He laughed, stopped pumping his legs, wiped his forehead with a towel and stepped off the machine. He was wearing a bright blue bikini brief and nothing else. I was surprised. Usually he wore nothing at all. A concession to age, perhaps? He saw where I was looking and looked there himself.

"Doctor's orders," he said. He didn't elaborate and I didn't ask.

"Interesting spot for the painting," I said as we met in the center of the room. He locked his arms around me in a bear hug of a greeting and kissed the corners of the mask I was wearing. Putting his arm around my shoulder, he led me to a sitting area in the corner. He smelled of sweat and camphor, with just a hint of alcohol.

"It's not valuable enough to hang with the others," he said, seating himself on an uncomfortable-looking hardback chair. I settled as best I could on the one opposite him. It was like sitting on concrete.

"Besides," he continued. "I rather enjoy looking at it; I enjoy imagining the embarrassment of the Americans who had it stolen from under them. That gives it a worth no other painting could have."

He laughed. Dieter didn't like Americans.

"That had to have been some caper," he continued. "I wish I knew how you did it. Even more, I wish I could have seen their faces when they discovered it gone. Ha! I would bet your President Bush was apoplectic."

"He's not my president," I said. "In fact, I don't believe he's the president at all. He didn't win the election. The court gave it to him."

"Yes," Dieter said with a nod. "Which just goes to show you that any public office can be obtained … if you know the right people. But that is politics, no? And you didn't come all this way to discuss politics."

He waved his hand in the air as if to dismiss the whole process. "What brings you from the safety of your island to see me?"

I considered whether or not to mention the trip from the airport, but I needed Dieter and every move Dieter made went through Helga first. Piss her off and I could screw up the whole thing. And, if Helga was being truthful and what happened had nothing to do with me, what did it matter? Dieter's problems were his own, let him handle them in his own way. I decided to cut to the heart of the matter.

"I have something in the wind," I shrugged. "Testing the waters. Nothing definite. But I do need a favor for which I'll gladly pay."

"No need, my boy," he said. "For the joy the Washington has brought me, I will give you whatever I can."

"I need to get to the States," I said.

There was the merest suggestion of him stiffening in response and a fleeting spark in his eyes. Then it was gone.

"The States?" he said. "This sounds like more than just something in the wind for you to risk that destination."

"It may well be, but I won't know until I get there and check out some things. Can you get me on one of your planes?"

One of the few holes in American airport security was that they rarely scrutinized airline crews, especially those on the many private and exclusive planes flying the rich and notorious from one party to another. Dieter owned such an airline and I hoped he would let me fly as one of the crew. It was a risk but a small one. Especially with the influence Dieter carried.

"Get you on one," he laughed. "Of course I can get you on one. When would you like to leave?"

"I was hoping tonight," I said.

"So soon?" he said, surprised. "I was hoping you could stay for dinner. If this venture of yours means you might return to your former profession, there are some acquisitions we could discuss. After your current job, of course."

"Well," I said. "This job is pretty iffy at the moment; I haven't really given much thought about what I might do afterward. We could, perhaps, talk later. Right now, I'm afraid time is kind of tight."

"I understand, of course," he said. "Any chance I might be interested in ... your goal?"

"It's not a painting, Dieter," I said. "I can tell you that much."

"There is more to life than paintings, eh Daniel?"

"True. But I already have a buyer … if the job even looks good to me," I added. "I won't know until I get where I'm going. If it's a go and things don't work out afterwards, well, we could talk."

"Good enough," he said, then clapped his hands as if to settle the deal. "I will have Helga make the arrangements. In the mean time, why don't you let Alix fix you a bite to eat. You look positively famished."

Chapter 5

There were only two passengers on the flight over, a half-stoned rock star I'd never heard of and a young woman who all but sat on his face the entire flight. Once we deplaned and were past all the check points, I shed the flight attendant uniform I wore and slipped into a pair of 501s and a flannel shirt. I had just under four hours to do what I needed to do and be back at the airport before the plane was scheduled to fly back to Frankfurt. I hailed a cab outside the terminal and as it hurtled its way up Highway 101 and into San Francisco, I felt an ache in my heart I hadn't expected.

I had the driver drop me off at the corner of Kearney and California. I wanted to walk to China Town, up the steep grade of California Street, stretch my legs after the long flight, enjoy some of that ocean breeze in my lungs. The sky was powder blue, dotted with delicate cotton ball puffs. A white wall of fog was moving in along the fog corridor. As I chugged my way up California Street, the clank and hum of the cable-car cable came to me like a distant tune I'd loved once but had forgotten. It brought a smile to my face to hear it again.

As I neared the end of the block I felt the first tendrils of paranoia return. The Interpol thing was nagging at me. Dieter hadn't brought it up which bothered me. Something was up and he knew more than he was saying. The odd thing was, I didn't think it was solely about me. If Interpol wanted me enough, they'd have taken me the moment I stepped off the plane in Frankfurt. What bothered me most was how anyone had known I was traveling at all. I hadn't told anyone.

Except Dieter.

And Helga. By default.

The worker bees were streaming out of their offices now, heading for the restaurants and cafés and dark bars in the financial district. A quick bite, a cappuccino or two, a couple belts of something hard and hot, whatever it took to get through the last half of the day. I watched a group of tourists go by on the cable car, laughing and pointing and poking cameras in each others' faces or up at the towering buildings.

I was seventeen the first time I rode the cable car. I carried a gold and jade buddha wrapped up in a paper Safeway bag. It was my first major score. Then, as now, I was on my way to China Town. Then as now, I wasn't sure what to expect.

My mother had died the year before. We'd been staying in a rundown transit hotel in the thumb of Michigan and I'd known the moment I walked into the hotel lobby that she was no longer with me, that this time I wouldn't find her boarding a Greyhound, or hanging around by the side of the tracks at some freight yard. It was almost as if one moment I could feel her there, floating amidst the dust motes in the dim yellow light, then the feeling was gone. I stuck around long enough to make sure her body was taken care of then headed west.

There were only two activities I enjoyed back then; reading and going to museums. Reading took me out of myself, out of my moment to moment existence. I had no formal schooling. I doubt I attended a year's worth of classes in my first sixteen. But I was a voracious reader, consuming words the way an alcoholic consumes booze. My mother claimed I was born with a book in my hand because of all the Sesame Street she had watched in preparation for my birth. Whatever the real reason, I found out early on that nothing was too insignificant to read; cereal boxes, soup cans, the billboards along the highways. When she stole the food we ate and the clothes we wore, she always stole a book or a magazine for me to read. Teaching me to read was my mother's paradisiacal gift. Libraries were paradise found.

Museums, on the other hand, centered me, calmed the frenetic flow of teenage hormones that coursed through my veins. The quiet, contemplative atmosphere, the leisurely stroll from painting to painting, statue to statue, the thought of how much money just one of those items would bring if I could only get it out of there. It became a game of sorts, casing whatever museum I found myself in, figuring out the security, memorizing the entrances and exits and, ultimately, selecting the item I would steal and how I would go about stealing it.

The only reason I hadn't stolen anything major up to that point was because I had no idea what I would do with the piece once I had it. Oh, I was sure I could get it. For me, that was never in doubt but I had no connections, no entrance, no union card for the Brotherhood of Thieves.

Then I met Octavio Wu.

I first observed him in a heated discussion with a younger woman in a small museum in San Francisco. A shotgun scattering of hushed Cantonese and English was passing between them to the accompaniment of violent hand gestures. His distress was obvious and she was trying to calm him down. From what I could make out, he was saying that a certain jade and gold buddha on display was, in fact, a family heirloom stolen from them in the communist takeover of China during the late forties. He wanted it back. The museum refused.

I decided then and there to steal the buddha. I had already cased the place, as was my habit. The museum was South of Market, in a shabby part of the City more at home with the night-train-and-McDonald's-hamburger set than the champagne-and-caviar crowd. The security system was a joke, even for a seventeen-year-old. The locks were simple deadbolts. The alarm system consisted of magnetic strips attached to the frames of windows and doors. A simple strip of metal, slipped between the magnet and the contact, would override that. On the roof was a skylight with a cheap Yale lock securing it. The lock even had the key code etched on its brass bottom. I had the buddha in three days.

Wu had stared at me as if I had appeared in a puff of smoke, the buddha in my outstretched hand. I had placed it on his counter, ready to bolt. After a very long and tense moment, he smiled and whisked the statuette from sight. As I had hoped, there was more to Wu than his dusty old shop full of things nobody wanted. He became my union card and we have been friends ever since.

Chapter 6

California Street has one of the steepest grades in the City and by the time I reached Grant Street I had to stop outside St. Paul's church to catch my breath. One whole side of the old brick building was embraced by scaffolding. A sheer black dust curtain hung from roof to sidewalk, undulating in the balmy breeze.

A homeless guy, wearing a worn and fading fatigue jacket with a 3rd Cav patch on the shoulder, stretched out a gloved hand. The gloves were tattered, stained leather, his blackened fingers poking through the ends. It was hard to say where the gloves ended and his fingers began. He was sitting on two battered skateboards bound together with silver duct tape. The stumps of his legs peeked out beneath the worn and dirt encrusted tails of his jacket. Johnny hadn't exactly come marching home. I gave him a five and turned up Grant Street.

China Town hadn't changed much since my last, ill-fated visit. Some shops had closed, some new ones had taken their place. I found the herb store I was looking for and ducked down the narrow alleyway beside it. China Town is laced with dark, dank alleyways, smelling of smoke and fish and rotting vegetables, the passages twisting and turning like a maze. Often they lead only to another street but on occasion, they will open onto sun-soaked, secret squares ringed by small shops that cater to the locals. Wu's shop was in one such square.

Just as I was beginning to think that time had erased my memory map to his location, I stepped from the cool, fetid darkness into the full warmth of the sun. A large, ornamental maple dominated the center of the square, its leaves a violent shade of red. Circling it was a deep pool filled with bright, colored koi. Wooden benches, their oak slats freshly varnished, wrought iron frames gleaming black, surrounded the pool. Across from them, beyond a wide expanse of inlaid brick, a thick ring of jasmine grew. The sweet smell permeated the air, the heady odor a relief after the dankness of the alleyway.

I scanned the courtyard. There was no one about. I could hear a radio playing and someone singing off-key. Birds fluttered in and out of the trees. Traffic was a distant hiss. Though the trim and clapboard side of Wu's shop were newly painted, the windowpanes in the door were all but opaque with dust. Not so the display window, though, which struck me as odd and caused me to step back into the darkness of the alleyway.

The last time I had been here the window had been as opaque with grime as the door, the display area containing little more than useless junk and cobwebs. Now the window was gleaming in the sun, a series of mirrors stretched across the length of the display area, each section tilting in a slightly different direction. I noticed that one section was catching the sun's rays and reflecting them back like a spotlight into the trees that fronted the building. As I followed the ray of light, I understood why. Wu was a devious man.

Stepping back into the sun, I hurried across the courtyard and slipped through the door of Wu's shop, setting off a tinkle of tiny bells. Inside, the shop hadn't changed at all. It was still gloomy and dust covered. Row after row of rusty steel shelves containing items so coated with grime, they were unrecognizable. But junk was not what had made Wu rich. He was a middle man for far more precious items and, crucially, the source of any information you needed on just about every secure building in the world. It was a hobby with him, collecting architectural drawings, security layouts and wiring diagrams. A very lucrative hobby.

"Either you are more insane than even I believed, or you have one hell of a job in mind."

I turned as Wu emerged from between heavy emerald green drapes that separated the front of the store from the back. We embraced. Wu is a thin man, all sinew, muscle and bone. He was wearing tan chinos and a tan chambray shirt buttoned to the collar. His thick, grayish-white hair was neat and trimmed and he had that talcum powder and lilac water smell that comes from old- time barber shops.

"Nice arrangement in the window," I said.

"Yes," he said, moving toward the counter. "I find it a constant source of amusement."

"How long have they had the camera out there?" I asked.

"Almost six months now," he answered. "They keep moving it around. I keep changing the window display."

"They're not being terribly secretive about it, are they?" I said.

"No," he replied. "It's more an intimidation game than an intelligence gathering one. I get few customers in the shop and they know this. Once, I repositioned the camera and pointed it across the courtyard. They were out the next day to turn it back. They made no attempt to hide their actions. If I complain, it goes away for a couple of days but then there are strange men lurking about the shadows. All in all, I prefer the camera."

"You bugged as well?" I asked.

"Of course. They plant them. I find and destroy them. It's become a game of sorts. One I believe they are tiring of."

"Going-away-tired? Or roust-you-tired?"

"The latter, I fear. My sources tell me they are narrowing their search. Apparently I'm on their short list. In another month the shop will be here but I will not."

"The White House job?"

"Indeed. Since they can't get the thief, they have grown quite persistent in determining who supplied him with the means necessary to bypass their security. There are not that many who supply what I supply."

"I'm sorry, Wu."

"Don't be, my son. Next to the return of the buddha, being involved in that heist was perhaps the greatest joy of my life. Besides, my children have been urging me to retire for years. So now they will get their wish."

"How are they?" I asked.

"Shawn is quite well. He owns a prosperous software firm in Taiwan and has just purchased another in Bali. Melissa, well, she has followed in her father's footsteps, only she uses a computer to do what I did for years behind this counter."

He swept his hand lovingly over the worn wood, a look of dreams in his eye. It passed as soon as it manifested.

"And how is Kastania?" he asked.

At the mention of her name I felt a trapdoor open in my chest. He saw the look on my face and hastened to change the subject.

"Bad topic, I see," he said. "Well then, perhaps we should turn to business. I assume you did not risk the dungeon's darkness to say hello to an old man."

I swallowed hard. "Kaz is fine as far as I know. We had ... a falling out, I suppose you could say. It wasn't very pleasant."

"I had heard something to that effect. You two were quite the pair. There are those who wondered who would kill whom first. Fire and fire often cancel out each other. Or consume completely."

"More the latter than the former, I think."

"I often suspected as much. So, to business then. What are you planning, Daniel?"

"I'm going to steal the Parthenon Marbles," I said, deciding there was no point in beating about the bush.

He nodded his head, not at all surprised.

"I see. So, as I've always suspected, you truly are insane. That is a good thing to have confirmed. What is next, Daniel? The Pyramids? I believe they could be considered impossible to steal by some. Do you have a buyer for these Marbles?"

"Well, no, actually. I plan to give them back to the Greeks."

"Of course," he said, making a 'what else' gesture with his hands. "How could I have thought otherwise. And what do you need from me?"

"Floor plans, security, the works. Anything and everything you have on the British Museum. And, if you have anything at all on the local London police, especially any disaster response or preparedness plans, airway codes, frequencies, that sort of thing, they would be helpful as well."

"Hmmm. The museum will be easy enough. And, I may have some small amount of information on the local police. All in all, your timing is perfect. Another week and this shop will be deserted. Melissa had all my paper files converted to something a computer understands. We plan to store all the data on tape and dismantle the computers soon. Come, let us see what I have."

I followed him behind the counter, past stacks of clutter, into the dusky back room. Wu removed a small black box from his pocket, much like the switch used to arm and disarm car alarms only this had a keypad on it.

"Let me see," he mumbled, holding the box at an angle to the dim overhead light. "What is this week's code?" He stared off into the distance for a moment then quickly punched in a series of numbers. There was a sharp click and a section of the back wall swung forward an inch.

"I have to keep those numbers straight," he said, tugging on the edge of the door and swinging it aside. "Get them wrong and the data on the computers self-destructs."

We stepped into a white-walled room with rubber mats on the floor. There was a strong smell of ozone. Old fashioned analog clocks lined the wall, giving the time in every time zone of the world. Several large Dell computers were giving off a plangent humming in a rack in one corner of the room. Opposite them a nineteen-inch flat-screen Dell monitor sat on an oak workstation. Wu sat down in a comfortable-looking chair and began running his fingers over a keyboard. The whole setup looked like something you'd find on the Starship Enterprise.

"Hmmm." He peered at the screen. "British Museum."

The screen filled with information. I could hear him sub-vocalize as he read.

"Not much has changed in terms of architecture. Some new security cameras. They've instituted a new key card system." He read some more. "The Marbles are situated primarily in room 18, ground floor. Good." His thin fingers played over the keyboard like a concert pianist. Leaning to one side, he opened a drawer, pulled out a blank CD and inserted it in the drive. He punched a few keys and I heard the drive whine up to speed.

"OK. Wiring and phones are pretty much the same though they have all new data lines for their network." He punched more keys. I watched the green light blink on the CD drive.

"Ahh … what's this?" He began reading again, his lips moving as his eyes traversed the words on the screen. "Their security system has gone through some changes in the last year." He punched a key and the CD drive began to hum again. "These drawings I'm giving you are perhaps four months old." More keys.

"Their cameras and key card system are tied into an outside security firm. Any alarm going off in the museum will trigger an alarm at the security company. The video signal from the cameras in the museum is processed on an internal computer, compressed and sent to the security firm every thirty minutes. Except for that burst, the inside computer is not tied into their network and not connected to the outside when idle. If the transmission does not occur, an alarm sounds at both the main control center in the museum and at the security firm."

That was a new wrinkle, one I hadn't anticipated. "Do you think someone at the security firm is actually watching the video 24/7?" I asked.

"I doubt it. It's probably more a cover-their-ass maneuver than anything else. However, it's going to be impossible to remove anything from the museum without it being picked up on a camera. That image is sent to the security firm every thirty minutes. Even if you take complete control of the museum you can't shut the cameras down without sounding an alarm. Whatever happens, they must continue to record."

"Well, what if I found a way to send, oh, I don't know, a Road Runner cartoon or something?"

"You probably could but you run the risk that there is someone at the security company actually looking at the video they receive. No. You will have to control that computer and what it sends to the firm. I see no way around that."

I bit my lip and began to pace the room. When I turned back to Wu, he was staring at me, a sly smile on his face."

"You know she can do it," he said. "I have a feeling you two will have to kiss and make up."

I laughed. "I'm not sure how well that's going to fly," I said.

He shrugged his shoulders. "Love," he said.

"Sucks," I answered.

"Perhaps," he said. "But what would life be without it?"

"Fewer emotional upheavals?" I said.

"And infinitely more forlorn." He turned back to his computer and I watched as his fingers picked up their dance over the keyboard. I felt strangely exhilarated. I had hoped from the beginning that I would need Kaz involved in this and here it was.

I watched Wu finish up his work. It fascinated me the way some people take to computers. I find the beige box useful but, more often than not, baffling.

The large Dell screen flashed several times, resolved, dissolved and resolved again. There wasn't much there that I could understand. The green light on the CD flashed again, the computer made a chiming noise and another set of diagrams resolved on the screen.

"This is the main headquarters for the local police in London," he said. "I've already downloaded the phone and security information to the disk as well as codes and frequencies used. This is the last of what you'll need."

Again the green light flashed. When the drive stopped turning, Wu removed the disk, put it in a slim purple CD case and handed it to me.

"The usual fee?" I asked.

"Well, since this will be my last official job and considering the good cause, let's call it half. Do you have the numbers?"

I produced the sheet of paper containing the account codes for the money Eleni had provided.

"You ready?" I asked.

"It'll be a moment," he said, his fingers flying over the keyboard. "What once was a simple task is now a navigational nightmare. I must first set my digital watchers off on a false trail. Okay, I'm ready to proceed."

I read the numbers off and he typed them in. Less than a minute later I was a hundred thousand euros poorer.

Chapter 7

Back in the front of the store, Wu pulled a bottle of Maker's Mark from a dusty shelf, wiped two crystal glasses with a terry cloth towel and poured us each a glass.

"To a new life," he toasted, then threw his head back and downed the shot.

"To the resumption of an old one," I countered and followed suit.

"Where are you planning to retire?" I asked him.

"Fiji," he said, refilling the glasses. "Construction is nearly finished on my new house. Walking distance to the beach, a small dock, a sixteen-foot sail boat and a barbeque large enough to roast a camel. The island has excellent Internet service. The weather suits these tired bones. What more could a man ask?"

"Will you miss it?" I asked. "Being at the forefront, I mean?"

"Probably," he answered, now sipping from the glass. "But it may take a while. This is a new millennium, Daniel, a new world, the world of computers. Melissa can do in moments what it took me hours to do in the old days. My old files took up the entire basement of this shop and then some. Now, all of it resides in a space not much larger than a pack of cigarettes. What with high speed scanners, digital cameras, the Internet connecting every point imaginable, we could have conducted this entire business with a single phone call with no need ever to meet."

"True," I said. "But I prefer the human touch."

"As I do. Which is why it is time for me to retire … make room for the young and up and coming."

I turned and stared out into the courtyard for a moment. "Sometimes," I said, sighing, "I feel the same way."

"But why, Daniel? You are a legend in your own time, one of the very best of thieves. Why would you consider retiring?"

"I don't know. I feel Old School, or something. I've watched Kaz do in a day what it might take me months to prepare and execute, without her ever leaving the bedroom. She can steal things with a computer I couldn't get near in a lifetime of planning. I watched her work, watched her taking the security barriers down as if they were little more than pieces of string strung between two poles. It got to the point where I began to wonder why I was even there – made me feel like a Captain Dunsel."

Wu nodded his head. "Ah, yes," he said. "I remember that Star Trek episode well. Poor Captain Kirk, made useless and ineffectual by a computer. I have felt that way myself these last years. But remember, Daniel, in the end, the computer failed and a human had to take control. A computer can never lift a painting from a wall or remove a diamond from its velvet-lined box."

"Yeah," I said. "I suppose you're right. Still, working with Kaz, it just felt like the edge was gone; the rush. It all seemed too easy. You know what I mean?"

"I do, indeed. Adrenalin is a powerful force. One however, which can cause as many problems as it solves." He laughed, clapping me on the shoulder. "Come, Daniel. Is it not better to be safe than languishing in a jail cell?"

I laughed as well, though I couldn't say for sure I felt the same levity. "Well, putting it that way does shed a different light on it."

"Of course it does. Now, are you planning to return right away or can you stay for dinner?"

"No," I said, looking at my watch. "I have to get back. I snuck in on one of Dieter's planes. It heads back in a couple of hours."

At the mention of Dieter's name, Wu's eyes grew dark.

"What's the matter?" I asked.

"You haven't heard, then? No, not so surprising. You have been out of the loop for too long."

"Heard what?"

Wu looked past my shoulder and around the shop as if he expected someone to be listening.

"Be very careful where you tread in Dieter's world, Daniel," he whispered. "Rumor has it there is a powerful storm brewing amongst the European crime syndicates and Dieter is at its center. Even within his own organization there is rumor of dissent. Did you hear of the bloodbath in Luxembourg this past winter? Like something out of the twenties' gangland era. Seven men, four of them Dieter's top generals, were gunned down in a busy restaurant. There have been similar executions in Bonn, Paris and Madrid. It would seem that Dieter may have irrevocably enraged too many people with his arrogance and iron hand."

"That explains a lot," I said. I brought Wu up to speed on what had transpired in Germany.

"How very interesting," he said. "And you're correct about Helga. That woman fears nothing, so her hesitation must be considered suspect. Were you able to determine who was following you?"

"No. She just said there were problems," I answered. "My first thought was Interpol but that didn't make any sense."

"Oh, perhaps it might."

"What do you mean?"

"There have been some interesting rumors about them as well. There is a Frenchman named Henri Marceau who, it is said, is building a small empire of his own within the organization. He has been after Dieter for years, with little success. Marceau considers himself something of an art collector, though his collection is minor in comparison with Dieter's. Perhaps he covets what Dieter has; perhaps more than just his art. It's all speculation at this point. Whatever the case, Daniel, I would be very careful if I were you."

"I always am," I replied.

"And beware when you leave the shop. The cameras and the bugs I can control but from time to time there are agents about. They want their thief quite badly."

"So I've heard."

We finished our drinks and Wu walked me to the door. He leaned into the window display, made a minute adjustment to one of the mirrors, then turned and embraced me once again.

"I have long enjoyed our friendship, Daniel. I hope this will not be the end of it."

"I don't see why it should be," I shrugged. "I mean, I've always wanted to go to Fiji so you being there may just be the incentive I need."

"And you will be welcomed as a king," he said.

We embraced once more and I left the shop, Wu's warning heavy on my mind; the CD heavy in my pocket.

Chapter 8

There were several small children sitting about the pool, intent on watching the koi, when I stepped from the shop. They were talking, pointing and laughing at the happenings beneath the water. A B. B. King tune was drifting from one of the flats. Moving briskly across the courtyard, I left by a different alleyway.

Rumors of Interpol. Rumors of Dieter. Empires rising and falling. The thoughts went round and round but found no slot to settle in. I was beginning to wonder if I had any part in this at all – or had I just walked into the middle of a grander scheme? And how would any of it affect my plans? Once I was back in Europe I would no longer need Dieter. If it wasn't me Interpol was after, then I should be able to leave the morass behind and go on about my business.

Sensing the tail put a dent in that hopeful thought.

Pausing at the end of the alleyway where it emptied out onto Waverly, I caught the reflection in a car window of something moving behind me. It was there and gone almost before it registered. I looked up and down the street. It looked to be the normal mix of local and tourist. I stepped out, cut between a dented Camaro and a truck delivering fresh fish and jogged across the street. I saw my tail reflected in a shop window as he appeared in the exit of the alley I had just come from. He wasn't very good at this.

I strolled down Waverly, peering in the shop windows, poking through the merchandise lined along the sidewalk. From time to time I could spot him half a block behind me. He stood out amongst the brightly-clad tourists like a Baptist minister in a Gypsy camp. Hard as I looked, though, I couldn't detect a second tail. Either the second guy was very good or there was no second guy. I didn't consider myself that lucky. If there was one, there was another somewhere.

I came to another narrow lane, one which I knew led to a maze of alleys. I knelt down as if to tie my shoes and, hidden by the sidewalk tables and a group of tourists, I crab-walked into the alley. Rising, I began to run. The noise from the streets diminished. I stopped, huddled against a wall and listened. Soon I could hear the light slap of leather against cement. He was following. I listened hard for a second set of steps but couldn't detect them. I slipped further down the alley, ducked around a corner and into a small alcove. I was growing tired of being the hunted.

I heard him pass where I had turned down. He slowed then stopped. I could hear the hiss of his breath as he considered his next move. He turned and made an about-face into my alley. I pressed myself deeper into the shadows and when he came abreast of me I sprung from the alcove and drove into him, slamming him against the rough brick wall. He managed to bring his elbow back and into my ribs. As I turned away from the blow, I hooked my leg into his and brought it out from under him. He fell to the ground like a sack of wheat. I was on him before he could recover, pressing my knee hard onto his spine just below his neck and pulling his head back by his hair.

"Who are you?" I said, giving his head a tug.

He grunted, squirmed and I eased the pressure just a little.

"Fuck you," he said through gritted teeth.

I bounced his head off the cement and then pulled it back with a jerk, pushing my knee deeper into his back.

"Foul language is a sign of ignorance," I said. "Who are you?"

At that moment, I felt something cold press against the back of my neck. I stiffened.

"Let him go," said a voice from behind me. It was deep, more a growl than a voice. I let him go. He squirmed out from under me as I rose to my feet, slowly raising my hands out to my side. The man I had pinned was beet red and as angry as a half-starved pit bull. He flew at me in a rage.

"No." The growl again. The man stopped as though he had hit an unseen wall, his face inches from mine. I could smell the cavities in his teeth.

"I'm going to fuck you up," he hissed.

I brought my knee up hard into his crotch. Growl slammed me into the wall while his foul-mouthed partner slipped, helpless, to his knees, his mouth agape, looking for all the world like the figure on the bridge in that Edvard Munch painting.

Growl spun me around and then pushed me back against the wall. He was a surprisingly thin man for having such a deep a voice. I had expected something in the lasagna range and here was fettuccine.

"Who are you?" I asked.

He reached into his pocket and pulled out his wallet. Flipping it open, he flashed his badge. "FBI," he said.

Nice try, I thought, glancing at the badge. It was a phoney. Themis had her sword in the wrong hand.

"What do you want with me?" I asked.

"Why were you at the Chinaman's?" he asked.

"He's Peruvian and Taiwanese," I answered.

"I don't give a damn about his pedigree," Growl said, pushing me again.

"You keep pushing me," I said, "and I am going to hurt you."

"You think so?" he smiled.

"I know so," I said. His smile faltered.

"What's this?" he said, reaching into my jacket and retrieving the CD.

"Relaxing sounds of the sea," I said.

"You're a real smartass," he said.

"High school dropout, actually," I said.

"Why were you at Wu's?" he asked again.

"What does that have to do with the painting?" I asked.

The question confused him for a moment. "What painting?" he asked.

Definitely not FBI. Foul Mouth groaned and began to struggle to his feet. Growl made the mistake of looking away from me. I swept his gun arm aside and rammed the heel of my other hand into his chin. His head snapped back so hard I thought it would keep rolling right off his shoulders. As he staggered back, I snatched the CD from his hand and turned to run. Before I could take a step, Foul Mouth was on me.

I doubt he heard the shot that took him down. In a heartbeat he was a weight slipping down my legs as the gunshot echoed through the alley. It sounded like a basketball being hit by a bat. Silencer, I thought. A second shot gouged a hole in the brick wall inches from my head. I dropped to the ground just as a third bullet hit the wall where my chest had been seconds before. I looked up at Growl. He was turning toward the sound of the gunshots. A bullet caught him high in the chest and he kept on turning until he toppled to the ground.

I crawled on hands and knees to the end of the passage as fast as I could scramble. Three more bullets pockmarked the brick wall in my wake. I rolled around the corner and rose to my feet, running before I was fully upright. I zigzagged up the alley, turning whenever opportunity presented itself, paying little attention to where I was. I knew I wouldn't hear the shot that killed me but I was unsure if killing me was in the plan. The shooter had taken out each guy with a single shot yet couldn't hit me with half a dozen? Not likely. The more I thought about it, the more convinced I became the shots were meant to miss me.

A Yellow Cab on Grant Street almost hit me as I dodged between parked cars. The driver leaned out the window to give me the finger, almost plowing into the back of a parked bakery truck. Ducking into the Chinese Emporium, I ran down an isle, scattering tourists in my wake, descended to the second level and ducked out the back door.

I was standing above the park now. Hundreds of children were screaming and laughing, human pendulums on swings and monkey bars. Old men played *mah jongg* on the wooden benches that surrounded the park. I straddled the playground, dashed across Kearney and cut through the park next to the Transamerica building.

Once in the financial district, I slowed my pace to match the crowds on the sidewalk. I angled across Commercial, turned onto Battery and headed in the direction of Market Street, glancing warily around and crossing the street at odd places to see if I was being followed.

Two blocks later I ducked into Sherlock's Haven. It was quiet inside, the smell of cigar smoke sweet and heavy in the air. I bought two boxes of Fuente Gran Reserva for Spiros and two boxes of Macanudo Portofino cigars and five cartons of Nat Sherman's Hint of Mint cigarettes for myself. The Sherman's were all but impossible to find on the island and having them shipped there doubled the cost. Given the risk I'd taken to get to San Francisco I was damned if I was going to leave without some.

Back on Battery, I looked up and down for any sign of a tail. Feeling confident there was none, I resumed walking toward Market Street. There was a Peet's coffee shop just shy of the corner and I stopped in there. The milling crowd hid me as I moved from window to window, sipping a cup of Major Dickason's while studying the people walking by outside. Again, no sign of a tail. I bought five pounds of French Roast and headed out. On Market I hailed a cab.

An hour later I was back in my flight attendant's uniform and passing through the private gate, out on the tarmac to Dieter's plane. Walking up the steel stairs to the door, the wind caught my jacket and hooked it on the railing. I stopped, unhooked it and, as I started to resume my ascent, a man ducked under the wing below me. I froze. Though I could only see the top of his head as he passed, I was sure it was Kellerman, dressed in a mechanic's blue coverall, the insignia of Dieter's airline sewn across the back.

Chapter 9

No one showed up to replace Foul Mouth and Growl until I arrived at the airport on Kefalonia. The new guy was easy enough to spot. His skin was the color of dried concrete, his suit dark blue and rumpled and several sizes too large for his frame. He was either too stupid to blend in well, or too confident to care. The island becomes a prime vacation destination in the spring and summer. Amongst the influx of tourists with their bright summer clothes and salon tans, he stood out like a coffee stain on a white silk shirt.

He didn't follow me as I left the airport but I noticed him muttering to himself as I passed him, speaking *sotto voce* into a microphone. I could just see the curl of white wire trailing from his ear and down the collar of his coat. My first thought was CIA or possibly FBI but I rejected it pretty fast. Sophisticated equipment: decidedly unsophisticated operatives. Interpol, maybe, but they looked more like thugs.

Things had become dicey in the last twenty-four hours. A cacophony of doubt rose in my mind as I crossed the parking lot to my car. At the rate the roaches were scurrying from the woodwork, I would soon need a scorecard to figure out who was who.

I took the long way home, making several stops and abrupt turns. Several times I caught a glimpse of a dark sedan but they never came close enough for me to make out any detail. The weather had turned unseasonably warm and I took my time driving up the long road to my house, glancing every few seconds at the rearview mirror. If they passed by on the main drive, I missed them.

I had shuttered the windows before leaving and the house was stifling inside. I started to throw them open to let in the evening breeze but stopped. The house is isolated, far from the nearest town. There is a steep drop to the Ionian Sea to the rear and thick groves of almond, fig and olive trees on the remaining three sides. No matter how diligent I was, I'd never see anyone approaching. Even this motley crew.

I made a phone call.

"Daniel!" Spiros's voice boomed out of the receiver, sounding as if he was standing a foot away from me instead of several miles.

"Spiros," I said. "It's been awhile."

"Indeed." There was a long pause. "I understand you are working again."

"Perhaps," I said. "More like checking out the possibilities at this point."

"Always good to be certain of the position you have in mind. Saves heartache in the end."

"I've always thought so."

"So, young Daniel, is this call business or pleasure?"

"Business, I'm afraid."

"Business it is, then. What can old Spiros do for you?"

I looked out the front door, down the long drive from my house, trying to formulate what to tell him. Never trust an open phone line was a prime directive.

"I picked up some strays earlier this evening," I said. "I'm worried they might be loose on the grounds and I don't want them messing with my other cats. I thought if Katrina's boys weren't busy, they could check it out, maybe round them up if it should come to that."

"Ah yes," Spiros said. "The cat population is a bad one here on the island. I'm sure the boys would be glad of an evening's work. Should I have them dispose of the creatures if they run across them?"

"No," I said. "I'd like to see them ... decide whether they would fit in with my collection."

"You have far too many cats already, Daniel. You are too easy a mark. But I will tell the lads to go easy on any strange felines they encounter."

"Thanks, Spiros."

"And you must come calling soon. I wish to hear more of this job you pursue."

"I had planned to. Soon."

"Soon it is then," and he hung up.

I knew it would take Katrina's sons a least a half hour to make their way to my part of the island so I headed for the kitchen. Setting water to boil, I scooped some Peet's coffee into the French Press and whipped up some scrambled eggs. When it was all ready, I set it out near the window in the kitchen. The cats started gathering without bidding.

"Whatta ya think, guys?" I said, spooning some of the eggs onto the window sill.

They ignored me and began to growl low in their throats, moving cautiously toward the steaming plate.

"No opinion, huh?" I asked.

Smokey Jo – an all-gray female with the disposition of an Amazon warrior and the sharpest talons I'd ever seen on a cat – speared a hunk of egg on her claws and leapt from the sill. That broke the impasse and in moments the eggs, and all except the little calico, had disappeared. I could hear the cats hissing and snorting somewhere below the window. I spooned the last of the eggs out for her. She sat looking at me for a moment with round, gleaming eyes, then dug in with a vengeance.

"Haven't seen the pasty guy from the airport, have you?" I asked her.

She looked up briefly, finished off the eggs and disappeared.

"I guess that's a no."

I stared out the window, sipping my coffee. I knew I'd see no sign of Katrina's boys when they showed. They might well be out there already. I turned my thoughts to this most recent event.

I knew I wasn't followed in Frankfurt and I knew there was no one on the plane who had shown any interest in me. Which meant they were here. Waiting for me. Which meant they knew my destination … but at what point? And who were the players in this evolving game?

Most important of all, where did I fit into it?

Dieter had to be the focus, but the focus of what? Wu had mentioned dissension in the ranks of Dieter's organization but what could that possibly have to do with me? With my plans?

Wu had also mentioned Interpol. Now there, at least, was a connection, though I had the impression that Interpol's interest in Dieter was not altogether on the level, leastwise where this guy Marceau was concerned. Were the guys who accosted me in San Francisco his? And what about Kellerman? I was sure it was him I saw at the airport and though I hadn't seen the shooter, I was fairly sure that was him as well.

And now there were at least two guys following me on the island, guys who were waiting for me to show up. How could they have known my final destination? Only Dieter knew that.

And Helga.

Would either of them have told Marceau? Certainly not Dieter.

Gordian knots, all of it, and my brain was growing tired trying to untie them. I decided to let it simmer a bit, see how the stew tasted at a later time. Turning to the material Wu had given me, I booted up the laptop and popped the CD into its slot.

As I studied the layout and wiring diagrams, I began again to question my sanity. The logistics on this job were a nightmare. The Marbles were spread throughout one large room and, though most of the pieces were quite small, they were mounted on the walls or cemented atop pedestals. And then there was the column from the Erechtheion and the Caryatid to consider, both of which were in an adjoining room.

I chewed on my lower lip until it was raw. This was a complicated affair. I wasn't looking at some diamond I could put in my pocket or a painting I could roll up and stuff in a cardboard cylinder. This was a lot of heavy rock that had to be dismounted, lifted, packed into a truck in such a way as to minimize damage, then hauled across five sovereign nations. Provided I could get it across the English Channel in the first place. I was going to need an immense crew, something that in my customary isolated way of working, I wasn't used to handling.

But I knew someone who was.

It was well past midnight and faint thunder echoed over Mt Ainos when at last I felt tired enough to sleep. I shut down the laptop, washed the dishes, opened all the shutters on the windows, and headed to my bedroom, sure now that I wouldn't be disturbed.

The little calico was curled up on one of my pillows. I don't let the cats in the house but I'd developed a particular affection for this one. Smaller than the rest, she stood her ground against them all. I did my best to crawl beneath the covers without disturbing her.

The morning sun was pouring through the unshuttered window when next I opened my eyes.

Chapter 10

From the back porch of my house I can see the Ionian Sea stretching westward like a sheet of dark glass, the sound of its waves crashing against the rocks far below, a distant drum pounding a lonely rhythm. I had bought the house from Dino some years before but this last year had been the first time I'd spent any length of time in it.

Stretching my arms high over my head, I bent low and touched my toes, bouncing a little to stretch the muscles in my legs. My skin felt tight, my bones brittle. As I rose to standing position I felt the dual sensation of being overtired and over-amped wash over me in a white haze of dizziness. Other than the occasional walk to the taverna up the street, I had been pretty sedentary this last year. I was long overdue for some exercise. Perhaps a stroll on the beach was in order.

The beach in question was black sand and ancient lava flow at the end of a narrow, winding, rock-strewn path that ran down the cliff at the rear of my property. Tidal pools were scattered about, filled with all manner of sea life; starfish, tiny crabs, the occasional small fish, shelled creatures clamped tight to the lava sides, vivid sea anemones spotting the bottoms of the pools. It was a peaceful place to walk, to think, and I needed both.

Given how tired I was, the treacherous trail seemed a risky proposition. There was a small, secluded road that led there as well and I decided on a little warm-up jog to get the blood flowing. Twenty minutes later, winded and hurting more than I should, or expected to, I came to the end of the road and stepped out onto the beach.

The sea was calm, the waves lightly kissing the ancient lava flow and hissing back through the black sand. Moving gingerly over the slick surface, I walked out to the tide line and began stretching my muscles. It felt good to bend and twist, feel the tension and fatigue leave my body. I loved this little patch of beach, this island off the west coast of Greece and have loved it from the first moment I saw it, standing on the bow of the ferry as it pulled into the dock at Sami so many years ago.

You'd be hard pressed to find a more varied landscape in such a confined space: mountains, hills and deep valleys; steep and wild cliffs which sweep down to windless white beaches. The color of the sea caressing those beaches is a blue-green no painter's palette could ever match. This was the land of Homer and the thick blanket of fir trees that covers the mountain tops are the same trees from which the ships of Odysseus were built.

I had never brought Kaz here and, standing there, the warm water tickling my toes, I felt a profound sense of regret for not having done so. Was the gulf between us too wide now? Shaking my head, I felt again the despair I had come to this beach to dispel. As I turned to head back home, two men, their arms crossed, stood several yards away. I recognized the one from the airport, his suit even more rumpled than the last time I'd seen him. His partner didn't look much better. I wondered where they'd spent the night.

I looked past them, up the overgrown road and could just make out a dark car parked there. From where I stood I couldn't tell if there was a third or even a fourth person waiting at the car. Seemed likely, though.

I looked back at the two men. The big guy looked to be packing firepower beneath his arm. The pasty guy's suit was so bulky, he could have been carrying a howitzer and it wouldn't have shown. In either case they hadn't drawn what weapons they had. Not here to kill me, then. Not yet anyway.

"Private beach," I said. "No swimming. No water sports." I pointed off to my right. "May I suggest Lourdas? A bit of a drive from here … but well worth it. Easy access. Clean sand. Pretty girls. An excellent taverna."

The pasty one turned to the beefy one and said something in French. So, they were Marceau's boys. The beefy one rumbled something back and took a step forward. He stared down at the meter or two of open water that separated them from me and scowled.

"You will come with us," he said.

"To Lourdas?" I said. "No thanks. I have too much to do this afternoon."

I took a step back and to one side. The beefy guy followed my move on his side of the water.

"You will come now," he said.

I glanced to my right. It was fifteen meters to where the cliff trail to the rear of my house started. The two of them would have to run at least twenty meters in the opposite direction just to clear the water and twenty more back to arrive where I now stood. That gave me a forty meter head start.

As if sensing my move, the beefy guy stepped forward. The moment the leather sole of his shoe hit the sea-slick lava, it went out from under him. Arms pinwheeling and bellowing like a bull elephant, he fell backward with a resounding thump, knocking over his companion in the process.

That was the cue I needed. I started to run.

Scrambling up the narrow path, I glanced only once over my shoulder. They were barely five meters up the path and having a hard time of it. The smooth leather soles of their shoes were no more useful in gaining purchase on the sand and rocks than they had been on the beach.

I made it to the top, my lungs bursting. Gasping for breath, I turned and looked back down the trail. The two of them had given up on their pursuit and were fumbling their way back down. The way they were dressed, they should never have tried chasing me on foot in the first place. The car would have been quicker. They might even have arrived there ahead of me. Or caught me later. Not the sharpest pencils in the box, this bunch. It was an island, after all. How far could I go?

I half ran, half limped, to the house, dashing in through the back door and bashing my knee on the jamb in the process. Cursing and hopping about, I grabbed the traveling bag I'd packed earlier that morning and hobbled out the front door. There wouldn't be time to change out of my running clothes. Those two, and possibly more, could be here at any moment.

I hesitated at the car, letting my gaze sweep the long entranceway to the house. Tree-lined, shaded and running a good distance from the main road, it was difficult to see if anyone approached. A pale plume of dust might rise into the trees if someone drove fast enough but, with the heavy tree cover and the twists and turns in the road, even that would be easy to miss. And there was always the possibility they might stop and block the road on the blind side of one of the several sharp curves in the road, although this didn't seem likely. These two hadn't struck me as the lay-in-wait type.

There was a smaller, rutted and rock-strewn road that meandered toward the cliffs before turning and eventually merging with the main road not far from the neighborhood taverna. My low-slung Fiat wouldn't like it but it was the safer route to take. I had a late afternoon appointment in Istanbul that had taken me half the night to set up and I wasn't going to let a couple of thugs in rumpled suits keep me from it. But first I would have to tie up my fan club long enough for me to make the plane.

Twenty minutes and a bent running board later, I pulled into the taverna parking lot, swung around the back and parked the Fiat near the rear entrance, out of view from the main road. Inside, Olma sat knitting by the front window and didn't give me so much as a glance. Her husband John just nodded when I asked to use the phone. That I was dressed in dirty shorts and T-shirt didn't give him pause at all.

"Katrina," I said when she answered. "Are Nikos or Kostas around?"

"Those two are wherever the food is," she said.

I heard her put down the phone and call to them. A moment later Kostas was on the line. His English is about as good as my Greek so it took several long and complicated moments to get across what I needed them to do. After a flurry of Greek, I heard Nikos begin to laugh and I knew they understood what I wanted. Kostas told me to lay low for an hour and he hung up.

Using the WC, I changed out of my running clothes. Back in the dining room, I ordered a plate of goat chops, nervously gnawing at them, as I glanced every few seconds at the wall clock. I waited the prescribed hour, got into the Fiat and went looking for my fan club. For this to work, I would need whoever was following me, to follow me. It didn't take long. As I passed my house, a black Mercedes was coming from the opposite direction, moving real slow. The driver pulled a U-turn as we passed and the pursuit was on.

I'd spent nearly a year cooling my heels on this island and in that time I'd probably driven every narrow back road and alley the island has. I lost them several times, once long enough to chat with some tourists in Metaxata and direct them to the house where Lord Byron once lived. When the Mercedes finally appeared down the block, I pulled around a corner, staying just far enough ahead of them so they wouldn't get lost again.

The beefy guy was driving and he looked none too pleased. I could just make out two other figures in the car, so there had been three after all. Time was growing short. The way the beefy guy was clinging to my rear bumper, I was sure he was getting ready to do something drastic. And my plane was due to leave in just over an hour. I had to hope Kostas and Nikos had been able to complete their end of the plan. I sped up and headed for Argostoli.

Once in town, I made my way to the square and over to the Premier restaurant. A young guy with close-cropped black hair, wearing a yellow jacket, raced out and opened my door, valet-parking style. As we exchanged places, he winked, smiled and sped off in a squeal of tires.

The Premier doesn't have valet parking. The first part of the plan was working. He would drive the car several blocks away and park it in an agreed upon spot. Once the fun began, I would make my way to it and head off to the airport unaccompanied. I found a table near the edge of the street with a good view of the square and ordered a cappuccino. The Mercedes and the coffee arrived simultaneously.

They cruised the square once. As they passed, I tipped my head and offered a toast with my cappuccino. The beefy guy slammed on the brakes. That was when I noticed there was a fourth guy in the back seat. He glared at me and then barked something at the beefy guy and the Mercedes lurched forward, threatening two tourists who had to scramble to avoid being run down. As I watched them pull around the square again, I had the strangest feeling I had just had my first look at Marceau.

They turned up the street they'd originally entered on, disappeared for a moment and reappeared down another street. Parking was a bitch around the square during tourist season. The Mercedes pulled over and two guys got out, one of them the pasty guy from the airport. Marceau, if it was Marceau, stayed inside.

If the beefy guy was beefy, the one walking with Pasty was downright elephantine. This was not someone I would want to meet in a dark alley some – or any – night. I prayed that Kostas and Nikos would be ready to roll. I flipped open my cell phone, quickly dialed and got a grunt for an answer. A moment later I heard the first sounds of the entertainment to come.

There was a soccer game going on in the middle of the square, forcing Marceau's thugs to make a wide swing around it. A muffled but growing roar began echoing across the square as they reached the mid-point. Tourists halted in mid-stride. Diners at the cafés began looking around. In moments the street was filled with motorbikes. Huge Harleys with extravagant paint jobs, extended front wheels and high bars, bright red and blue and green Kawasaki racing bikes, battered Mopeds and scooters and knobby-wheeled dirt bikes. There had to be fifty or more.

As the procession of bikes turned onto the road that circled the square, half a dozen of them broke off and headed for the Mercedes, circling it so closely there was no chance of opening the doors. At the same moment, while six or seven more bikes jumped the curb onto the square, the soccer game broke up and the kids rushed to surround Pasty and Elephant Man. That was my cue to hit the road

Dashing up the street, I quickly found my car. I pulled out, tires screaming and headed south toward the marina. No sign of my pursuers. I followed the coast road around the tip of the island, checking my rearview mirror every few seconds just to be sure.

I arrived at the airport as they were making the final boarding call for my flight. Thankfully there was no delay in taking off and soon we were banking over the island heading east toward Athens. The flight was short, just long enough to finish the cold Spaten I'd ordered. Before I knew it, I was boarding another plane, this time bound for Turkey. At least I'd managed to slip out of Marceau's grasp for the time being.

Marceau would catch up with me sooner or later, of that I was sure. Next time, though, it would be on my terms, not his. Maybe then I could make some sense of what was going on, but that was a worry I could slide further down my list of things to do for now. In the meantime I had a long day ahead of me, convincing the first member of my crew that I was not completely out of my head. And, if my suspicions about my potential second member were right, a long night convincing him not to kill me.

Closing the blind on the window, I stuffed a pillow against it and was soon fast asleep.

Chapter 11

Mackenzie Zaganos was a Turkish Indiana Jones who dealt exclusively in artifacts. If you wanted a Sumerian scroll or Egyptian hieroglyphs, and had the money to pay for them, Mac was the guy to see. He'd been dealing in pieces of the Dead Sea Scrolls years before they were officially discovered. His network circled the Mediterranean and extended deep into Europe, China and Russia.

Like the fictional Indiana Jones, Mac, too, taught archaeology. I had met him in a most unusual way, in a museum in Tel Aviv, at the unlikely hour of three in the morning. The museum, of course, was closed and we were not exactly paying customers. I was there for a painting, a small Monet to which a Belgian industrialist had taken a liking. Mac was there for a small Babylonian clay tablet he wanted for his private collection. One of us tripped an alarm. We barely managed to escape before half the Israeli army showed up. The argument has raged for years as to who screwed up. I knew, of course, it was him. Just as he was sure it was me.

I awoke as the plane dropped slowly through a layer of heavy clouds, touching down in Istanbul in mid-afternoon. There were few people on board so disembarking was quick and effortless. Customs gave me a bored glance and passed me through. As I was traveling light with only my carry-on bag, I made it out of the airport in short order.

It was warm outside, the sky overcast. I found a cabby asleep at the wheel of his cab, startling him with a knock on the window. The promise of a fifty euro tip settled him down and convinced him to humor the extravagant American by circling the airport several times. Once I was convinced I wasn't being followed, I had him head into the city.

Istanbul was lively chaos. Cars, trucks, motorcycles and cabs all jostled for space on the wide streets. The bazaars were in full swing, tourists of all races and nationalities mingling amongst the bright, colored stalls. Vendors hawking their wares competed with street musicians. The air was heavy with the redolent scents of spice and incense. The cabby dropped me off at my location and I walked into a busy café. I spotted Mac immediately.

Mac's my height and maybe five kilos heavier. His black hair in ringlet curls, brushed the collar of his vibrant shirt, a shirt that exactly matched his brilliant blue eyes. His skin was the color of dark olive oil and just as smooth. Born of an English mother and Turkish father, he's a handsome man, devilishly charming and I was surprised to see him sitting alone, without the entourage of beautiful women that always seemed to hover around him.

His rugged face broke into a broad smile when he spotted me weaving my way past the crowded tables. He laid a gruesome-smelling cigar in the ashtray on the table and stood. "Many years," he said.

"Indeed," I said, and took the proffered hand.

He snapped his fingers in the air and a waiter magically appeared like a djinn from a tarnished lamp, minus the cloud of smoke.

"Greek coffee," I said.

The waiter scowled, took Mac's order and left.

"Turkish coffee," he said in the waiter's wake.

"Well," I answered, "the Greeks would argue with you over that."

"The Greeks," he laughed, "would argue over anything."

"True," I admitted. We made small talk as we waited for our drinks to arrive. I glanced around the café. It was filled with tourists.

"The war jitters seem to be losing their grip," I said.

"To an extent," he replied. "The Kurdish problem is causing some concern; for the time being things seem to be returning to a semblance of normality. But you didn't come to talk of politics, my old friend. What sort of fiendish plan are you concocting?"

"To the point as always," I said.

"Life is too short," he replied.

"Okay," I said. "Straight out with it then. I'm planning to steal the Parthenon Marbles from the British Museum."

His eyes widened and I thought I saw a glint of interest there.

"And who, if I may ask, might be interested in these artifacts?"

"Well …" I said. "… the Greeks certainly are."

"You're stealing them for the Greeks?"

"Well, that's where it gets a bit complicated," I said.

"Complicated in what way?" he asked, leaning forward, intrigued.

I cleared my throat. I could pull the job off without Mac but it would be a lot easier with him on board.

"I'm not exactly stealing them for the Greeks," I said. "What I mean is, it's more like I'm stealing them period. And, since I don't have a lot of room about the house to show them off, well, I thought the Greeks might be interested in having them."

A smile broke across Mac's face. His eyes glittered. "In other words," he said, "you're bored and this is a self-commissioned job. And, of course, I'm sure the

Greeks would pay a handsome ... reward … for such a return."

"Yeah," I said, letting him think what he wanted to think. "You could say that."

"And you need my help to pull this job off."

"Yeah … I've never really dealt with artifacts, leastwise not on this scale. I have some ideas but the logistics are a nightmare: freeing them from their mountings, packing them for safe transport, that sort of thing. There won't be a lot of time for fancy crating, at least not at the time of the heist. But I don't want to show up in Athens with a load of marble dust, either."

"You're thinking take them somewhere safe first, then attend to securing them for the long trip."

"Something like that," I said.

He stared off into distance, his forehead furrowed, lips pursed in thought. "The Brits have nearly half the sculptures, if memory serves," he said.

"About that," I answered. "Of the original hundred and fifteen frieze panels, ninety-four are left: thirty-six in Athens, one in the Louvre and fifty-six in London. The metopes don't seem to have fared as well. There are only fifty-four left of the original ninety-two. London has fifteen, the rest are still in Athens."

"And there are the pedimental figures to consider."

"Seventeen in all – all in London."

"Those could be troublesome."

"I thought that myself," I said. "They have some architectural bits and pieces I'm not going to bother with. It's the items from the Parthenon itself I'm most interested in. The four slabs of the frieze from the Temple of Athena Nike and the column from the Erechtheion are in another room, as is the Caryatid. I could live without the four frieze slabs and even the column but I'd hate to give up on the Caryatid."

"Ah, yes. The Lady." He plucked the now-dead cigar from the ashtray and relit it. The foul blue smoke swirled about his head. "You know," he continued, "a Roman soldier carved his initials into one of them. Goes to show that graffiti is not a recent phenomena."

"Animals piss on trees to mark their territory. Men carve their names. Byron carved his into one of the pillars at Poseidon's temple on Cape Sunion."

"And wrote something of a nasty poem about Elgin, if memory serves."

" 'Childe Harold's Pilgrimage'," I said. "And yeah, it wasn't what you'd call real flattering."

"It's hard to imagine they've been fighting over those things for nearly two hundred years."

"The Brits are bulldogs," I said. "They get a hold of something, they tend to never let go. It's their opinion that they saved the Marbles from sure destruction."

"Reluctant as I am to compliment the Greeks, they can be as tenacious as the Brits where their Marbles are concerned. I seem to recall they gave supplies to the Turks to keep them from tearing apart the columns of the Acropolis."

"Close," I answered. "It was during the war of independence against the Ottomans. Your ancestors were breaking up the surviving walls of the *cella* to get at the lead shielding around the clamps so they could melt it down into bullets. The Greeks offered to give them bullets if they would refrain from destroying the Parthenon."

"Tenacious, foolish and brave," Mac said. "They had to know those same bullets would soon be flying back their way, drawing their blood, burying their own."

"Amazing what some folks will do to protect what they consider their heritage."

"Indeed."

The waiter arrived with our drinks. He set them on the table along with a plate of Turkish pastries and departed. I took a sip of my coffee. It was bitter and harsh. A couple of these and my stomach would feel like it'd been scoured out with coarse steel wool.

Mac took a bite from a pastry and set it down. "I assume you've acquired floor plans, security layouts and the like?"

"I have," I said. "And a number of other items as well."

"Need I ask from whom?" he asked.

"The usual," I replied.

"How is our friend?"

"He's well but the pressure on him is increasing. He'll soon go to ground."

"Pity. He's an invaluable source of information."

"He's passing the business on to his children so the source will remain, just a different proprietor."

"That is good to know. Services such as that are always in demand."

"Not to mention expensive."

"The cost of doing business, my friend. So, you think you can steal these Marbles?"

"I think it's a possibility," I answered.

"What kind of time period are we talking?" Mac asked. "To remove them, I mean."

I set my cup down. "Eight, maybe ten hours," I said.

"Whew," he said in an exhalation of breath. "That's cutting it damn close. It took Elgin, what? Five years? Six?"

"More like eleven all told," I answered. "Keep in mind, though, that he wasn't just after the Marbles. He had his people digging all over Greece for artifacts. But the Marbles were the prize, the fifth century BC being the height of Greek art, with the Marbles the finest example of that period. And he had, what, in terms of technology? Hand saws, ox carts and sailing ships? And he had to remove them from the building, remember. All that work's been done for us. They're all but sitting around loose now."

"Loose or not, you're still going to need an army of help," he said.

I smiled and shrugged my shoulders. "That's why I'm here talking to you. This army would have to know what they're doing. I don't know those kinds of people. I'm hoping you do."

He nodded, sipped his coffee. "How do you plan transporting them?" he asked, setting the tiny cup in its saucer. "That's a lot of rock."

"I was thinking truck," I answered, "with a ship diversion to draw off the heat while I sneak across the channel. Find a safe spot to lay low long enough to recrate everything and then over the continent and into Greece. That's a rough sketch. I haven't really thought out the whole plan. I'm still gathering intel."

"You have a driver in mind?"

"I'm working on that."

He leaned back in his chair, his fingers steepled. "I understand the Albanian is back in Athens," he said.

"I'd heard that, too," I answered. "Actually, that's my next stop."

"Be wary, my friend. He's none too stable since his escape from that hellhole in Iraq."

"I've never thought of Andreas as being stable to begin with," I answered.

"You're right. But still a talented man. There isn't a machine on this planet he cannot look at once and know how to operate."

"Exactly. But more important is what's inside that shaggy head of his. The man's a smuggler's smuggler, a walking road map of every country he's been in. I'm going to need him or a case full of Michelin and Rough Guides to get me safely from England to Greece."

Mac looked across the café, staring out the window at the traffic in the street. I knew he was thinking things over so I sat back, sipped my coffee and waited until he turned his attention back to me.

"So tell me, old friend. Why would I want to help the Greeks get back what Lord Elgin stole from them?"

"You mean what the Turks allowed Elgin to steal."

"Well, there is that. But I'm not responsible for the actions of my ancestors."

"True enough," I said. Removing a Sherman from the pack in my pocket, I fiddled with it a moment before lighting it. "I can think of half a million reasons why you might want to help them get their artifacts back," I said, grinning through the smoke.

He looked at me for a long moment, his eyes twinkling. A line of sun crossed his face. He didn't even squint. "You can't mean ...."

"Oh, but I can. Plus expenses. The half mil is clear."

He sat back in his chair, reached up and pinched the bridge of his nose. He nodded. He was in.

"I can't help but wonder what your take in this must be," he said after some thought.

"You wouldn't believe me if I told you, Mac." I looked down at my watch, sipped the dregs of my coffee and rose from the chair. "I've got to get going," I said. "My plane leaves in an hour."

He rose, took my hand. "Tell me anyway," he said.

I smiled, shook his hand and stepped away from the table.

"Not a dime," I said. "Not a single dime." And I turned and walked from the café. He was still standing there when I finally hailed a cab and disappeared down the street.

Chapter 12

The flight back to Athens was turbulent and I was beginning to feel a little raw. After landing, I caught a cab into the city, marveling yet again at the stone edifices of a lost time that appeared briefly amongst the hodge-podge of modern architecture.

Because I was back in Greece, I bumped my usual vigilance up a notch and directed the driver on a random journey through busy tourist areas, down the narrow roads and *culs-de-sac* of quieter residential areas and into the seedy slums where Gypsies and refugees pitch their tents. Satisfied I hadn't picked up a tail, I finally directed him to Hadrian's Gate. I paid the fare and watched as he drove off, continuing to inspect the traffic as I did. Foolish, perhaps, and not a little paranoid – but a healthy amount of paranoia is what distinguishes the thief from the prisoner.

Andreas once told me the only place he felt completely safe in Athens was within the confines of what was once known as the Albanian quarter, better known today as the Plaka. Easy enough to see why. Spread out along the northern and eastern slopes of the Acropolis, the Plaka has arisen atop the ancient residential areas of old Athens. Hundreds of thousands of tourists visit its labyrinthine streets and neoclassical architecture every year. Motor vehicles are heavily restricted, with most streets too narrow to accommodate them.

Checking traffic, I made my perilous way across Leoforos Vasilissis Amalias and turned up Lysikratous. Slipping in amongst the tourists, I wandered the narrow, shop-lined streets, taking in the heady, spiced scent of roasting lamb, listening to the babble of voices and straining to detect if anyone took more than a passing interest in me. When I was reasonably sure I was just another face in the crowd, I stopped to consider whether I should find a room for the night, or look for Andreas now.

As I knew, and had shared, most of his favorite watering holes, finding him would prove easy enough but I was tired and travel-worn and certain he'd be drunk and belligerent when I did find him. Then again, were I to wait until morning, I could well spend an entire day trying to find where he'd holed up. When I did find him, he'd be hung-over and belligerent. All things considered, I preferred the belligerent drunk to the belligerent hung-over.

With all its twists and turns, the Plaka is a confusing place. On more than one occasion I found myself approaching a café or bar I had just visited. Twice I thought I was being tailed but with all the milling tourists it was hard to tell. I reasoned that my anonymous friends couldn't know where I was, so who was there to tail me? Still, it always paid to be cautious, so I made my way to the outer fringes of the old city. Coming to the Church of the Metamorphosis, I ducked quickly around the corner and into the entrance.

The door was locked. The area was deserted, the street dim. I concentrated on the sounds around me; the soft wind in the bushes, the chirp of the crickets, the distant sound of traffic. Once I thought I heard the scraping of leather on stone but no one appeared on the street. I moved to a small bench, sat down and lit a Sherman. It tasted raw on my tongue. I'd already had three today and two was my limit.

Throughout its entire length not a soul passed up or down the street. Satisfied, I crushed the cigarette beneath my heel and continued my search.

Back in the heart of the Plaka, I checked out one or two more cafés and several bars with no luck. I continued walking the twisting, narrow streets, past the many souvenir shops and restaurants, all of which looked vaguely alike; the same postcards in the twirling racks, the same T-shirts pinned to the walls, the same antiquities lining the shelves.

I was looking now for a particular place but after my wanderings, I was completely disoriented. Finally I turned onto Herefontos Street and spotted the Adams Hotel. This brought a flood of memories I didn't need at that moment. Two weeks in a second floor room and wandering the Plaka like a tourist with Kaz on my arm.

I walked to the entrance of the building, shaking off the memory as I did. Turning, I spied the corner of the Acropolis and the route to my destination fell into place. In moments I was walking up Adrianou Street, the oldest street still in use in Athens, and turning onto Kydatheneion, a street with which I was intimately familiar. My destination was a short distance away, wedged between a small theater and a shop selling jewelry. One of the places Andreas haunts when he wants to be alone, as well as the place where I buy my ouzo. There is none finer in all the world.

The Brettos distillery and bar was old and weather-beaten; a colorless artifact amongst its colorful neighbors, the oldest distillery in Athens and the second oldest bar in Europe. The display windows, though beautiful in their simple arrangement, look as though they haven't been changed in years. The inside of the store has a marvelous array of multicolored liqueurs lining the back wall, from the worn wooden floor up to the gloom of the nine-meter-high ceiling. Along the right wall are old wine barrels stacked three high, the oak dark and encrusted with age. Long plastic tubes extend from their spouts to spigots spaced along the shelves where they nestle. The left wall contains many of the wines and brandies that the Brettos family has been making for generations.

There is a counter that runs along the left side of the room and along the back wall below the liqueur display. It's a small space with barely room for the three bar stools set against the counter. As my eyes adjusted to the darkness, I spotted Andreas sitting on one of those stools. He had his head down on his folded arms and was singing softly to himself in a thick, hoarse voice, an almost-full bottle of ouzo less than a meter from his hand.

I glanced over at Mr. Brettos who had looked up from his paper when I entered the shop. He shrugged his shoulders with a what-else-is-new look in his eyes.

"How long?" I asked in Greek.

He shrugged. "Two, three days," he answered. I nodded and walked to the back of the shop.

Moving the bottle farther from Andreas's reach, I shook him lightly but he didn't respond, just kept singing into his shirt. Mr. Brettos brought me a glass and I poured a shot from Andreas's bottle. I could see this was going to take some doing. I downed the shot and resigned myself to a night in Athens trying to wake the dead.

I ordered strong Greek coffee from the taverna across from Brettos and told the guy who delivered it that I wanted more every twenty minutes until I told him to stop. His mouth agape at the twenty euro note I gave him as a tip, he went away smiling, telling me in his best English that it would be a pleasure to serve me.

I had a hell of a time forcing the coffee past Andreas's lips but I managed to get most of it down. I had just set aside the fifth one when he suddenly reached across the bar, grabbed the bottle of ouzo and managed to chug a quarter of it before I wrenched it from his hand, the clear thick liquid splashing a line across the counter and onto the floor. He cursed me, tried to take back the bottle and then collapsed on his arms again.

Andreas has always been a drinker. Some of his alcoholic feats are legendary in the trade. But I had never seen him this bad. I had only the sketchiest details of his capture and imprisonment in Iraq. I think I was seeing firsthand the aftermath of the year he'd spent beneath the heel of Saddam Hussein.

I've known Mr. Brettos for years and he has known Andreas even longer than that. When it was time to shut down the shop, he simply said a soft '*Kalinicta*' and rolled down the front shutters, tossing me the key before he left.

"What do you want?" Andreas asked some time later.

The sound of his voice made me jump. I was almost asleep, my head lolling against my chest.

"You sober?" I asked.

"Too close," he said. He raised his head, swayed on the bar stool for a moment and then regained his balance. He reached for the ouzo. I moved it away.

"If you're going to be a prick," he said, "you can leave now."

"Good to see we're still friends," I said, sliding the bottle to within his reach. He grabbed it, hesitated, pushed it away and then grabbed it again.

"I owe you," he said. "I don't like owing anyone anything." He tilted the bottle back and took a long draw from it.

"You don't owe me anything, Andreas," I said, pulling the bottle from his hand and pouring myself a shot.

"Bullshit," he said. "It was you paid the mercs to get me out of that place. I owe you a life. That is not an easy burden for a man to carry."

I sipped the ouzo, staring off into the colorful depths of the back wall. It was true that I had put up the money to have him sprung but it hadn't been my idea alone. Though the news of his capture and imprisonment had come through Spiros, I suspected it was Kaz who had informed him and asked for his help.

Whether Spiros told Kaz of my involvement I didn't know. I could have asked. Just as I could have used the opportunity to talk to her. But this was less than a month after the Washington theft. I was still being bull-headed and, I suppose, a bit ashamed.

"Look, Andreas," I said, dropping the thought and turning back to him. "I'm sorry you feel that way. I wasn't the only one involved in that."

"I know of this," he interrupted. "But it was you, your money, your connections, that made it happen. Kastania only wished for it. She had not the means to free the cuckold from his chains."

"Goddamn it, Andreas," I shouted, surprised at the sudden anger that rose in me. I wasn't the quick-to-anger type and swearing was something I rarely, if ever, did. "I did not cuckold you. Kaz and you were finished long before I came on the scene. The relationship you have with her is more in your mind than in reality."

He stared at me for so long that I thought he had passed out, sitting up with his eyes wide open. At last he shook his head.

"The past is the past," he said. "Allah in his infinite wisdom chooses to shit upon his people from time to time. I can do little more than accept his gift."

"Oh, bullshit, Andreas. You're not even Islamic."

He laughed and reached for the bottle. I let him have it.

"Had you going there, didn't I, Daniel?"

There were too many false notes in his sudden turnabout but I thought it better to let him have his out. There were times when I didn't understand the machismo of the Mediterranean Man.

"So," he said, finishing the last of the ouzo. "You have come bearing gifts. What is it you need from me?"

I leaned over and grabbed another bottle of ouzo from the back wall. This was going to take a while and a bit of lubrication couldn't hurt. The plan had been coming together since my talk with Gerasimos. Now, with my trip to America behind me and my meeting with Mac, I pretty much knew how I planned to pull off the job. Andreas, with his knowledge of all the back roads of Europe would be the next key element. I gave him every detail I could think of. We sat in silence after that. Him nodding, his head inching back to his folded arms; me waiting, anxious for his answer. When it came, he delivered his *coup de grâce*.

"Rocks," he said with a snort. "You ask me to help you steal rocks? You are fucking crazy, do you know that my American friend?"

His head hit his arms and he began to snore. I took one last sip of ouzo and slid from my chair. He was in. It was time I made it back to my island.

Chapter 13

I was weary of all the traveling. I'd been out of the game too long, holed up on my island with nothing to do. There was no sign of my tail when I arrived back at the airport. No men in rumpled suits, no black Mercedes following me home. My head was pounding from all the ouzo, my ears ringing from all the coffee I'd drunk to chase the ouzo away. Dawn was an hour away when I pulled up behind my house.

The cats were waiting for me. They wove in and around my feet as I made my way to the front door. I filled their bowls with food, topped up their water bucket and went inside. I could hear them squabbling as I closed the door.

When I turned, the little calico was sitting on the floor looking up at me, her yellow eyes shining. We stared at each other for a moment then I stepped around her and headed for the kitchen. She followed close behind.

I was hungry but there was little food in the house. I'd been traveling so much I hadn't had a chance to shop. I found a can of tuna, opened it, gave half to the calico and ate the other half myself. I longed for a hot shower but feared I would either fall over or be wide awake.

In the bedroom I closed the shutters and lowered the slats, hoping to keep as much sun out of the room as possible. Then I went around the rest of the house and shuttered the other windows as well. And, for the first time since buying the house, I locked the doors. Shedding my clothes, not bothering to hang them up, I fell onto the bed and was asleep before my head settled into the pillow.

It was well into the afternoon when I woke. The calico was curled up at the foot of the bed. I found some Advil on the dresser and dry swallowed them. My head felt like a bell tower on Easter morning. A shower helped.

The small house was trashed. The garbage can overflowed in the kitchen, towels piled in the corner of the bathroom, dirty clothes strewn about the bedroom. And there was still no food. Where were the damn elves and fairies when you needed them?

I rummaged about in the cupboards and came up with some stale bread and half a bottle of local olive oil. I poured some of the oil in the last of my clean dishes, sprinkled it with oregano and began soaking it up with pieces of bread. That was breakfast, or lunch, or an early dinner, I wasn't sure which.

Stepping outside, I watched the sun take a dive through a mare's tail pattern of pink clouds on its way to the Ionian Sea. I flipped open the cell phone and called a woman I knew who did laundry and housecleaning. She agreed to come the following morning.

I checked the food and water bowls and, deciding they were filled enough to keep the little felines happy, I made my way to the car. I had some shopping to do and some thoughts to go over. A beer and something hot and filling would help that process along.

I stopped at the Lido, filled a basket with eggs, coffee, tuna fish and enough cat food to feed half the feline population of Kefalonia and headed into Argostoli. I parked the car down the street from Katrina's taverna, found a table and ordered a large bowl of mutton stew and a bucket of cold beer.

I spotted the man I surmised was Marceau while walking from the car to the taverna. He was sitting at one of two tables outside a small café across the street, watching me. The mutton stew came and went and the empty bowl returned to the kitchen and still he didn't move. I was just opening my second Heineken when he paid his check, rose, brushed off the dark suit he wore, and walked in my direction.

There was a Renault parked in the shadows at the end of the lane. I noticed a figure inside perk up as Marceau rose from his seat. I turned my head. There at the other end of the lane sat another shadowy figure in a small Fiat, equally alert. Neither seemed familiar. I inched my hand beneath the notebook in which I'd been writing. There was nothing there but an ashtray but I was betting Marceau wouldn't know that.

He stopped at the curb, looked both ways up and down the lane and crossed casually. He was smaller than he had appeared in the back of the Mercedes – just under two meters – on the shy side of sixty kilos. Well dressed in an Italian-cut suit, Gucci loafers and a subdued red tie edged in gold trim, he had a dainty step that made his dark curly hair bounce against his skull.

"You won't need the six-shooter, Mr. Samsel," he said. He pulled out a chair and joined me at my table.

I stared at his eyes. They were a deep shade of amber, with no malice in them. Nor much of anything else. Glancing over at the two cars parked at either end of the lane, I looked back at him.

"Actually," I said. "It's a Beretta. Thirteen shots with one in the pipe."

"Which I'm sure is occupied," he answered.

"Always," I said.

I had just such a gun in a box at the house and though the clip was loaded, there was never a shell left in the chamber. I doubted the gun had been removed from its box more than half a dozen times in the ten years I'd owned it. Hand guns scare the hell out of me, though I'm loath to let anyone know that.

He looked up and down the lane in the directions I had just looked and then turned back to me. "You have nothing to fear from them. They are my ... security. Nothing more."

I eased my hand out from beneath the notebook and took a sip of Heineken.

"So. To what do I attribute the honor of this meeting, Monsieur Marceau?" I said.

His eyebrow arched at my knowing his name and a small smile turned the corner of his lips.

"You are a difficult man to arrange an audience with," he said, eyeing the bucket of Heineken on the table. I slid the bucket in his direction and he removed one from the ice.

"You should try the direct approach more often," I said, as he flipped the cap off a bottle. "I believe it works better than sending goons to deliver your invitation."

"Goons?" he said, taking a sip of the cold beer.

"The guys in the Mercedes," I said. "In Frankfurt. The three you sent when I got back to the island."

"Yes," he said. "You did make them look rather foolish with your little prank."

I cocked my head and smiled. "I don't like being followed," I said. "It makes me nervous. I tend to become a little playful when I'm nervous."

"Playful." He laughed. "Yes. That must have been some spectacle for the tourists: a hundred hoodlums roaring into town, surrounding my men while you made your escape."

"It was effective enough," I said, noticing that he wasn't including himself in the embarrassment. Did he want me to believe he wasn't there, or was it just some ego thing? The dress, the hair, the way he carried himself all screamed of ego.

I finished my beer, reached for another and opened it with a soft pop. I waited for him to bring up the shooting in San Francisco. The silence stretched out. Could he be unaware of it? Was it possible they weren't even his men? They certainly weren't FBI. If I was correct that it was Kellerman who had taken out the other two, then what did that say about where Kellerman's loyalty lay? Or Dieter's? All the questions came rising up again. Just what the hell had I stepped in?

"What do you want, Marceau? What does Interpol want?" I asked after a lengthy pause.

"Interpol?"

"You do work for Interpol," I said, taking a sip. "Or is this visit ... unofficial, as it were?"

"Official, unofficial. Is there a difference?" he said, eyeing me over the top of the bottle.

"I think there is. But why don't you clarify it for me?"

He sat back in his chair, staring a hole through me. He finished his beer in three quick gulps and set the bottle on the table. A nervousness had come over him, a sudden stiffness which gave the lie to his insouciance. Something was up and I had no idea what – but he had no idea that I had none – and he was unsure of just what to say to me.

"I'm curious," he said, seeming to find a degree of composure, "why you decided to leave the ... relative freedom of your island to visit the Dutchman? I mean, half the United States is looking for you. That would seem a dangerous trip to make."

"You mean the half that's over here, or the other half over there?" I said.

He laughed. "You have something of a flagrant disregard for authority, Mr. Samsel," he said.

"Yeah, well. Slum upbringing will do that to you," I answered.

He reached for the last beer in the bucket. I turned and caught Katrina's attention and ordered another round. When she brought it out, I gave her a look that told her I needed more than just a bucket of beer. Smiling, she returned inside, pulling a cell phone from her apron pocket as she disappeared into the gloom.

"What do you want, Marceau?" I asked again.

"Why did you go see the Dutchman?" he said, his demeanor turning serious and dark. Again, no mention of my meeting with Wu.

"It was his birthday. I always like to wish the old man well."

Marceau's face hardened, his lips pursed tight. "Are you working for him?" he growled. "Some nefarious job to fill the gaps in his gallery?"

"Gallery? What gallery? I'm afraid I haven't a clue what you're talking about, Marceau."

"I could arrest you here and now, Samsel," he said, his voice edgy. "Turn you over to the Americans. They would love to get their hands on you for that White House job."

His attitude was beginning to piss me off.

"First, I doubt you have the authority. There's no warrant for me in Europe that I'm aware of. As for the job you mention, from what I've heard – and I know little more about it than that – the Americans haven't yet determined who the thief is. Why they would want me in connection with it is beyond me. What exactly is your game, Marceau? What is it you want?"

"What do you have going with the Dutchman?" he said, his voice curt.

"I told you," I said. "I was just wishing him ..."

"Bull," he said, interrupting. "Why are you teamed up with him? What is he up to?"

I relaxed in my chair, the anger flowing out of me along with the tension I'd been feeling for days. It wasn't about me after all. The whole thing revolved around Dieter – and Marceau's mistaken belief that I was somehow involved. Why my involvement might worry him was bothersome but, it didn't seem like something I needed to worry about. Provided I could convince him I had nothing to do with whatever Dieter might be up to. I needed Marceau off my back if I was to continue pursuing the Marbles in safety, so I decided to tell him the truth. Or at least a portion of it.

"I needed something," I said after a pause. "Dieter was able to supply it. That's all there is between us. I'm not involved with anything Dieter might be involved in. I don't walk that walk. If you've read my jacket, you'll know I tend to work alone."

"You're lying to me, Samsel. I can see it in your face."

My anger returned in a flash of heat. Marceau was flustered now and irrational. His face was flushed and beads of sweat had appeared on his upper lip, making it gleam. So much for dissuasion.

"I really don't care what you think, Marceau," I said. "I've told you all that I'm going to tell you. Dieter and I have nothing going. You can believe it or not. I really don't care."

"And if I brought you in? Would your story change in a few hours, perhaps?"

"First off," I said with deliberation, my anger increasing exponentially. "You don't have the authority."

I reached under the notebook, laying my hand across the cold glass of the ashtray, throwing the little Frenchman a bluff, wondering if he would call it.

"Second, you don't have the balls."

Apoplectic, his face bloomed bright red, his eyes bulged. He raised his hand and snapped his fingers. I could hear car doors slam but I didn't turn my gaze from his face. He stood abruptly, his chair falling backward to the ground.

"I will have my answers," he demanded.

I sat back in the chair, my hand still beneath the notebook.

"I doubt it," I said.

Maddened, he turned first in one direction then the other. Six men had entered the lane, three at either end. The man in the Renault was spread face down across the hood of his car, his arms behind his head. The man in the Fiat was lying sprawled on the ground surrounded by three men armed with baseball bats. Marceau turned as three more men walked lazily from across the street, fanning out behind him.

"So," he said, turning back to me, with malicious calm. "You elude me again."

"It would seem so," I said, taking a sip from my Heineken.

"Why did you go see the Dutchman?" he said.

"You have your answer already, Marceau. You won't get a change in the story now."

I picked up a piece of bread, dipped it in the *dip me spanaki* the waitress had left and popped it in my mouth. The taste was tart and cold.

"I would suggest you leave, Marceau. While you still can. And take your boys with you. The next time I see anyone following me, I won't be so playful."

He glared at me, one of those you-have-sealed-your-doom looks short tyrants seem so fond of. I smiled back. He turned without ceremony and stalked off up the street, disappearing around a corner.

I felt the tension seep out of me. As I removed my hand from beneath the notebook, the three men who had come from across the street nodded and faded into the gloom. At either end of the lane, the men there disappeared as well. I heard the Fiat start up and drive away. The Renault fired up soon after and the man drove by at a menacing pace, a grim smile on his face. He was wearing a blue beret and looked vaguely familiar but was gone before I could remember who he was.

I leaned back in my chair, gazing out over the tops of the buildings across the lane without seeing them. Something about that blue beret. And then I had it. The driver of the Mercedes who had pursued me in Frankfurt. There was something else. I had seen him again later without making the connection. He'd been one of the guards outside Dieter's compound.

I let the front legs of the chair come down with a bang. Did Marceau have people working for Dieter? Was Dieter aware of this? Were the two of them working together on something? That didn't seem likely. If so, what was the point of Marceau's little visit? His threats? And why hadn't he said anything about the men who had accosted me in San Francisco? Something very weird was going on and somehow I had stepped right into the middle of it.

Katrina came out, bringing a small plate of *kritikos dakos* with her.

"Thank you, Katrina," I said.

"My pleasure," she answered, sweeping away the empty bottles and plates. "The boys and their friends have so very little to do. It is good for them to flex their muscles from time to time."

"Yes. And be sure to put the added expense on my tab."

"Oh. There is no charge, Mr. Samsel. What you plan for Greece is payment enough."

I smiled as she walked away. Word spreads fast on a small, isolated island. Spiros knew what I was up to therefore the entire island would know as well. I had no fear it would leak to anyone who could stop me. The islanders are close-mouthed and wary of strangers.

I took a bite of the *kritikos dakos*. The tomato was fresh and juicy, the cheese soft and smooth. This fretting over the Dieter/Marceau mystery was going nowhere and would continue in that direction until more clues revealed themselves. If it did have something to do with me, I'd find out sooner or later. If not, it would just blow over and become a non-issue.

Either way I couldn't let it stop me now. It was time to have a talk with Spiros.

Chapter 14

The following morning was warm and moving with rapidity toward another hot day on the island. The breeze off the Ionian Sea was tinged with the smell of salt and seaweed baking in the sun. I shut down the computer, gathered up my notes and stuffed them all in a backpack, which I shoved in the back of my closet. I heard a car pull in behind the house, heard the car door slam and a moment later there was a knock on the back door. It was the woman I'd hired to clean the house.

Voula was a statuesque woman, late forties I guessed, with dark, reddish hair tied in a tight bun at the back of her head. She had a soft voice for a woman so big and a smile that lit up every inch of her face. The light shining from her eyes was infectious in its nameless joy.

She had an armful of cleaning supplies and two young girls in tow, one carrying a broom, the other a rag mop and a large galvanized bucket. The two children eyed me inquisitively, peeking out from behind their mother's long skirt. I smiled. One of the girls giggled. The other hid her face in her mother's apron. I bid them enter and between my broken Greek and Voula's broken English we managed to come to an understanding of what I needed her to do. I paid her up front and headed out to my car.

I drove inland, checking my rearview mirror from time to time to see if I was being followed. There were few cars on the road and none of the drivers seemed at all interested in me. I cruised southeast, passing through the town of Keramies and then turned toward the southern end of the island. I had the windows down and the air was hot and smelled of sheep and goats and dry grass.

Once past Keramies the land flattened out and dipped a little toward the sea. The temperature became a bit cooler and I could smell just a hint of salt in the air. As I rounded a long curve, I spotted Spiros's spread about a mile ahead. I knew it was likely he would be out there, tending his vines.

Spiros had what was probably the finest Robolla vineyard on the island. It yielded maybe a hundred barrels a year tops and the wine was damn near hallucinogenic. What Spiros himself didn't drink, was offered to favored guests and one or two select tavernas around the island. Robolla didn't travel well and there were damn few places beyond the island where it could be found. Many a visitor to the island came there for the sole purpose of tasting his wine.

I found him where I expected, out in the vineyard, stripped to the waist, wearing sweat-stained chinos and a red kerchief around his neck. A broad-brimmed straw hat covered his balding head. Black hair, laced heavily with gray, fell from the sides grazing his shoulders. His nutmeg skin glistened with sweat as he hoed the chocolate-colored earth around each gnarled vine. The ground was empty of weeds, the vines exploding in a riot of green.

A flash of golden fur streaked close by nearly bowling me over. It stopped in a cloud of dust, turned and looked up at me with enormous brown eyes, a red tongue lolling from its panting mouth. Recognizing me, I swear the dog smiled and the next thing I knew he had planted his big paws on my chest, licking my face, trying with all his might to knock me down to wrestle with me.

"He has always liked you," Spiros said. He pulled a kerchief from his pocket, leaned on his hoe like a cane and wiped his brow.

"I've always rather liked him as well," I answered, rubbing the big dog's head while trying to avoid another sloppy doggy kiss.

Treacle, which Spiros claims means sweet poison, is a Golden Retriever/Irish Setter mix with the color and looks of the former and the sleek, boundless energy and puppy-like disposition of the latter. He's a gentle and affectionate dog and, when he wants to lick your face, your face will be licked, one way or another. Giving in to the inevitable, I accepted his ardor. Satisfied, he pushed off and was gone in a blur of motion.

"Mischievous beast," Spiros chuckled, as we both watched the dog reach the end of the row, turn and disappear. "I lock him in the house to keep him from his mischief but he has learned to jump up and bounce his front paws off the door until the latch springs free. Then away he flies to wreak his havoc upon all that comes before him."

I looked over at Spiros. His eyes were moist and the lines at their edges turned up in a smile. His tone was that of a father talking of his son. He caught me looking, swiped the kerchief over his face and stuffed it back in his pocket.

"Global warming," he said, staring up at the sun, thick, calloused fingers shielding his eyes. "Good for the grapes," he continued. "Not so good for the grower of grapes. I had a feeling I'd be seeing you soon." He looked over at me. "Your ventures thus far have been prosperous?"

"Things are working out," I said. "How are you, Spiros?"

I reached for his outstretched hand. He pulled me into an embrace, hugged me hard and then held me back at arm's length, his huge, weathered hands clamped to my shoulders.

"Another job," he said. "Why do you risk it?"

I stared into his anthracite eyes which were, in turn, searching mine.

"It's what I do, Spiros."

"Of course it is," he said, slapping my shoulder. "And about time, as well. I was beginning to worry about you. A man must work. It's all he has. An ancestor of mine helped salvage some of the Marbles from the *Mentor* when she sank in the harbor of Kithira after a storm. Have I told you this? No, of course not. I have wine chilling at the house. Come."

He laid the battered hoe against the guy-wires holding the vines and turned away. I followed him up the narrow row between the vines. The air was sharp with heat and the smell of dry earth and snipped leaves.

We turned out of the vineyard and walked across a short expanse of browning grass to his house. A billy goat and his mate watched us for a moment and then returned to their lawn-care duties. The veranda was alive with plant life. Cyclamen and ivy hung from sphagnum moss baskets. Roses, irises, various lilies, plants I had no name for, lined the waist-high barrier that kept awed, often quite drunk, guests from falling a hundred meters or more into the Ionian Sea. Spiros nodded to a wicker chair and then turned into the darkness of the house. He returned a few moments later with a chilled bottle of Robolla and two glasses.

He poured the wine and sat across from me. "You will want to know of Kastania," he said. Spiros wasn't one for wasting time. Unless, of course, the subject turned to politics. On that subject he could, and often did, go on forever with no regard for the circular movement of the clock's hands.

"I have to find her, Spiros," I said.

"I thought you might."

He sipped his wine, smiled and took another sip.

"A fine crop, this one," he said. "Fine indeed." He set down the glass, leaned forward, knitting his fingers together and laying his arms on the table.

"She will not be happy to see you," he continued. "But, of course, she will as well. She is a willful child, full of passion and fury. Much like her father and dear mother, rest her soul. Corsican, Greek and Gypsy. You will find no more volatile combination. She will likely wish to kill you for abandoning her."

I felt ashamed and cornered. I muttered something about having no choice.

"Of course you had a choice. You made a choice. Was it a foolish one? Who am I to judge? A man does what he does, telling himself he has no choice, then lives with the regrets as well as the rewards. But women do not believe there are places where a man has no choice. Women are the stronger of us, though we men like to think otherwise. We spend our lives trying to make them believe they are the weaker sex. We never win in the end. They know. Men think they rule the world but without women, where would a man be, eh? Helpless, hungry and wallowing in his own filth." He laughed hard and took a long drink from his glass.

"She's pretty pissed, huh?" I said.

"She is murderously pissed, Daniel. You will be lucky if you retain half your hair when you again approach her."

"Have you spoken to her?"

"Kastania? No. I am told she waited for you after the White House heist. A week or more. You didn't show

100

and no word came from you. I understand two men paid her a visit during that time. Interpol? Perhaps. Perhaps some American agency. My informant knows not. Whoever they were, they arrived at her door with the illusion they were an authoritarian force to be reckoned with."

He smiled, took a sip of wine.

"She left one with a broken arm, the other so battered he was airlifted to a hospital. After that, she headed to Africa for a time, doing God knows what. There is rumor that a software project in Spain was infiltrated … that all the proprietary information ended up in the hands of an Austrian company. Was she a part of that? I cannot say for sure. Later, she was spotted in Gibraltar and then disappeared again."

I sipped my wine, taking it all in, staring off toward the horizon, watching a ship in the hazy distance crawl across the sea. "Do you know where she is now?" I asked.

He sipped his wine, looking over the rim of his glass at me.

"I warn you again, my friend. A meeting will not be pleasant. Kastania is not the type to take rejection well. No woman is, but especially her. She loves you deeply, you know."

"Does she?" I asked. The taste of the wine turned sour in my mouth. "And I damn well didn't reject her, Spiros. I didn't ... okay, so maybe I did have a choice of sorts but it didn't feel like one at the time. She's so smooth and confident at what she does, cutting through every obstacle and security barrier with no more effort than waving your hand through the air. Compared with her, I felt like an amateur. How long do you think she'd love an amateur? Tell me that."

I put down my wine glass, careful not to slam it on the marble-top table. Spiros was looking at me with a sorrowful, almost pitying, gaze and my momentary anger subsided.

"Okay, so maybe the White House job was a mistake," I continued. "We argued over it for weeks. She didn't want me to do it. She thought I'd botch it. I couldn't not do it. The idea was too deep in my blood. I had to prove to her I could, didn't I? And I did. I beat it, Spiros. I got the painting."

"And ended up a prisoner to it."

"Yeah, well, there is that."

"And now that you feel her equal once again, you feel she will take you back with open arms, a new respect for your skills? You believe this in your heart?"

Shaking his head, his gaze drifted off over the vineyards. "I find that quite sad."

"What does that mean?"

"I think you are mistaken about where your thoughts and feelings intertwine with those of Kastania," he said. "But it is not my place to untie that knot. The true nature of your relationship with Kastania is something you must take up with her."

"You know where she is then?" I asked, not wishing to delve further into Spiros's speculations on my psychological makeup.

He sipped the last of his wine, and refilled his glass.

"With the Corsican, her father. In Bize-Minervois. She is staying in the apartment the two of you own there. Across from his restaurant. She has been there a month or more. As far as I know – and I checked just this morning in anticipation of your visit – she is still there."

"I don't suppose the candy and flowers approach would work?" I asked.

"The candy she would throw at you and the flowers she would make you eat. No, I fear your only recourse will be to present yourself and take what she has to dish out to you."

I finished my wine and Spiros went back into the house for fresh supplies. I turned in my seat and looked out over the sea. From this distance it looked like a textured piece of glass the color of charcoal. I watched another ship make its way along the horizon, fighting to keep my thoughts on it and not on Spiros's words.

He saved me from the struggle by returning with a plate of *taramasalata* and a wicker bowl of hard, crusty bread. We ate, drank more wine and spoke of everything but Kaz or the job. That was Spiros's way. Once a thing was settled, it was settled. No point in picking it to death. That was fine by me.

Sometime after the sun dipped its last dying rays into the sea, I bid him farewell. He wished me luck and I headed back across the lawn, cutting through the now-dark vineyard. Somewhere along the way I picked up a golden shadow as Treacle appeared out of nowhere and followed me to my car. He accepted a pat on the head and I accepted one last lick on the face. Then he was gone again in the same swift way he had come. On the way home I called the airlines and booked a flight to France.

Gerasimos had said I needed a woman to share my bed. He was right, though it wasn't just any woman and it wasn't just to share my bed. It was Kaz I wanted. My life I wanted her to share. If only I could prove myself worthy.

Chapter 15

I've been a thief nearly all my life.

As a kid, I never stole the usual things a child steals, the bubble gum and baseball cards, soda pop and candy. I remember at seven or eight watching an older boy being led from a dime store in handcuffs by two burly blue-clad cops. He'd been caught snatching a yo-yo and a pack of Doublemint. The lesson I should have learned, watching the boy being folded into the patrol car, his face sweaty and caving in on itself, was that stealing was wrong. But I wasn't a normal little boy living in a normal family. My only thought at the time was the kid was stupid for pocketing something so frivolous and getting busted into the bargain.

In my early years it was my mother who was the thief, while I was just the distraction. She would send me into stores where I would wander about, pulling items from the shelves, carrying them around and setting them back on other shelves. While I attracted the attention of the clerks and what security the store might have, my mother would stuff whatever she thought we needed – food, clothes, the occasional candy bar and a book for me – beneath her long, bulky coat.

She never stole things she could have fenced for money. I don't think she understood the value of money and, very likely, would have given it to some homeless person she met on the street or misplace it as she misplaced her keys, her purse, sometimes even the clothes she was trying to put on in the morning. My mother was scatterbrained, alone, deeply paranoid and saddled with a second mouth to feed when she was barely able to put food in her own.

I learned early on never to stray far from her sight as I was never sure she would be there when I returned. Once, when I was nine or ten, I lost myself in a book at a local library, unaware of how late it was, until the library announced it was closing. In a panic, I ran home and found the house empty, what few belongings we had, gone. I ran back into town, first to the Greyhound station, finding it as empty as the house had been, then out to the freight yards. There I found her, off in the shadows, waiting for a slow-moving freight. She hugged me, then scolded me for getting lost. Before she could say more, lights swept over us and, with little more than a short run, we were rolling north.

I've always wondered if she was waiting for me then, or if she would have jumped that freight without me if I hadn't arrived in time. It was a question that plagued me for years but I was too frightened of the answer to ask it. As the years and miles passed, our roles reversed. I became the thief, she the distraction. By the time I was fourteen, I operated alone while my mother retreated further and further into her imaginary world.

I've had a fascination with the impossible for as long as I can remember. While most kids collected comic books and baseball cards, I collected discarded locks and spent hours learning how to pick them. I couldn't enter a building without figuring another way out, or how I would get into it if I didn't have a key.

My early skills as a thief were honed in mom-and-pop groceries and five-and-dimes, and, though I never stole more than what we absolutely needed to survive, there was always a shadow of guilt that coated me like sweat. Often I would return at night and wash their windows or clean up the alleyway behind the store.

The feeling had nothing to do with morality. I never developed the sense that stealing was wrong. It was survival and one did what one had to do in order to achieve that goal. Picking the lock, penetrating the building, slipping in silence through the empty gloom to possess that which was not mine to possess, was a high I couldn't get enough of, but stealing from those who were as poor as I was blunted that thrill.

Though I've never been to a shrink, I've read enough psychology over the years to recognize how my mother's flighty and unpredictable behavior affected me. It forced me to don the mask of extroversion, to hone my social skills to a sharp and witty edge, which in turn allowed me to move in any social group with an enviable ease. This, coupled with my fascination with the impossible, laid the world at my feet and led me, invited or otherwise, into the homes and secret galleries of rich and powerful men. I am very good at what I do. Perhaps the best there is.

Throughout my adult life I have lived alone, traveled alone and, most important of all, worked alone. I have few close friends, most of them within the brotherhood of thieves. There were women in my life as well but I always kept them orbiting at a safe distance, never letting them see my true face.

Then I met Kaz and that was when the trouble began.

Chapter 16

I first saw Kaz at a party, in a sprawling mansion within walking distance of the Eiffel Tower, hanging on the arm of a dull, well-dressed man, all soft and attentive to his every word as he guided her through his phalanx of guests.

She turned at some point and our gazes met. It felt as if the lights had dimmed. I saw her mouth open, a look of surprise cross her face and then she abruptly turned away. I groped for a chair and sat down, short of breath, my heart beating much too hard.

I fought the shakes, trying without success to understand what had just happened. Love at first sight? Absurd! I set the untasted champagne I'd been holding down on a table and resumed my exploration at the fringes of the party. This was not a leisure evening for me. I was working, here to check out security, memorize the entrances and exits of the place while looking for clues to the host's hidden gallery. There was a Van Gogh in there for which a man in South Africa was willing to pay a handsome price. I was determined to find a way to it.

But after that singular moment it became hard to concentrate. Instead of seeking clues I found myself seeking her, spending long moments just watching her move. There was a knot in my stomach I couldn't dislodge. Then I recognized it. Envy. Envy for the colorless man in his thousand-euro tux, carefully-coiffed hair and too-white teeth. He was close to her – where I wanted to be.

They were moving about the room like bees in a field of clover. I tried to avoid a meeting but it was inevitable. They cornered me along a wall of leather-bound books I had been inspecting. I felt the light touch on my elbow and turned, all but falling into her gaze, my breath catching in my throat. To my amazement, she seemed as unsettled as I was, her gaze breaking from mine with an almost audible pop. We chatted for a moment, though for the life of me I couldn't say what words passed between us.

When they turned to move on, I felt as if something precious was slipping from my grasp. I almost reached out to stop her. Instead, I watched her walk away, my eyes seeing only her in the room. They were several yards away, about to engage another couple, when she turned her head and leveled a look at me which made me step back as though I'd been shoved. A faint smile touched her lips and she turned away.

The evening came to an end for me. I was too shaken to work. I turned and was heading for the door when I saw her place her hand on the host's chest, kiss him on the cheek and move off on her own. She slipped through a door and was gone. Without a thought, I followed.

A long marble hallway. Ornate marble pedestals every three meters along one wall. A Roman helmet, a Ming vase, a Greco bust with one ear missing and a chip from the nose. On the opposite wall hung lesser but by no means inexpensive paintings, each in its own hermetically sealed, pilfer-proof case. I caught the sound of slippered footsteps and followed in their wake.

Rounding a corner, the footsteps vanished. I stopped, perplexed. There were several doorways down the hall and a stairwell leading up to my right. I was about to take the stairs when I heard a door click shut ahead of me. I followed the sound to the last door before the hallway turned again. Cautiously, I opened it and stepped into a small pantry. A dim light shone across the room. I took several more steps when, without warning, there was a knife at my throat.

"What are you doing here?" her voice hissed in my ear. The scent of cinnamon and lavender filled my nostrils, making me feel heady.

"Following you," I whispered, deciding that a sharp blade against bare skin called for a certain level of honesty.

"Why?" she hissed.

I faltered. I couldn't think why. Or rather, I wasn't sure I could explain it. I began to swivel around to face her. She resisted at first, then let me. When we were face to face, scant inches between us, I told her so.

"I don't know why. I just wanted to see you."

Then I did something I would never have expected. I kissed her. I'm not sure who was more shocked, me or her. Stepping around her, I headed for the door.

"Café du Monde," she said. "Noon. Be there each day. I will find you."

We did meet, three days later, and were lovers before the day was out. By the end of the week we were partners in crime. I had the Van Gogh while she acquired a chunk of computer code worth as much as the painting.

Her mastery over the computer was beyond my comprehension but by the time she was done, stealing bubblegum from a candy store was riskier than snatching that priceless work of art. I was in awe of her talents and heady with the thought of the treasures we could steal. Had anyone told me my exuberance wouldn't last, I would have laughed in their face.

Chapter 17

Sunrise found me with little to do. The cat bowls were full, the water bowls replenished and I'd arranged for a friend to watch over them while I was away. My bags were packed and in the car. The little calico was sitting on the kitchen table watching me as I finished off the last of my morning coffee.

"Well," I said to her, as I rinsed out my cup and set it in the drainer, "I'm off to the slaughter."

She looked at me with those amber eyes of hers, a curious tilt to her head, stood up, stretched and ran off on her own private adventure. I headed for the door and my own.

The plane touched down in Montpellier at a little past nine. Despite the early hour, the airport was filled with holiday travelers queuing up at ticket counters and loading gates. There was a noisy buzz in the air like a classroom of kids when the teacher is late. It took me several minutes to wend my way through the crowds and over to the area devoted to car rental.

I was anxious and deep in thought. Details of the plan, worries over what to expect from Kaz. Fearful of rejection. Not only of the job, but worse, of me. I was so preoccupied that I nearly gave the woman behind the Europcar counter a credit card that didn't match the passport and driver's license I was carrying. Luckily, I caught the mistake in time, jerking it out of her hand and replacing it with another.

I had to get a grip.

As I hurried across the lobby, keys in hand, I spotted a poster that slowed my step. It was Edvard Munch's *The Scream*. Kaz and I had celebrated our second anniversary with the theft of a notebook of his early drawings and had returned to Paris where we had met. It should have been a happy celebration.

"Who is this Captain Dunsel?" Kaz asked. "Is he military? Police?"

"It's nothing, Kaz," I answered. "I'm sorry I brought it up. Let's just drop it, okay?"

"No. I do not wish to drop this. We drop too many things. We have made a good score and are back in Paris and you mope about as though your best dog has died. I am not understanding this. And then you tell me you feel like this Captain Dunsel and when I wish to know of this man you say to drop it."

I sighed, knowing she wasn't going to let it go.

"He's not a real person, alright? He was just some character on an old TV show I saw a long time ago. I mean, he wasn't even a character. Just someone referred to. That's it, Kaz. I didn't mean anything by it."

"Then why did you say it? What was he that you think you are?"

"Useless," I shouted. "Okay? He was useless. It was a term the show's characters used to describe someone whose skills were no longer of value because something better had come along. There, are you satisfied now?"

"And you feel this way? Useless?"

"Yes. No. Yes. I do, dammit. I mean, Jesus, Kaz. Stealing that damn notebook was about as difficult as walking into a public park and snatching a piece of paper from a trash can. A trained chimp could have got in there and out once you were finished with your magic tricks."

It hadn't been our first argument; it wouldn't be our last. I pulled my gaze from the Munch poster and made my way out to the car lot. Within minutes Montpellier was receding in the rearview mirror of a silver Peugeot.

111

I decided to take the N112 along the Mediterranean coast rather than the A9, despite the fact that with all the tourists on the highway it would delay my arrival in Bize. As I was dreading every kilometer that slipped beneath my wheels anyway, adding time to the equation didn't seem to matter.

I pulled off the highway at Sète to get a late breakfast, driving slowly through the small coastal town until I found the apartment building Kaz and I owned there: three flats and a small restaurant overlooking the canal. I pulled the Peugeot over, killed the engine and sat staring at the building, remembering a time when I'd been busted by the local gendarmes.

"Why, Daniel?" Kaz asked me after presenting the cops with the ownership papers proving that I did own the building I'd been accused of breaking into.

"Why what, Kaz?" I said, as I hurried away from the police station. I was sore and angry and needed a shower.

"Why did you break into your own building?"

The car door was locked. I bounced my fist off the roof and turned to face her. "Don't you mean why did I get caught breaking into my own building? How did I get caught? The great thief, tripped up by a two-bit alarm system? Isn't that really your question, Kaz?"

"Why are you so angry with me, Daniel? And why the alarm? Where did it come from, this alarm?"

"I put the damn thing there, okay? I had them installed on all three of our places!"

"But why, Daniel? I do not understand this? If you put them there, why were you trying to disarm them?"

I spun around in frustration, arms in the air, fists clenched, wanting to scream at the sky. "Will you please unlock this damn thing so we can get out of here? I just want to go home."

We drove in silence. I knew she was chewing her lower lip, a habit when she was trying to be patient, patience not being one of her stronger traits. It wasn't until we turned inland that she let out a great sigh and I knew her patience had run out.

"What is wrong, Daniel?" she asked. "Are you ill?"

"Great," I said. "That's just great, Kaz. This is the perfect time to bring that up."

"Bring what up? What is wrong with you, Daniel? I only meant ..."

"I know what you meant, Kaz. Dammit. How insensitive can you be? I was tired, stressed out. And it was just that once. And what the hell does that have to do with now anyway?"

"What are you talking about, Daniel? I am asking only about the alarm."

I found a small café by the water and ordered breakfast, took a long time to eat it, and stared out over the canal. Afterward, I took a long stroll along the waterway, stepping in and out of the small shops. Despite Spiros's warning, I considered flowers, candy, a gift of some kind but ended up rejecting them all. He was right. Nothing I could give her would make up for what I'd done.

Back on the road, I followed the coast until just past Agde where the N112 turned inland. As I passed through Béziers I remembered it was here that I first got the idea to steal the Washington painting. I'd been spending more and more time away from Kaz and on that day I'd visited a small art gallery, half casing the place and half just enjoying the paintings. In the gallery in the small café, I overheard two snobs discussing the White House and the art that was on display there.

"You would think," said one man, "that in a place such as that, so secure, they would have paintings

113

worth seeing. Who would dare steal them? And yet, all that hangs there is trash. Who would even want such stuff?"

I'd raced home after that. I'd known exactly who might want one of them. It had taken me an hour to track down the Dutchman. I hadn't intended to tell Kaz of my plan. I hadn't wanted her in on it. It was one I was going to do myself – as in the old days – but she'd walked in during my conversation with Dieter.

"You cannot be serious, Daniel," she said, after I hung up.

"Oh, but I am serious," I said. "Very serious."

"But it is insane to do such as this. The painting has no value."

"It has value to Dieter," I said. "What's the matter, Kaz? You don't think I can do it, do you?"

"It has nothing to do with how I feel about if you can do it. It is senseless to steal something so worthless, with so much risk involved."

"A risk I can handle."

"That is not the point. You steal what you can afford to be caught with. That you have always told me. The higher the risk, the higher the value of the piece needs to be. To steal this, this Washington, it is insane, Daniel. It threatens not only you but us."

"You're so damned convinced I'm going to get caught, aren't you? Thanks for the vote of confidence, Kaz."

Lost in thought, I nearly missed the turn onto the D11. The traffic was surprisingly light and it wasn't long before I spotted the single-pump gas station and bar that marked the road to Bize. I made the right and pulled over to the side of the road across from the L'Oulibo Olive Cooperative.

The argument had begun that day continued late into the night and resumed the following morning. It raged on and off over the next three days until I walked out on her and caught a plane to San Francisco. That was fourteen months ago.

Sitting in the Peugeot, staring out the windshield, I thought of my conversation with Spiros, of the things I'd revealed and those I hadn't, even to myself. Was it just that Kaz made me feel inadequate or was it more than that? I felt as if I were turning to stone. No job I've ever pulled, including the Washington, frightened me as much as the idea of confronting Kaz.

I smoked a Sherman, then another and finally a third before my anger overcame my fear. I put the Peugeot in gear and let it creep, well below the speed limit, all the way into Bize.

Chapter 18

The ornately carved wooden chair came crashing through the French doors and landed with a shattering squeal on the flagstone patio outside the restaurant, a shower of broken glass cascading around it like glittering hail. Curses followed in a mixture of English, French, Italian and a language I'd never heard.

What tourists there were began leaving as soon as the yelling started from the second floor apartment, across from the restaurant. One couple braved it out but they too fled after the chair had taken flight.

"I warned you, Daniel" said the Corsican. "She is not happy to have you here."

"I noticed that," I said, wiping at a small trickle of blood on my cheek where a piece of flying glass had nicked me.

"That door will be impossible to replace," he sighed.

"Not to mention the chair."

I looked over at what was left of the Louis XVI chair, now in splinters on the patio.

"I suppose it was real," I said.

"Kastania doesn't abide fakes, I'm afraid."

I watched the wind billow the lace curtains through the shattered panes. Kaz had a temper only a god could endure. Or someone hopelessly in love. She took that moment to walk out on the balcony. Seeing her again took my breath away. I'd almost forgotten how beautiful she was. Deep red hair that flowed in tight waves across her shoulders and back like the rolling inferno of a forest fire; eyes so deeply green they made emeralds blush with envy. At that moment both eyes were smoldering and both were directed at me.

"You bastard," she screamed and hurled a coffee cup at me. It hit the patio several feet away. Kaz was good at a lot of things but, thankfully, pitching coffee cups wasn't one of them.

Before I could respond, she whirled around and disappeared into the apartment, a trail of curses in that strange language spinning off in her wake. I turned to look at her father. His expression was pained.

"What's that language she's speaking," I asked. "I've never heard her use it before."

"Romanian," he answered. "Her mother, rest her soul, was a Gypsy. I hadn't realized she had taught Kastania so much of the ... the old traditions."

He poured half a glass of Eau de Vie and downed it in a single gulp, still looking up at the place where his daughter had been standing.

"What's she saying," I asked.

He poured another half glass and handed me the bottle, looking at me as if he expected me to disappear in a puff of smoke at any moment.

"You don't want to know, Daniel," he sighed. "You really don't want to know."

A loud thud and the sound of breaking glass belched from the splintered French doors and echoed up the narrow streets. More cursing erupted followed by another crash.

"The china cabinet?" I asked.

"Probably," he answered.

I looked up at the balcony. Kaz was standing there again, her red hair brushed and glowing against the pale marble backdrop of the apartment walls. She was wearing jeans and a white blouse, buttoned only at her breasts. I caught glimpses of her midriff as the wind off the river whipped the tails of the shirt. The ache I always felt when near her blossomed in my chest. I heard her father's chair scrape on the fieldstone, heard him walk away.

"Why are you here, Daniel Samsel?" she asked. Her eyes burned holes through mine. "And do not dare to speak of love or desire. And do not apologize. I spit on your apology. And do not say to me that you have come because of one of your capers. Surely I will slit your throat where you sit if you came for my aid."

I opened my mouth, closed it, opened it again, feeling like a sturgeon on ice at the local market. "You're not leaving me much room here, Kaz," I said.

"You do not deserve room, betrayer! You do not deserve my boot heel after stepping it in dog shit!"

I let my head sink into my hands, kneading my forehead with the tips of my fingers, my eyes closed to stop the tears I could feel gathering there. After a moment I threw my head back and with a deep sigh, rose from the chair. I looked up at Kaz. We stared at one another for a moment, then I turned away. I had reached the arch that separates the old city of Bize from the new when she spoke.

"If you step beyond that arch, Danny Samsel" she said softly. Her whispered voice seemed to fill the square. "I will hunt you down this time and kill you."

When I turned back at her words she was gone. I felt as if a net had opened up beneath my feet. I returned to my chair and sat down, staring up at the balcony where she had been.

The Corsican appeared, a small pillow in one hand, a bottle of Eau de Vie in the other. He handed me the pillow and set the bottle and a small, thimble-sized glass on the table beside me. "Welcome home," he said and turned away.

I wedged the pillow behind my head, filled the thimble and picked it up. It felt warm in my hand.

Sipping it, I watched the shadows lengthen until all was dark, before slipping into a restless sleep.

Chapter 19

I awoke stiff, dry-mouthed, my head pounding like an eight-cylinder engine firing on six. The grating noise that had invaded my dreams turned out to be the sweeping of shattered glass across rough stone, into a metal shovel. A young man in baggy blue overalls was hunched over his broom several yards from where I sat. He looked up at me, a scowl reiterating the resentment in his thin lips.

Hearing voices, I looked up. Two men were removing what was left of the French doors. I sat up, pulling my legs from the chair opposite me and settling my feet on the stone. The muscles in my thighs and calves ached as if I'd been running all night. My knees popped when I bent them.

Save for the scowling sweeper, there was no one about this early in the morning. The restaurant was closed, though I could make out movement in the shadows to the rear of the place. I turned back to watch the workers up on the balcony.

Just as I was thinking that I would kill for a cup of coffee, I heard a door open behind me. A young girl stepped out. No more than fifteen, dressed in tight red jeans and a man's baggy white shirt, her coal-black hair twisted around in a knot and pinned to the back of her head. She had a silver tray in her hand. A silver pot steamed, the smell of coffee hitting me like a fresh breeze on a hot day. The tray also contained a dish of croissants and a cut glass bowl of dark jam. She set the tray down, made a slight bow and, blushing somewhat, turned away.

I poured the coffee, added sugar and milk and dug into the croissants, not realizing till that moment how hungry I was. I was pouring my second cup of coffee when Kaz's father came out and sat down. He was holding a huge, brown coffee mug with the words *Chien de Café* circling its middle. He hadn't yet shaved and the gray stubble on his face glistened in the morning sun.

"So," he said, taking a sip, "I see you are still alive."

"Were you worried I wouldn't be?" I asked.

"There were moments, yes."

We both looked up at the balcony.

"Have you seen Kaz this morning?" I asked.

"She was down earlier," he replied. "She has gone for a walk with the dog. Down by the river. I believe she wishes you to seek her out."

"Ahh, the river. Yes. The better to dispose of the body."

He laughed. "Had she wished you dead," he said, "she could have done it at any time while you slept."

"She was down here?" I asked. "During the night?"

"Several times. Where do you think the blanket came from?"

I had wondered about that on waking but, like the pillow, I thought it had come from him. The Corsican sipped his coffee, watching the men working on the balcony. I polished off the last of the croissants and jam. Pouring what was left of the coffee from the pot, I finished that off as well.

"Well," I said with a deep sigh. "I suppose I should go look for her. You didn't notice if she had anything sharp or breakable with her, did you?"

"Nothing sharp. And only the dog is breakable. I doubt she would throw him at you though. More for his sake than yours, I'm afraid."

"Thanks for the vote of confidence," I said, and headed off to the river.

It was a beautiful day, the cigales chirping softly, the heat not high enough yet to be uncomfortable. The lush green foliage of the trees curled out over rushing water the color of onyx. Lilies bloomed along the river's edge; maroon fuchsias and multi-hued irises stretched as far as the eye could see. The air was heady with negative ions and the smell of river mud and moss. I followed a well-worn trail that angled away from the river, cut through a field of lavender and meandered back through a grove of almond trees to the water's edge.

I had been out for about half an hour when I spotted the dog. Pinkerton, was his name. Pinkerton J. Snoopington III to be exact. He was an old dog, sixteen years or so, shaped like a barrel with long, thin legs, mostly black and tan and white patches over each eye that always made me think of Little Orphan Annie. Pink was one of those Heinz 57 varieties which never falls ill and goes through life with the stoic disposition of an all-knowing and disillusioned cleric.

He raised his head as I walked into the clearing, peered at me with a bored look, as if asking 'What took you so long?' Raising his leg over the spot he'd been sniffing, depositing a few drops of urine, he moved on to another spot, nose buried in the leaves like a pig searching for truffles.

"Hey, Pink," I said, moving toward him. "What are you up to there?"

"He's reading his pee-mail," came a voice from behind me.

I nearly jumped out of my skin, looked around but couldn't see her. Hearing a splash, I parted the weeping branches of a willow tree that blocked my view of the river and stepped out onto a small, sandy beach. Kaz was treading water about a meter off shore, her red hair fanning out behind her like a shawl.

"P-mail?"

"Yes," she said. "Like ..." She muttered something in French. "I think of it like email for dogs. Pee-mail. They wander about, find a spot and leave a little pee. It is a message to another dog. This other dog comes along, sniffs the message, understands what is being ... " – French again – " ... said and, with a little pee, he, or she, replies. And on it goes for each dog. They all can read what the others have left and they all reply with whatever is on their mind. Pinkerton has many friends. They all know the importance of communication."

Wincing at that last remark, I sat down on the soft sand.

"Kaz," I said, trying to force words past the lump in my throat. "I'm just really ... "

"No, Daniel, no apologies. Apologies will not bring back the days and nights we have lost."

I felt anger stab at my chest. "Lost because you had no faith in me, in my abilities."

"No, my thief, lost not from lack of faith. Lost because you felt you had to prove something to me you were never in need to prove. Yes, I was furious when you stole the Washington. Furious that you would not listen to me; furious that you threatened what we had. But never was I in doubt of you. And when you disappeared – and I have always known where you were – do not think otherwise – my fury was greater still. But so, too, my sadness: sad that you thought our love too fragile to endure."

I stared down at my feet nestled in the sand, unsure of how to respond, unsure if I even could.

"I was never the better thief," she said, her voice as soft as the water lapping against her shoulders.

My head jerked up so fast that my teeth clacked together. "What?" I gasped. "How could you ..."

"Know what you are thinking?" she finished. "Your Captain Dunsel told me."

"My who? How?"

"I spoke many times to Spiros and Eleni."

"They didn't mention that to me," I interrupted.

"Because I bid them not to. They told me things of your past, things you had never spoken to me of. It was Spiros who explained this Captain Dunsel to me. He sent me a tape. Watching it, I began to understand. I knew then the reasons for your alarm, your reason even for the stealing of the Washington. What I could not know were your reasons for keeping this from me, or why you wouldn't come home to me. Not until Eleni told me of your mother, of the demons she harbored. It was then I understood you were afraid. Not of me but of our love. Afraid I would one day leave you, as you always feared your mother would."

I stared off across the water, tears clouding my vision, memories clouding my thoughts. Afraid – was that it? Was I afraid to love for fear of losing love? Afraid to accept that I might be worthy of being loved – for myself alone?

"What is it you want from me, Daniel?" she asked.

For a moment I was confused, unsure of what she was asking. There must have been a strange look on my face for she laughed and said, "I don't mean that. I mean the job. And yes, I know that is one reason you came. Spiros told father and father told me, though not the details. What are you planning?"

I shook my head, unsure of what to say. "I shouldn't have come," I started. "I mean, it's not that I shouldn't have come. I wanted to come. I never should have left. Now, I'm not sure of anything. Yeah. I'm planning

124

another job. In some ways it's worse than the Washington. And I'm not sure why I latched onto the idea."

Kaz laughed, the water jostling around her. "My dear Daniel, have you grown so unsure of yourself that you cannot see you have come to this idea because you are a thief?"

"No," I said. "I came to this idea to find a way back to you."

"Oh, *mon voleur*, you still do not understand. You never needed an excuse to come back to me. My heart has always been open, from the moment I met you. I know this as surely as I know the color of night. I am a Gypsy, no? Gypsies know these things. My mother told me that the instant my father appeared before her, she knew he was the one only Mother Death could part her from. She told me I would know this truth as well when my time came, when the man I was to be with always, entered my life. I knew you were him that night in Paris. As with my mother and father, none but Mari can separate us now and even then but for a short time. Now, tell me of this job you have come to me for aid, before I shrivel up like a prune."

I felt a cold nose on my neck and then a shove, as though even the dog was forgiving me.

"I need a hack," I said. "Several of them."

"And you thought I would do this ... hack for you?"

"I was hoping."

She stared at me for a long moment.

"And what is it you plan to steal, *draga mea hoț*?"

"The Parthenon Marbles," I answered.

She began to laugh. "You are such a beautifully demented dreamer."

She stepped from the river. I watched the water cascade from her breasts, her nipples hard and glittering

125

like ice. Stepping onto shore, she reached for my hand and pulled me to my feet. In the same motion she pulled me to her and then, turning, sidestepped us into the water.

It was cold, but only for an instant.

Chapter 20

It took me the better part of the day to convince Kaz I was serious about stealing the Marbles. She paced, drank Pepsi like it was water and told me I was crazy well into the evening.

Later, sitting on the balcony of our apartment overlooking the restaurant, sipping tea, I continued laying it out for her. It had been coming together in my head throughout the afternoon. That was how it had often been in the three years we were together. I would have a goal in mind, with only sketchy ideas of how to reach it. We would talk it out and, in the talking, the plan would resolve itself. I had forgotten that aspect of our relationship; overlooked it in my fear. But it was happening that way again and gradually she was beginning to see it.

Midnight came and went. The long day was taking its toll and I fell asleep in the chair. I awoke to the sun in my face and the murmurs of early morning tourists drifting up from the tables below. Kaz was gone. Her laptop was sitting on the glass table next to me, a multicolored ball bouncing lazily off the sides, changing colors as it drifted across the screen. I tapped the space bar and the ball disappeared and the security diagrams from Wu appeared in its place.

The table was littered with empty Pepsi cans and tea bags. Sheets of paper with neat notations in the margins were scattered about. Most of them looked like articles printed off the Internet. There was a stack of papers next to a small Epson printer. Pulling the pile into my lap, I began going through it.

The first sheet was a list of names, security personnel working for the museum, complete with pictures. Kaz had highlighted several with a hot pink marker. Following that were data sheets on the names she had highlighted: credit histories, school records, employment background, addresses and telephone numbers, not only theirs but those of their neighbors as well.

As I was shuffling through the pictures, one caught my attention. The hair was wrong. The mustache. Still. But it couldn't be, I thought. A guard? At the museum? Before I could give it more thought, Kaz came into the room. I returned the picture to the pile with the others.

"The museum hosts overnighters from time to time," she said.

I looked up at her. She was carrying a silver tray with a steaming coffee pot and a plate of pastries on it. Using her arm to clear a spot, she set the tray down and began to pour coffee into two mugs.

"Overnighters?" I asked.

"Yes." She dropped two sugar cubes into one mug, poured in milk and handed the mug to me. "Sometimes a social event. Sometimes a high school class. They section off a portion of the museum and everyone gets to have their own private exhibition."

Pouring milk into her mug, she grabbed a pastry and sat in the chair next to me.

"And we can use this?" I asked, reaching for a pastry.

"Security doesn't like the practice. I read a number of emails of complaint. Seems that management likes the overnighters as a promotional device but refuses to increase security personnel on those nights. The museum is strapped for cash and can't afford it."

"So security is drawn away from the rest of the museum to cover the event," I said, seeing where she was going with this.

"Yes. Can't have drunk patrons, or young children, roaming the dark halls at night."

"Sounds perfect for young thieves, though," I said.

"Not so young anymore, I think. But yes, perfect. And there is one coming up."

"When?"

"Thirteen days."

"Thirteen days," I repeated. "That's cutting it close. When will the next one be?"

"Several months," she answered.

"Too long. Where will the group be?" I asked.

"The lower floor, directly beneath rooms eighteen and nineteen, where we will be."

"Oh. That's dicey. What about the loading dock? The gates?"

"One guard. The courtyard is covered by camera. The entire museum is covered by cameras, all recording to a bank of video recorders in a locked room. Thirty minutes of video are compressed and transmitted to an outside security firm on the half hour, which you already know. It is all quite automatic and this could be very troublesome. If there were a way for us to obtain previous recordings, well, we could possibly find a way to transmit those."

She took a bite of pastry and continued.

"I do not know if such recordings exist and I have not yet been able to penetrate the security firm and would prefer not to. Their security will be much tighter than that of the museum. I will need more time to investigate."

"What about the loading dock gate?" I asked. "Anything there?"

"The gate is controlled from the gatehouse and from the central security room. At night, there is one guard on duty in the security room."

I sipped my coffee, finished the pastry and reached for another. "Are the guards assigned to sections or just roam at random?" I asked.

"Sections. There are two who patrol the part of the museum we are interested in."

"Hmmm." I stood up and started to pace the small balcony. "We're going to have to take the guards out, replace them with our own people."

"I was thinking this myself. What do you propose? Surely you don't mean to harm them?"

"No. I don't want any bloodshed. I was thinking more along the lines of them taking an unexpected nap."

"Drugs?"

"Something like that."

"Still, someone is going to have to take the security room and control those transmissions before anything else can be accomplished. All security and communications take place in that room. Without it we can do nothing."

I looked over at her. There was a gleam in her eye; a look she gets when she knows what she's going to do. And knows that it's dangerous as hell.

"I have the feeling you're starting to think this is doable," I said.

"You know I am the one most qualified," she said. "It is all computer operated in that room. Computers are what I do."

"I know," I said. "It's just that, well, it's ...."

"Dangerous," she interrupted. "I know. But what is the point of stealing, if stealing were not so?" She smiled. This was part of why I loved her so, I thought.

The doorbell rang at that moment and we both leaned over the balcony rail to see who had come calling. Two men in work uniforms, tool boxes at their feet were standing at the door. I yelled down to them that we'd be there in a moment.

"I'm going to call Mac and Andreas," I said, loading up the serving tray with our empty mugs and as many of the Pepsi cans as it would hold.

And make another call as well, though I wasn't planning to tell Kaz about that one just yet. I had to be sure. Kaz began gathering up the papers, closed her computer and hauled it and the printer into the apartment.

Setting down the full tray by the sink, I grabbed the phone and made my calls. Mac came on after only two rings. I told him where I was and that I needed him up here yesterday. He put me on hold while he called the airport and came back on within minutes. There was an afternoon flight. He could be here by evening.

Andreas was harder to track down. By the time I reached him, Kaz had let the workers in and they were already measuring the length and width of the French doors. It was a cell connection and Andreas's voice kept cutting in and out. I told him that I needed him up here as soon as possible.

There was a long silence on his end and I started to think that either I had lost the connection or he was going to back out. One of the workmen plugged in a saw and hit the switch several times. Over the clatter of the saw blade I thought I heard a scuffle then the squeal of an animal or a small child. Then Andreas was talking in a rush, telling me he would catch the first plane he could and then the line went dead. I stared at the phone, puzzled, and laid it back in its cradle. The last call I would save for later, when I had more time.

Chapter 21

Mac arrived late in the evening, looking as dapper and fresh as though he had just walked out of his house instead of flying for several hours and driving several more. He was anxious to hear the plan but I put him off, not wanting to go through the whole thing again once Andreas showed up. I gave him the printouts Kaz had made together with her notes and left it at that. We had a late dinner, shared a bottle of wine, then retired to the apartment, putting Mac up in the small guest room.

Mac, Kaz and I were sitting in the back booth of the restaurant when Andreas arrived the next day. It was nearly noon when I spotted him standing in the square looking lost, a battered tartan suitcase in his hand. I rushed out to greet him. Though he was clean-shaven and sober, there were dark circles beneath his eyes and what looked like a fresh bruise near his temple. I asked him about it but he brushed it aside with some comment about running into a door.

After depositing his suitcase at the apartment, we walked over to the restaurant. Andreas greeted Mac nervously and became tense when Kaz walked in from the back room. Mac was eager to hear the plan but I was keeping it to myself for the time being. I didn't want to discuss it in the restaurant. Too many tourists.

The workmen were installing the French doors and repairing the damage Kaz had wrought inside the place, so the apartment was out. I gave Narbonne a thought. There were a number of large, outdoor eating places where I was sure we could find a remote enough table to discuss the project.

Instead, I opted for St. Chinian. Narbonne was spread out over a wide area and always crowded with tourists, whereas St. Chinian was compact and drew fewer tourists, especially during the week. It was also a bit closer, tucked away in the foothills where the narrow, winding roads leading into town would make surveillance easier. Besides, I loved their local wine and the food at the restaurant I had in mind was excellent.

It was late afternoon when we arrived. The cafés, bars and restaurants in St. Chinian all line one side of the N112, with the serving area across the busy street in a large, shaded park. Each café or restaurant displays its own colorfully designed tablecloth to distinguish it and from a distance, the arrangement looks like an intricate mosaic nestled amid the trees. I found a parking spot and the four of us made our way to a far table.

A group of men were playing *pétanque* in the court a short distance away. A line of locals and tourists hugged the fence, shouting encouragement and snapping pictures. We hadn't been sitting but a moment when I spotted a young woman, her hair tied back in a loose braid, threading her way across the busy street with a tray of drinks in her hand. Considering the insane way the French drive, I wondered how many waitresses were run over in a year. Waiting tables was dangerous work in St. Chinian.

I watched her make her way through the scattered crowd, moving through different cultural groups like a bee in a field of wild flowers, leaving nectar behind instead of collecting it. When she noticed us sitting at the most distant set of tables, her tired smile dipped, replaced by something resembling a frown. Sullen, her empty tray hanging at her side, she walked to our table. We ordered lattés all around, except for Kaz who opted for her usual Pepsi, and asked for menus. She found two on an empty table, brought them to us, then left to get our drinks. I laid the plan out quickly, going over the things Kaz and I had discussed the previous day.

"How many guards do you think we'll need to replace?" Mac asked, scratching notes in a small spiral pad.

"The one in the control room," Kaz answered. "I'll take that one."

"I may have something going there," I interrupted. Everyone turned to me.

"Someone inside?" asked Mac.

"It's a possibility," I said. "A slim one. I'm going to have to move real slow on this one, but I'll know more before we hit the place."

Kaz laid her hand across mine. "You recognized one of the guards," she said.

"Maybe," I answered. "It's been a long time. I'll have to consider if it's worth taking the chance."

"It would be good to have someone inside," Mac said.

"I agree," I answered. "But only if it's worth the risk of approaching him. Like I said, it's been a long time."

"Do what you can," said Kaz, giving my hand a squeeze. "As for the rest, the two guarding the room we are interested in, they will need to be replaced and we may need to eliminate the rest on that floor as well."

"And we should have at least one of our own down on the floor below us," I added, "to keep an eye on the overnight party."

"What about communication between us?" Mac asked.

"Ear plugs and lapel mikes," Kaz answered. "Scrambled and on a secure frequency. With a very limited range, so it won't be picked up by accident outside the museum."

"What about communications from outside the museum?" Mac continued.

"There should be very little that time of night," Kaz answered. "What calls there may be are routed through a central system. I will control that system."

"I like your attitude," Mac quipped. "What about the video burst to the security firm?"

"I have some ideas," Kaz said. She turned to look at me. "And perhaps our potential insider could help in that area?"

I didn't comment, as I was still uncertain if my contingency plan would amount to anything.

Andreas sat quietly through this phase of the discussion, cleaning his nails with a small penknife. The waitress arrived with our drinks, took our food order and left. I started in on the rest of the plan. Andreas closed the knife and slipped it in his pocket.

"Is this realistic?" he asked, a hint of scorn in his voice. "How are we to gather all these things and carry them from their place?"

I started to say something but Mac jumped in ahead of me.

"It may not be as unrealistic as it sounds," he said. "If you separate the whole of the Marbles into their individual parts, it becomes less of an impossibility. Overall, the metopes and panels themselves are quite small. Heavy … but quite small. Even the pedimental statues should give us little problem. The Caryatid," and here he waved a hand in the air, "well, she may be problematic, as will the column from the Erechtheion. That is something we will have to deal with when the time comes."

Andreas shrugged his acceptance and I continued.

We would need two tractor-trailer rigs and a Range Rover, I explained. The Range Rover would carry spare fuel, food, first aid items and the few weapons we might carry. One of the tractor-trailer rigs we would have filled with crated rocks and send it off to the docks as a diversion.

"Why rocks?" Andreas asked.

"Because we're going to drop a dime on that rig once it's loaded aboard ship and out to sea," I explained. "The phone call will divert them to the docks and well away from our escape route, which will take some of the heat off us. The container, filled with rocks, will be welded shut, forcing the authorities to use a scanning device to check the contents. I want them to see what they expect to see. The manifest for the load needs to match the weight they'll expect. The more time they waste dealing with that, the more time we have to disappear."

"My cousin Eddie has a quarry north of London," Andreas said. "It would be the perfect place to fill a truck with stone. No questions. And I get a discount." He smiled for the first time since he'd arrived.

"The discount I'm not worried about," I said. "The discretion, however, is excellent."

"The trucks," he continued. "Would it matter if they came from Belgium?"

"Not so long as we can get British plates for them. These wouldn't be hot trucks, would they? I don't want to run that risk."

"Oh, no. Legitimate they would be. My uncle deals in heavy equipment. He could get us anything we need."

"At a family discount, no doubt," I said, smiling.

"A man's family is all he truly has, is it not?"

"In that case, look into the Range Rover as well."

"I will need drivers for these vehicles," he said.

"I've already spoken to a woman who runs the taverna I frequent, back on the island. She has several sons, all out of work. They could use the money. Her twin sons Kostas and Nikos are waiting for a call. I'll have them meet you in Belgium," I said.

I mentally checked off another point and went on. We would need an experienced crew: those whose only job would be to help with loading, plus a few extra to fill the guards' positions. That was where I hoped Mac would come in.

"I know some people who could do the job and keep their mouths shut," Mac offered. "I've used them on digs before. They know artifacts, how to handle them, crate them. But they won't be cheap, or easy to come by. I'll need to do some traveling. These aren't the sort of people you call on the phone."

"Money's not the issue," I said. "Nor the travel. We have some time yet. But I don't want them to know what the job is until they show up on site."

"That won't be a problem," Mac answered. "I'll start rounding them up … get them on their way to England."

"And I have people in London we could use to replace the guards," Andreas added. "Very trustworthy if the money is right."

"Good. And it will be. The same admonition goes for them, though. They are not to know what's going on until they are inside the museum."

The waitress arrived with our food and we set the planning aside as we dug in. Andreas seemed to lighten up as he ate, even telling a few off-color jokes that had both Kaz and Mac laughing so hard they spewed food all over the table. When the last plate was clean, we returned to the discussion.

"What about defensive measures?" Mac asked. "This isn't going to be like sneaking into an empty gallery and stealing a painting."

"I've given that a lot of thought," I said and pushed my plate aside. "The one thing I don't want is bloodshed. If there are any deaths linked to this heist it's going to make it hard, if not impossible, for the Greeks to keep the Marbles once we get them there. I would just as soon cut and run if it comes to that. That's why I'm opting for these."

I reached beneath my chair, pulled out a battered briefcase and laid it on the table. Looking around to make sure no one was watching, I opened the case and removed an unusual pistol and a plastic container of dull-colored darts.

"Ketamine darts," I said. "They're used to subdue large animals. Fast acting, fairly harmless, unless you consider a pounding headache afterwards as life-threatening. We'll use these to take out the guards. They should also give us enough time to get away if something goes awry. I'm hoping it doesn't come to that. They may also come in handy as we make our way to, and through, the Chunnel. There will be less risk once we're in France, provided Andreas can keep us to the back roads. But, if we encounter a cop or two, the Ketamine should do the trick."

"There is much ground to travel from London to the channel," Andreas said. "And beyond England, as well. You seem not so worried of this."

"Oh, I'm worried enough, but I'm counting on the embarrassment factor to help us out in that department."

"The what?" Mac asked.

"Embarrassment," I said. I leaned forward, studying each of their faces. "When I stole the portrait of

138

Washington from the White House, I couldn't have been out of DC by the time the theft was discovered. Yet I managed to get it on a plane and over here without being caught. Why? I think it was embarrassment. The authorities weren't willing to face the humiliation of admitting someone had broken their security, snuck into the White House and stolen a famous painting right out from under their noses, so they kept it close to the bone."

I returned the dart gun to its case and set the case beneath the table.

"Even now they're not certain who stole the painting," I continued. "They have a short list and I'm on it, but there have been no official warrants issued. They don't want so much as a peep of the theft getting out. I'm counting on the same thing happening with England. They're not going to go public with the fact that the Marbles have been stolen right out from under them. They'll keep it to a small group … try to track us down themselves. That gives us an edge. At least for a while. And if they bite at the decoy we're setting up, all the better."

The waitress returned to the table, offering us an assortment of desserts. I ordered a *crème brûlée*, Mac and Kaz ordered the mousse and Andreas a lime sherbet. I had the waitress include a bottle of Clos Bagatelle Saint-Chinian La Gloire de Mon Père.

My recitation over, it was now time for comments. We spent the rest of the evening going over the fine details, working out hitches, smoothing the plan to a fine gloss.

"One last thing," I said, reaching beneath the table and retrieving five wrapped packages from my briefcase.

"How thoughtful," Mac said, reaching for a package. "A present."

"Of sorts," I said. "More like an insurance policy."

Kaz was the first to unwrap hers. Holding it up she said, "A balaclava?"

Andreas and Mac followed suit with the same puzzled expression on their faces.

"The embarrassment factor will only go so far," I said. "The Brits are going to be mad as hell and looking to vent their anger on anyone they think may have the expertise to pull off such a heist. We five are too well known to avoid scrutiny. Once on site, we'll need to wear these at all times."

We were the last to leave the outdoor dining area, leaving the harried waitress a pile of dirty dishes, empty glasses and a hefty tip for her troubles.

There was silence in the car on the return trip home, all of us deep in our own thoughts.

Chapter 22

Exhausted, I was nearing the turnoff to Bize before I realized I was being followed. Or thought I was. There was something about the lights shining in my rearview mirror that set off warning bells. Was one of the headlights flickering? Had I noticed that flickering before? I couldn't be sure but I didn't want to risk it so I bypassed the turn-off to Bize and continued up the highway.

Several miles later I made a quick, unannounced left onto an unmarked vineyard road. The car following me seemed to slow and then sped past. I relaxed somewhat but still took a random route through the vineyards, looking for any sign of another vehicle and not spotting one.

Eventually I found my way back to the main highway. No one in the car seemed to notice but I was still troubled. Mac and Kaz were busy in the back seat going over the security system of the museum. Andreas was enigmatic and silent, staring out the open window, smoking one cigarette after another. Of the four of us, he was the only one who hadn't sampled the wine. Even Kaz had drunk a glass, a rare occurrence for her.

It was just past nine when we arrived in Bize.

This time of year the tourists crowd the town and take up all the parking spots, so I dropped everyone off at the arch and went looking for somewhere to stash the car. When I got back to the apartment, Kaz and Mac were hunched in front of her laptop looking through the security diagrams. Andreas was nowhere to be found. I was more than a little worried over his distant mood. In my past encounters with Andreas, he had never been a laconic man, drunk or sober, so his current silence was perturbing.

I hit the Corsican's place first. It was a madhouse of tourists but no Andreas. I made my way through the narrow streets of old Bize stopping at every restaurant, tavern and small café that was still open. Still no Andreas. Finally, I spotted him sitting at a table outside a small tavern frequented by the locals.

It was off the beaten path, a semicircle of gravel in front of a weathered store front, the faded letters of its name barely legible, even in daytime. There was a scattering of rough cut, wooden tables, their surfaces stained and carved with initials and pledges of love. Only one of the three lights illuminating the outdoor area was lit. Andreas was sitting at the farthest point from its feeble rays.

"Is there something wrong, Andreas?" I said and joined him at his table. His head was bowed, his hands wrapped about a half-full glass. There was a bottle of cheap Marc on the table. A cigarette smoldered in a chipped glass ashtray. He looked up at me, raising his head until his gaze was level with mine. His eyes were haunted, the dark circles beneath giving them a hollow look.

"Wrong?" he said. "Nothing is wrong. Why would you think this?"

"I don't know," I answered. "You seem ... off. Not your usual self. That kind of thing."

"Myself?" he said, his expression harsh. "And what is my usual self? The drunk? The jokester? Do you think you know me at all?"

The bitter words reverberated around the empty square.

"Look, Andreas," I said after a moment. "If there is a problem here, we need to deal with it now."

He stared at me for some time and then laughed. It sounded forced and insincere. "You worry too much, Daniel," he said.

"There's a lot here to worry about," I said. "Is this about Kaz and me?"

He laughed again. This time more like the old Andreas I knew.

"I really rattled you with ouzo's words back in Athens, didn't I old friend?"

His laughter faltered and sadness eclipsed his smile like a shadow crossing the moon.

"No," he said, his voice a whisper. "This is not about Kastania."

He looked around him, swept his arm out to encompass his environment, then looked back at me.

"I am growing too old for all this. Too many miles, too many beds not my own, in too many places I will never see again. My family hardly recognizes me on those scarce occasions when I venture to my home. My mother weeps and tells me I look like my father before he died. My father was seventy when he passed, Daniel. I am forty-eight. How is it a man of forty-eight looks twenty years more than his age?"

Pushing the bottle in my direction, he reached into his shirt pocket and withdrew a pack of Turkish cigarettes. Lighting one with a kitchen match, he broke the match in two and cast it aside. The smoke from the cigarette wreathed his head in a blue cloud. He was silent for a long while. I took a sip of the Marc. It was harsh stuff and scalded my throat.

"Have you ever considered what you give up for this life?" he asked, the words soft and far away. He downed the remainder of his glass and refilled it. I'd known Andreas long enough to know to let him speak.

He wasn't looking for answers from anyone but himself.

"The sacrifices?" he continued. "Living in shabby hotels and dark back-street hovels. Moving, always in darkness, always on the run. Never marrying. Never having children. A family. Family is all a man has, all that he truly is. Family and friends."

His voice trailed off and he was silent for a long time. I was on the verge of speaking when he said, almost under his breath, "Family. Friends. Which is the greater do you think?"

He looked up at me, his eyes trying to focus on my face. I felt he was trying to tell me something but I didn't know what.

"Which would you give up, Daniel? Your family for your friends? Or would the friends be those betrayed for family?"

Family? Friends? I had no family. My friends, limited as they were, were all the family I had.

"Why does it have to be either way at all?" I asked.

He stared at me for a long moment and then looked away, chuckling deep in his throat.

It wasn't a cheerful laugh.

"This will be my last job, Daniel," he said. "It is time to go home."

He pulled another cigarette from the pack on the table and lit it off the butt end of the one he'd been smoking.

"Do not worry so," he said into the smoke. "It is a good plan … we will make it work. But now, I must be alone to think, to go over the plan. Do not take offense, old friend."

"I wouldn't think of it," I said. I rose from my chair. He reached out his hand and I took it.

"We have been good friends over the years," he said, clasping my hand in both of his. I swear there were tears in his eyes. "I can never thank you properly for what you did for me."

"Andreas ..."

"No," he said, waving his hand in the air. "Let it be said. It must be said."

He let my hand go and I stepped back from the table, leaving him there amidst the darkness of his questions.

Chapter 23

I walked back to the apartment. The lights were out when I got there. Mac was snoring on the couch. I grabbed a beer from the fridge and stepped out onto the balcony. Andreas's words were going round and round in my head. He still hadn't returned by the time I finished the beer. I went into the bedroom, undressed and crawled in next to Kaz. She sighed in her sleep as I curled myself around her.

The following morning, Andreas was nowhere to be found and I assumed he'd left for Belgium before anyone else awoke. Mac left several hours later, after going over – again – Wu's security data with Kaz. He had to return to Istanbul first, then make several trips to places he wouldn't name in order to gather his crew. He assured me that he, and they, would be safely in London in three days.

I made a call to the island and arranged for Katrina's sons to fly to Belgium to meet up with Andreas. My third call to London connected me to the man I wanted to reach. An hour later I was convinced he could be of some help to us, though not in the way I had hoped. The pieces of the plan were settling into place. If only my thoughts would do likewise.

Shortly after noon, I found myself ravenous and started to head downstairs to the restaurant. Kaz begged off lunch, opting for a long, hot bath and a nap. I declined her invitation to join her. She had been up most of the night working out the final security details with Mac and was dead tired. I, on the other hand, was feeling wircd. The hot bath might have done me some good in that department but I doubted Kaz and I would have managed much bathing. The stint in bed would have been anything but a nap.

So, after a lingering kiss that almost made me change my mind, she ruefully started to draw her bath, while I went off to the restaurant where I sipped a cold Spaten and nibbled on a baguette spread with *pâté rouge* at one of the outdoor tables of the restaurant.

Alone with my thoughts, I wondered why I hadn't told Mac or Andreas about my encounter with Interpol or my little café meeting with Marceau. I hadn't even told Kaz. Except for my momentary fear the night before, there hadn't been a hint of a tail since leaving Kefalonia. Up until I'd called Mac and Andreas, no one but Kaz and I, and Spiros of course, knew about Bize. I had no reason to believe that I was in any danger and yet I could sense Marceau's presence as though he were sitting at the table behind me.

I didn't like the feeling.

With the plan now in full motion, I knew the moments would begin to slow their inexorable pace. It was always that way with me before a job. In the days, weeks, months after a score while I'm living high, traveling, enjoying the cafés and restaurants, not even close to thinking about the next job, time becomes a thing of beauty, to be savored in its passing. When a job is at hand, time begins to lose all meaning and form amidst the feverish planning, the research cutting across days, or weeks, when three in the morning could be the same as noon. When the final moment is upon me and I am on the job, time becomes the silent enemy. The blink of an eye can be fifteen minutes, a heartbeat ten. The hands of the clock race about its face like something chased by the Devil himself.

It's the moments between the end of planning and the start of the job I find the most unbearable. Time becomes the endless ticking of a clock in the hour before dawn when sleep eludes you. I become agitated, chain-smoke, pace until I've worn paths in the floor. Under normal circumstances those stretches are mercifully short. That wasn't going to be the case here. I was not used to working a job like this. Most of my thefts were solitary affairs with one, maybe two accomplices at most. Here, I felt like little more than the money man with others doing the actual work.

It's also a time when my innate paranoia is at its zenith, which probably accounts for why the guy sweeping the street beneath the arch attracted my attention. There was something off about him but I couldn't identify what it was.

There are several street sweepers wandering the streets of Bize. They're hired by the restaurant and shop owners and are a constant, if unobtrusive, sight throughout the tourist season. Usually pensioners, looking to supplement their income; sometimes a young foreigner working his or her way across Europe.

I tried to remember when last I'd seen one of them. They're easy enough to spot if you're looking; dark blue coveralls, a bandanna or hat to keep off the sun, sneakers or heavy work boots plus a small cart, a broom, a shovel and whatever other implements they need to collect the detritus that accumulates when tourists are about.

When the guy stepped out of the shadows for a moment, it came to me. He wasn't wearing sneakers or work boots but loafers. Polished loafers. And his cart was nowhere near. I'd never seen one of the street sweepers very far from their cart.

As I stood up from the table to investigate, he spotted me. He didn't run or even turn from his task as I approached him, which gave me pause. I stopped halfway across the court. He moved back into the shadows, then disappeared beyond the arch, his broom over his shoulder.

I started to return to my table, gave it a second thought, and walked over to the arch. By the time I got there, the man was nowhere in sight. Nor, I noted, was there any sign of a cart, though the broom was leaning against a wall. I stood there for several minutes, listening but heard nothing but the birds and distant traffic noise. Troubled, I passed back through the arch.

There, off to the side near my apartment wall, was a small pile of wrappers, bottle caps and dirt. A sound made me look back over my shoulder. A man in blue overalls, the same man I'd seen sweeping the street the morning after my arrival in Bize, came around the corner pushing his cart.

I looked down at his feet. He was wearing work boots. Turning, I stared back at the arch where the man in loafers had disappeared, an unwelcome frisson running up my spine.

Chapter 24

Several days passed without further sightings and I began to think I had imagined the man in loafers. I was also slipping deeper into agitation and frustrated frenzy. Impatient, snappy, I paced not only the floor of the apartment but the entire village of Bize.

I spilled drinks, left cigarettes burning in ashtrays and on the edges of tables. Out for a walk along the river one afternoon, Kaz became so infuriated with me she pushed me into the cold water. When my head broke the surface I glimpsed her turning up the trail and disappearing through a grove of almond trees. Pinkerton stood on the shore, staring at me in his stoic way, a look on his face that had 'idiot' written all over it.

Near the end of the third day, Mac called. He had made the rounds and gathered his crew. They would be flying to London in twos and threes over the next few days. He was already in London, holed up in a small apartment he'd rented on a weekly basis. It was one of those timeshare places that catered to the traveling businessman, equipped with all the amenities, including a high-speed Internet access line that Kaz could use when she arrived. He had already toured the museum once and planned to return that evening just before closing time.

Andreas called the following morning. The twins had arrived and he had made the deal for the trucks and the Range Rover. Except for some confusion at the Chunnel, when the Range Rover was forced to take a different railcar from the trucks, and Kostas, who was driving the Rover, got lost for several hours because he couldn't understand the English road signs, the trip into London had been uneventful.

After stashing one of the trucks, the Rover and the twins at an empty warehouse, Andreas had arrived at his cousin Eddie's house, safe and sound. The truck, he explained, was being loaded as we spoke.

At long last I felt the chaos of the last few days swirl into calm. Kaz was scheduled to fly to London first thing in the morning for a closer inspection of the security system. I would stay in Bize until the last moment. Next to the States, Britain was the most dangerous country for me to be seen in. It was thought best all around if I showed up the day of the heist and forsook any plans to do the town.

Pity. I rather liked London though most of my time there had been spent casing a target or stealing something.

Still, with Kaz gone, it would leave me with several days on my hands and I wasn't looking forward to that. The tourist season was in full swing so the Corsican wouldn't have much time to sit around and drink and talk. That left me to my own resources.

The night before Kaz left, we lay in bed, the sheet thrown to the floor. I was exhausted from days of waiting. I fell asleep listening to her breathe, feeling her fingers as she slid them through my hair, her fingertips on my face, touching my eyes, my nose, my lips, as though trying to memorize them.

I drifted into a strange dream. I was in a dark room or a tunnel. There were others there but I couldn't see them, just hear them as they moved about in the gloom. I kept calling for Kaz but my voice had no sound.

In the morning when I woke, Kaz was gone.

Chapter 25

I took a long hot shower, letting the stinging spray run through my hair and down my body until the water ran cool. I found a pair of chinos and a white T-shirt with something obscene written on it in Greek, and took Pinkerton out for a walk along the river.

While he read his pee-mail, I pulled the petals off flowers, chanting the age old 'she loves me' verse, skipped pebbles across the water, built a castle in the sand and, in general, moped. Now that I had her back, I didn't want to let her out of my sight. I was beginning to feel like a schoolboy whose girl had gone off on summer vacation without him. It was ridiculous. I found Pinkerton and persuaded him to follow me back to the apartment.

I found a fresh pack of Shermans and headed down to the restaurant for breakfast. There was a moment of shock when I thought I saw Kaz stepping into a shop further up the road. Telling myself I was being foolish, I bypassed the restaurant and headed to where I thought I'd seen her. It was a small store barely the size of a walk-in closet. Three racks of postcards sat outside the door. Inside, the wall and every available shelf space was filled with local trinkets. A low, glass-topped freezer full of ice-cream bars of all kinds worked double duty as a counter. Along the back wall stood an upright cooler, full of soda pop and Heineken beer.

What wasn't there was Kaz.

A young, dark haired woman, sitting on a small stool behind the freezer, looked up when I entered. She was reading an old James N. Frey paperback novel. I smiled, mumbled an apology in French and backed out into the street.

This was idiotic, I said to myself. Kaz was in England. In the restaurant, I plopped down in the back booth and ordered something from the menu. The food was as good as always though it seemed dry and tasteless to me; I left most of it unfinished. Before I finished my coffee, the tourists began to show up and it wasn't long before I could no longer tolerate their chatter or their stares.

It was just past noon when I made my way back to the apartment. There was a message from Mac waiting for me. Kaz had arrived and the two of them were off to tour the museum, which proved that it couldn't have been her I saw earlier. It bothered me that Kaz hadn't called but I shook that off. Everything was in place. What was there for me to complain about?

Feeling hungry, I warmed some cinnamon rolls smothered in butter in the microwave, made a pot of coffee, grabbed my notebooks and set everything out on the patio. I was going stir-crazy and if today was any example, I had to find something to occupy my mind. Since I enjoy the planning and the preparation as much as I enjoy the actual theft, I thought that going over it all might calm me down, center me.

It didn't.

I had gone over it all so many times that I knew it by heart, knew that it was as perfect as it could be. There was only one false note and it had nothing to do with the planning or the preparation.

The false note was Dieter.

I still couldn't figure the angle there, which bothered me. Any blind spot is potential trouble and the whole Dieter thing was a black hole. If, as Wu had said, this was an organized crime squabble, why the interest in me? I have no organized crime connections. I may have stolen a painting or two for one Don or another but it

153

was always an independent thing. I worked for no one but me and that was well known.

After an hour or more of pounding my head against the problem, I came away with little more than a headache and a ravenous thirst for something cold. I stood up, stretched and just as I was turning away from the balcony rail, something in the shadows in the lane next to the restaurant caught my eye.

My first thought was that it was Kaz. But that was impossible. Kaz was in London. Shaking my head, I stepped away from the railing. I tried to convince myself it was pre-job jitters as I stepped back into the apartment. But try as I might, I couldn't shake the feeling that she had been standing there watching me.

I ran downstairs and across the lane. One of the local dogs was snuffling around a garbage can. I disturbed a couple kissing in a doorway, the woman turned away, embarrassed, and buttoned her blouse as I made a hasty apology in broken French to her boyfriend. Following the lane, I made my way into the old part of the city, way past where the tourists venture. It was growing dark by the time I found myself coming up on the opposite side of the restaurant. No sign of Kaz. But then there couldn't have been, I told myself. This was insane.

The Corsican was in a jovial mood when I returned to the restaurant. The place had been packed to the rafters all day and the late dinner crowd was just beginning to arrive. I sat at the back table reserved for family and friends and drank one beer after another, trying to shake the image of Kaz and the mystery of Dieter and Marceau from my mind.

The Corsican and I played several sets of dominos in-between him making the rounds of customers, holding forth as he loves to do and pouring thimble-sized shots of Eau de Vie for everyone.

Sometime after midnight when the last of the tourists had left, I staggered back to the apartment. Pinkerton was lying on his cushion, back legs out to one side at a strange angle, his front legs straight out, his head between them. He looked up at me with limpid brown eyes as I stumbled through the door.

"Sorry, pup," I said, realizing I had forgotten to fill his food bowl before I left. I went into the kitchen and grabbed his food from the cabinet next to the sink. I was about to pour it into his bowl when I saw that the bowl was half full already. I tried to think, the beer I'd drunk making that little task trickier than I cared, or was able, to contemplate.

Had I fed him before I left and forgotten it? No. I was sure I hadn't. Then maybe he hadn't finished what I'd given him that morning? No. I remembered stubbing my toe on the heavy ceramic food bowl earlier in the day and it had been all but empty then. So when had I filled it?

My alcohol-befuddled brain couldn't work it out so I closed up the bag and put it back in the cabinet.

Like Scarlet O'Hara, I would think about it tomorrow.

Chapter 26

The following morning I woke up frustrated, the sweat-soaked sheets twisted about my body. Sleep had been elusive and during those moments when it had taken me, my dreams had been frantic and not a little frightening. The harder I tried to retain their shreds, the faster they slipped away until there was nothing left but a dull ache behind my eyes and the rancid taste of last night's beer and cigarettes on my tongue.

I managed to brew a pot of coffee without spilling or breaking anything. With a mouth like the bottom of a parrot's cage, I watched, with voracious need, the black gold drip into the pot, and swore off beer and cigarettes and late night domino games, not necessarily in that order. Midway through the second cup of coffee I forsook one of those pledges and lit up a Sherman out on the balcony, watching the sun paint the tops of the buildings in golden light. I had four more days to kill and if I didn't do something with my time I was going to go batshit.

It was essential for me get motivated, pumped up. With the Dieter/Marceau mystery preying on my mind, I needed to do a little research to make it less mysterious. Kaz had taken her laptop with her, so I would have to find a computer. I rummaged around in the closet and found some maps and a phone directory. There was an Internet café in Béziers and one in Narbonne. I opted for the one in Narbonne, called, took the hours and directions and prepared to go.

I've been to Béziers and Narbonne many times and enjoy both, though I have to say that of the two, I prefer Narbonne. The Canal du Midi locks in Béziers are an architectural wonder. Wandering about the Park of the

Poets is a day well spent but, for me, there is something dark and brooding about the town. Perhaps it was the sacking that took place in the early part of the thirteenth century during the Albigensian Crusade. Maybe the ghosts of all those killed the day Béziers was all but burned to the ground by the crusaders still linger in the back alleys and narrow streets. Seems ridiculous when I think about it but the fact remains that oft times, especially at night, the town gives me the willies.

Narbonne is the site of the first Roman city in France. The town was always bright and sunny with many narrow, twisting streets lined with beautiful old buildings, many in the architectural style of Narbonne's Roman ancestry. Kaz and I had spent many a day there, haunting the cafés and shops, doing the tourist thing, as she liked to call it. I even owned a building near the heart of the city, overlooking the canal. A restaurant, café and bar inhabit the ground floor while the three above are rented out as flats. I could do a little sightseeing, play landlord and see what I could dig up on the Internet.

Pinkerton's walk took up an hour of the morning. Despite my impatience to get going, I let him read all his pee-mail and reply in kind. Once back at the apartment, preparing for the day-long trip took another hour. It was nearly eleven when I passed through the arch and headed toward my car. I kept looking over my shoulder, half expecting to see Kaz. It seemed that the hallucinations of yesterday were gone.

It was a beautiful, clear day, the sun bright in a stainless blue sky. The air smelled of jasmine and suntan lotion and rang with the sound of children's laughter coming from the river. Once on the main highway, I felt buoyant and happy. Nothing like action to dispel the moody blues.

Except for some idiot who believed that running his front bumper several inches from my rear bumper at 120 kilometers an hour somehow made him more of a man, the trip to Narbonne was leisurely enough. It felt good to be doing something. I was beginning to wonder how I had spent over a year cooped up on the island without going out of my head. Finding a parking spot down near the canal, I made my way over to the bridge and into the main square.

A bandstand was set up on one end of the square, huge black speakers at either corner, bright bunting across the top of the stage. Four guys in leather pants and vests were setting up smaller speakers, a set of drums and microphone stands.

I hurried across the square, past a pharmacy and turned up a small street. Par for the course, it turned out to be the wrong one. I really needed to work on my French. The day was getting hot and my shirt was beginning to sag with sweat. I backtracked, got lost and after a couple more false turns I managed to find the Internet café.

It was down one of the shabbier streets of Narbonne, off the beaten tourist path. Gaming posters hung in the window. Several cases of empty Coke and Pepsi bottles, Mountain Dew and some French sugar beverage I didn't recognize, lined the sidewalk beneath a heavily-curtained window. There were few people in the street as I crossed. The air smelled of garbage stewing in the heat. Two cats, screeching, darted out from a small alley and crossed in front of me in a blur of fur and fury. When I looked up, Marceau was stepping from the alley where the cats had run.

"I told you we would meet again," he said.

Before I could turn and run, rough hands grabbed me from behind. I brought my foot down hard on the instep of one of my attackers, heard him howl in pain. As his hands slipped from my shoulder, I swung my elbow into the ribs of the other man but missed.

Twisting furiously, I tried to break away from my second attacker but before I could get free I felt a sharp prick in my upper arm. My attacker let go, pushed me away – hard – and stepped back. I recognized him as one of the men who had been following me on the island.

My arm felt as though it were on fire and refused to respond to my mind's commands. It hung, limp, at my side as if finding itself attached to something it didn't understand and didn't want to be near. I could see my fingers twitching in a wild display. It reminded me of Jerry Lee Lewis's fingers on the piano keyboard during a rendition of 'Great Balls of Fire.'

A great heat spread across my chest, down my torso, up my neck to my face. I felt as if I were dissolving. The man standing across from me split into two and then into two more. When the heat reached my legs, they buckled and I fell to the rough pavement, feeling nothing as my head cracked against stone.

Chapter 27

When I awoke, I felt as if I were back in the dream of the previous night. It was dark. I couldn't make a sound other than a grunt. And I couldn't move. The only thing that convinced me it wasn't a dream was the pounding headache that threatened to split my skull.

I was tied to something, a chair probably, though it could have been a medieval torture rack for all I could tell. Whatever it was, it wouldn't rock in any direction I tried to move it. The thing was bolted to the ground. Pushing my tongue between clenched lips, I discovered that my mouth was taped shut. The darkness was a hood pulled over my head but I could tell the room was dark as no light filtered through the cloth of the hood.

That Marceau had achieved his desire to have me alone was not in doubt. I could still see him in my mind's eye, like the after-image from a flash bulb. Where I was, or how long I'd been out, was anybody's guess. I squirmed about, testing the bindings on my ankles and wrists. They were tight, unforgiving and painful, cutting deeper into my flesh the more I tried to move. Not that movement of any kind was easy. I felt as if every muscle in my body had been drawn taut and then beaten with rubber bats. Weak, shaky, I slumped back in my chair and tried to think.

There were faint, scurrying noises in the room. I tried hard not to visualize what those furtive noises might be. The old horror movie Willard kept popping up in my mind faster than I could banish it. I could hear water running, a faint gurgling sound that seemed to be coming from my left. The air was dank, cool, smelling of mildew and motor oil mixed with dirt that had been around for a long time. An old garage, in all probability. Somewhere quiet and out of the way.

At some point I dozed, or passed out from the pain. My arms were pinned back awkwardly and the muscles in my shoulders were beginning to spasm. When I came to again, I found myself needing to pee like a racehorse. I was just coming around to the unpleasant idea of pissing in my pants when the lights went on.

I discerned several sets of footfalls moving about. Two sets split up on either side of me. The hood was yanked from my head and I sat for a moment blinking and twisting my head away from the harsh light that was shining in my face. As my vision cleared, I was able to make out a blurred shape standing across from me. The shape resolved into Marceau.

He nodded to one of the men who came over and pulled the tape from my mouth. The guy was anything but gentle and it felt as if my lips were being ripped off. Tears sprang to my eyes and the only thing that kept me from crying out was the vision I had of crushing the little Frenchman's throat. I forced myself to calm down, to find what center I could. Anger is only useful in certain situations and this didn't seem like one of them.

"Dr. Livingstone, I presume," I said. The words felt like wadded-up paper in my mouth. "Sorry I don't have a beer to offer you. The service here is lousy and the place is a bit dingy."

"Ever the smartass, I see," he answered. "I have a few questions for you, as you might imagine."

"Yeah, well, I have a few for you but somehow I doubt you'll be very forthcoming."

"No, Mr. Samsel. I think not. Your questions are of no importance to me. The answers to mine are."

"Like daddy always said, it ain't a fair world."

"As I understand it, your father died when you were quite young."

"See what I mean?"

Marceau's lips quivered and he dipped his head a fraction. The guy standing to my right turned and slapped me hard across the face, stepped back and resumed his position by my side.

"I am tiring of this useless banter, Mr. Samsel. I wish to know of Dieter's plans."

My head was ringing from the slap and it took me a moment to focus my eyes. I could taste the blood on my tongue, feel it sliding from the corner of my mouth.

"Were those his vacation plans or the ones for world domination?" I said when I was able. "I'm afraid I'm a little confused at the moment."

"Now, now Mr. Samsel," he said, shaking his head and tsk-tsking as though trying to maintain his patience with a small child.

"We can make this very hard or, we can end this *toute de suite* with your cooperation. It really is your choice. Either way I get what I want. I do hope you are smart enough to see that."

The way he said 'end this' shot through me like an arrow. The 'very hard' part didn't make me feel any better either. This idiot was seriously deranged. As I watched, he moved from the shadow into the light. He was holding a small riding quirt in his hand, tapping it against his leg. There was a bead of sweat on his upper lip and a gleam in his eye Torquemada would have recognized. He was breathing like a lover breathes before the dance of the beast with two backs gets into full swing. I decided to shift gears.

"I already told you, Marceau," I said. "I have nothing going with Dieter."

"Lies," he spat through clenched teeth, spittle flying across the room. He nodded his head and one of the guards turned toward me again. This time it wasn't a slap. The blow caught me on the point of the chin. Had I not been turning my head away, it may well have broken my jaw. As it was, my head felt as if it had exploded, my brain bouncing around inside its womb of protective fluid like a soccer ball at a hot World Cup game. Looking back at Marceau, my vision clearing, the look on his face gave me a sinking feeling that the old protective fluid was going to get a real workout.

Spitting blood to one side, "If you think that's a lie, Marceau," I said, "then we have a real problem."

"No, Mr. Samsel, it is you who has the problem. One which I will rectify when you tell me what I want to know."

He was breathing heavier now, the quirt dancing off his leg. I swear, the guy had a hard-on, he was enjoying this so much.

Genuine fear began to maul my usual sarcastic detachment. This was a no-win situation for me. I didn't have anything going with Dieter but Marceau wasn't going to believe that, no matter what. And I couldn't just make up something as I didn't have the slightest idea what the sick fuck was looking for. On the other hand, if I told him about the Marbles, about needing Dieter only to get to the States, he wouldn't buy that either. He would just think I was being evasive and set his goons on me again. He was convinced I was involved in something, something that had to do with him. If I was going to have even a ghost of a chance to get out of this in one piece, I needed to find out what that something was.

"What have you got going with Dieter?" I asked.

That took him aback. He stared at me for a long moment, the rhythm of the quirt slowing. I thought maybe I had changed the direction of things, then he smiled and nodded his head again. Pain exploded in my side when the guard's fist plunged into my lower rib cage. I nearly ripped my arm from its socket trying to bend into the white hot pain. He backhanded me with a right and brought his left around, landing a meaty fist just over my ear. By the time my eyes began to focus again, I was gasping for air, fully aware for the first time that I might not survive this meeting.

"I will ask the questions, Mr. Samsel," he said.

"Whatever," I muttered when I was able, still flippant despite my mounting fear.

"Why do you protect him, Mr. Samsel?" he said. He began to pace. His voice was soft now and I had to strain to hear him over the loud buzz in my ears. He wasn't nodding to his men to break the rest of my ribs over the snide remark. Maybe he didn't hear it. Maybe the direction of the conversation had changed.

"Dieter Schulz is an evil man," he continued. "A crime lord of the first order. His kind must be brought down, eliminated. My job is to see that such men are dealt with, removed from civilized society."

So you could replace him, I thought, but knew better than to say it.

"You leave your island refuge to see Herr Schulz," he continued. "You have a private conversation with him, something few are privileged enough to be offered."

That was true enough, I thought. Dieter saw very few people in person. The germ thing was a big deal to him. Most had to sit in a glass-enclosed booth and talk to him through microphones. I was one of the few he opted to see in the flesh, so to speak. I had never understood why, but who was to say what went through the paranoid mind of a man like Dieter Schulz?

The import of Marceau's words hit me. He knew I'd seen him in person and in private. How could he have known that? Did he have someone planted inside Dieter's organization? Someone deep enough to know the details of Dieter's inner sanctum?

"Shortly after," Marceau continued, "you boarded one of his private, overseas flights accompanied by a man named Kellerman."

"What?" I said.

"Do you deny that you went to the United States?"

I breathed a small sigh of relief. He hadn't caught my surprise at the mention of Kellerman's name. Now I had confirmation that it had been Kellerman I'd seen upon boarding the plane for the return trip. That it was likely that Kellerman had taken out the two thugs who had accosted me in China Town.

"No," I said. "I told you before that I went to see Dieter because I needed something. That something was a trip to the States."

"To see the Chinaman, Wu," he said.

I started to correct him then thought better of it. Marceau didn't care about Wu's pedigree anymore than the two guys in San Francisco had, nor did he have a sense of humor. I'd probably just get another kick in the ribs for the remark.

"Yeah," I said. "I went to see Wu."

"Your Mr. Wu seems to have disappeared," he said.

"Disappeared?" I tried to plaster a look of concern on my battered face. "He was just a harmless old man," I continued. "You didn't have to hurt him. He couldn't have told you anything."

"You misunderstand me, Mr. Samsel. It was not I who did anything to him, though I would very much like to talk to him. Do you know where he's gone?"

"I have no idea," I said, tensing for the blow I was sure was coming. "He didn't say anything to me about disappearing. But then he wouldn't. I hardly know the guy. He's just a source of information. Nothing more."

"What of the two men I sent to intercept you there? I suppose you know nothing of them as well?"

Thoughts raced through my head. Marceau seemed to know things he couldn't know and not things I expected he would know, like the fate of his men. I decided to give it to him straight. What did I have to lose at this point?

"Foul Mouth and Growl," I muttered.

"Pardon?" Marceau said.

"Your two guys … yeah, I ran into them. They took a bullet for you, Marceau."

"You shot them?"

"It wasn't me," I said. "I was busy being their punching bag at the time."

"Kellerman, then," he said, thoughtful. "I will deal with him soon enough."

Marceau had stopped his pacing. The quirt was quiet at his side. He began to rub his chin with the fingers of his left hand, staring off into the corner of the room.

"You said that you went to Wu for information. What sort of information were you seeking?

"Floor plans, wiring diagrams, that sort of thing. I'm a thief. Those are the kind of things I need to do a job."

"The job with Dieter," he said.

"I told you, I have nothing going with Dieter."

Big mistake. The blow caught me on the jaw before I could twist my head away. The guy was wearing a ring and it slashed across my cheekbone like a hot

166

knife. Blood dripped down my cheek and into my mouth. Before I could spit it out, he hit me again, this time in the ribs. The only satisfaction for me was that the blow caused me to spit the mouthful of blood in his face. He stepped back, wiping at his eyes. The other guy moved in. He hit me high in the rib cage with his left, followed by a right to my jaw. He was pulling back for another roundhouse right when Marceau stopped him with a barked order. With obvious reluctance, the man stepped back, a look of disappointment washing over his face.

"There is an interesting rumor in that nefarious world your kind inhabits," Marceau said. He was pacing again, the quirt slapping against his leg in a slow rhythm. "The rumor is," he continued, facing me now, "that you managed to steal a painting from Herr Schulz. Two, in fact. Picassos. Where does he keep his paintings, Mr. Samsel?"

Despite the pain, the question almost made me smile. Could that be what this was about? Was Marceau after Dieter's paintings? Was I going to end up a dead man because Marceau was lusting after Dieter's art?

I could feel anger taking the place of fear. None of this was making any sense. I had nothing going with Dieter and, though I did know where he kept his paintings, I also knew he had tightened his security considerably since last I'd been inside the vault. Marceau would have to nuke the place to get at them and what would be the point of that?

"There is, or was, a section of his underground bunker designed to house the paintings," I said, feeling no guilt for giving the location away. If Marceau was that deep into Dieter's organization, he would find out about the vault soon enough, if he didn't know already. And, for all I knew, Dieter may well have moved it.

"I understand you did some security consulting for him? After the theft of the Picassos. Though, of course, I'm sure Herr Schulz was not aware his thief and his consultant were one and the same."

Again, inside information. I doubted there were five people who knew I had discussed security with Dieter after the theft.

"Yeah. I spoke with him a bit about that," I said. "He asked. I gave him some advice. Whether he took it or not is anybody's guess."

Marceau was pacing again. He was looking off into a dark corner of the room as though thinking. The quirt slapped against his thigh.

"I will humor you for a moment, Mr. Samsel, and say that it might interest you to know that his collection remains where it was prior to the theft of the Picassos. However, he does plan to move it very soon. I understand the preparations are being made even as we have this pleasant little chat."

This little revelation made me hope I was up-to-date on my life insurance policy premiums. Marceau would never have revealed this to me if he had any intention of letting me walk away from here alive. He wanted Dieter's collection and he thought I knew where it was going. I could feel the anger building in me again over the hopelessness of the situation I was in. He stopped, turned toward me, pointing his quirt in my face.

"I want to know where it is going and when the shipment will be made," he said through bared teeth.

"Look, Marceau," I exploded. "I don't know. I'm not working for Dieter. Why won't you just accept that fact and stop asking me questions I can't answer? Then maybe we can go off, have a friendly drink and you can set your bulldogs on some schoolchildren while you get your rocks off watching."

I could see this little retort wasn't going to go over well. I swear, there are moments when I can be stupid beyond belief and this was going to be one of the finest of those moments.

And probably my last.

The color rose in Marceau's face. Veins at his temples and neck swelled and throbbed until I thought they would burst. He slammed the quirt against his leg and the two men moved toward me.

I was searching for suitable last words when the loud roar of an engine came to life nearby.

Chapter 28

Marceau, and the men who were about to pound me into chicken fried steak, turned. The wall on the other side of the room exploded in a shower of wooden splinters and rusty nails. A large, American-made SUV plowed midway into the room, crushing the huge klieg light that had been focused on me. The room was plunged into near darkness.

I saw a figure emerge from the driver's seat, recognizing her at once. It was Kaz. I thought for a moment I was hallucinating, that the final blow had been struck and I was suffering brain death, seeing Kaz in the last feeble firings of my neurons.

But it wasn't brain death.

And it was definitely Kaz.

With a twirl and a high kick, she sent Marceau sprawling to the ground. An arc of blue light crossed the room like twin lightning bolts and two metal prongs buried themselves into the chest of the man on my left. He screamed as Kaz gave him the full benefit of taser technology. The third man rushed her. She caught him with a heavy boot between the legs and then beat him to the floor with her fists.

Hell hath no fury like a woman whose boyfriend is tied to a chair and being tortured in a dingy garage.

Marceau was groaning and trying to rise. She kicked him in the head and he slumped hard to the floor, quiet. A quick poke in the ribs of the guy she'd beaten confirmed he wouldn't be moving anytime soon so she walked over to the guy she'd tasered and gave him another quick jolt. His body arched off the floor but I doubted he was feeling any pain at that point. Then concern replaced the stern look in her eyes and she strode over to me.

"Are you all right?" she asked.

"I've had better days," I managed to mumble through pulped and bloody lips.

She pulled a knife from a sheath tied to her ankle and slit the bonds at my feet and wrists. There were a thousand questions flooding my mind. None of them could find their way to my mouth.

I doubled over in pain, puking off to one side when she tried to help me up from the chair. She set me back down, muttering harsh words in Romanian under her breath. I thought for a moment she was going to walk over and crush Marceau's head flat with her heel.

"We must go," she whispered.

She slipped her arm beneath mine and tried again to help me rise from the chair. Midway up, the room flashed white as a lightning storm with me the center of its attention and my legs went as boneless as Harry Potter's arm when hit by Lockhart's spell. I pissed my pants but managed to stay on my feet.

Over what felt like a week of agony, she helped me stumble across the floor to the car and eased me into the front seat. I bit down through the skin of my cheek trying to keep in the screams of pain. My mouth was filled with blood, which was leaking out and dripping down my shirt. Through a blur of tears, I watched Kaz hurry around the front of the SUV. She hesitated at the door, gave Marceau another good crack of her boot in the ribs, then got in and guided the truck back into the street.

I gritted my teeth, my eyes squeezed shut as she made her way through the streets of Narbonne and out onto the N113, heading in the opposite direction from Bize. At some point she handed me several Ibuprofen and made me chase them down with water. I nearly gagged on them but managed to swallow them. Between them and the endorphins flooding my system, the pain seemed to subside somewhat. I finally managed to open my eyes and unclench my teeth long enough to look over at her.

"How?" I managed to gasp.

"For a man who prides himself as a watcher of others you are quite unaware that others watch you as well," she said.

She looked over at me. Seeing I wasn't exactly up for a Zen Koan moment, she continued. "The drive back from St. Chinian: I saw your reaction to the ones you thought were following us. All day you had been looking about as if you expected your worst enemy to appear from behind a tree. And I knew you were holding back from me. From your friends. You men will never learn that a woman knows these things. Father always admonishes me that I must learn to trust my man, so I considered that you had your reasons for keeping this from me. Still, it bothered me, so I called Spiros. He did some checking around the island and called me back. He told me of the problems you had there with this Frenchman."

"But I thought you were in England. The message from Mac …"

"I told Mac of my fears, that these men would find you if they had not already. He wanted to confront you, convince you to come to England early but this I knew you could not do. So I persuaded him to remain silent, to say I had arrived. Then I watched you to see what would crawl from the dark spaces in the woodwork."

I lay back in the seat, listening to the car's tires humming over the pavement. I felt weaker than I ever had in my life. The smell of urine and sweat and

172

lingering fear was pungent. I thought, not for the first time, of throwing in the towel on the job. Then Marceau's sneering look came to mind, the easy way with which he nodded his head to have his minions deliver pain. The anger came back in full force, riding atop the pain and fatigue.

"Where are we heading?" I managed to say when she turned off the main highway.

"A friend's place. He is away on business. We can use his place to get you back on your feet. I don't wish to risk the apartment. I don't know where those men acquired you."

"Acquired? How James Bond of you." I said, making a vain attempt at levity. "Spy novels are not a good way to increase your English skills."

She stuck out her tongue and gave me a look that, despite my immense pain, caused a shiver of desire to cascade across my nether regions.

"Uh," I said. "Friend's apartment. Right. Good idea. Then what?"

"I must get to London," she said, a hint of playful mirth in her voice. "I am behind in the schedule. You will stay at my friend's place, out of sight. Rest. You have only a few days to ready yourself."

We made the rest of the trip in silence. I guess I dozed. It was nearing dusk when we passed through Capestang and turned off onto a narrow, one lane road.

We soon pulled up beside a small cottage not far from the village of Poilhes. There was a car parked ahead of us, a small, mud encrusted Jetta with a dented rear fender and stickers from all over France plastered to the trunk and rear bumper.

I could smell grapes as Kaz helped me from the SUV. I looked around in the receding light and realized we were in the middle of a vineyard. The sound of the cigales matched the buzzing in my head.

The front end of the SUV was pretty mangled, the bumper bent back into the front fenders and angled down, pointing toward the ground. The headlights were smashed, the hood buckled and the grill was a twisted maze of metal slats. Still and all, it had held up well considering the thickness of the garage door it had gone through.

"At least you found some useful purpose for an SUV," I remarked through gritted teeth. "Where did you manage to find one?"

"It's tourist season," she said and left it at that. I decided not to pursue it. Someone would no doubt be majorly pissed when they returned from lunch to find their gas-guzzling Goliath gone.

Kaz got me inside with a minimum of pain and started a hot bath going, pouring in half a box of Epsom salts. Helping me undress, she eased me into the tub. I tried to swallow the scream that came with the heat and the movement without success, bellowing like an embattled bear as I slipped beneath the steamy water. Soon, however, the heat and salts began to draw the torment from my limbs. I suspected a lower rib was broken but there wasn't much I could do about it. Kaz disappeared for a while. I could hear her talking to someone on the phone but she was too far away for me to understand the words.

When she returned, she had changed her clothes, replacing the leather pants and heavy shirt for a loose blouse and pair of jeans. She was still wearing her shit-kicker boots.

"I must go," she said, her lips brushing my forehead. "Your flight is booked through Montpellier but you must not go there now. Marceau will be expecting you to fly away. I will book you on the TGV out of Toulouse to Paris, using your other passport. There is a small airport outside the city. Very private. I have arranged for someone to fly you to London. A friend will come and pick you up and drive you to the train station. Do not leave this house for any reason. I have brought things from the apartment you will need and there are many supplies here for you. Oh, and I have called a friend of father's. He is a doctor, one we can trust. He will come by tomorrow to look at you."

"Kaz ..." I started to say, wanting to thank her.

"There is no need to say the words you have in mind. I love you, Daniel Samsel. If you promise never to keep things from me again, then I will forgive you as well." And with that she turned away. I could hear her zipping up a suitcase in the front room, heard her heels click across the tiled floor of the kitchen, then the creak of the front door as it opened.

"Oh," she called. "One last thing. Remember to feed the dog next time you are left in charge of him. He does not like to miss his mealtime."

So much for the mystery of the full dog bowl, I thought, as the door closed with a soft click.

Chapter 29

I slept fitfully that night. It seemed no matter which way I tried to lie, something hurt. The brandy I found in the house helped a little but I was reluctant to rely on it. I had to be up and about in three days and though the booze might dull the pain, it would also slow the healing.

The doctor came by early the next morning. He looked me over from head to toe and assured me I was still amongst the living. Reluctant as I was to agree with him, I knew he was right. Death couldn't possibly be as painful.

He was as sure as he could be, without x-rays, that the rib I thought was broken was merely bruised. Merely indeed. Stephen King said the road to hell was paved with adverbs. I felt as if those adverbs had been used to pound my ribs back into place.

After sampling a glass of my brandy, the doctor handed me a bottle of Ibuprofen, wished me *bon voyage* and left. I hobbled to the bedroom and stood naked before the full length mirror. Marceau's boys had certainly gotten in their licks. I was swollen and discolored from the middle of my pelvis to my shoulder. This, at least, I could cover. My face, however, was going to be a problem. I looked like a raccoon that had been hit by a truck.

The eye above the cut was swollen and almost shut; the purplish discoloration extended to my lips. The other eye had fared better, though the skin around it looked more the color of a steak that had been left out too long. My ears were ringing like steam whistles at lunchtime, while little guys with big sledgehammers were scampering about inside my skull, trying to force their way out. I wouldn't be riding in the Tour de France anytime soon, I thought, but then I had never been inclined to ride it before my meeting with Marceau, so it didn't seem like much of a loss.

I spent the next three days taking long hot baths, sipping on the brandy when the pain was sharp and thinking about my encounter with Marceau. In my more far-out fantasies, I hoped Kaz had killed him, or at least done serious, debilitating harm, as otherwise I had a bad feeling I would be seeing him again. But then, were that the case, Kaz would be in a world of hurt I wouldn't want to see her in, so I relented and wished him only the world's worst headache.

Not one to find silver linings in dark clouds, at least I had a better idea of what Marceau was up to. Wu had been right. Marceau wanted Dieter's collection for himself. That he wanted to bring Dieter down was also apparent, though I doubted it was for humanity's sake. He wanted to seat himself on Dieter's throne. There was a power grab going on and Marceau had someone high up the food chain giving him intel on the comings and goings of Dieter's inner sanctum. My suspicions kept coming around to Helga but they wouldn't stick there. She was devoted to the man. Helga betraying Dieter would be like Christopher Moore's Biff dropping a dime on Jesus.

What still confused me was Kellerman's role in all this. Marceau had mentioned him in passing and I didn't see Kellerman as the mole. He wasn't in deep enough for one thing. And it looked like they were working in opposition anyway. Wu had said there was a power struggle going on. Perhaps Kellerman represented some other group that wanted the same thing as Marceau?

I went around and around the little I knew and, in the end, came away more mystified than when I started. I gave some thought to calling Dieter, to warn him, but there wasn't a phone in the small cottage, so I had to let it go. It wasn't that I felt I owed Dieter anything. He was the kind of guy who would have me killed in a heartbeat if an advantageous reason arose. It was more the thought of pissing off Marceau that prompted the thought of a call to Dieter. I'd do a lot to ruin just a single moment of his day.

Midway through the morning of the day before I was due in London, a lanky guy dressed in tweeds, complete with hunting cap and sporting a clipped, British accent showed up at the door. His face was flushed as if he had walked through the vineyard to get here. His nose was narrow, once broken, with a downward hook on the end that nearly touched his thin, pursed lips.

He was not the talkative type, preferring to puff on a long, slim, rather sweet-smelling cigar, looking about the small cottage and nodding his head here and there as if he were considering buying the place. I gathered my things, did one last check around and then he led me out to a battered, camouflage-painted Toyota Land Cruiser. Somehow the car didn't fit his personality; I was expecting a Bentley or something, but he seemed to handle it well enough. We made the trip to Toulouse in relative silence with only the sounds of Bach drifting from the speakers in the dash.

Chapter 30

The English air was heavy and stank of jet fuel as I stepped from the airport at Stanstead. The sky was a uniform gray with dark clouds crowding the eastern sky, the sun a dull white wedge struggling up from the horizon, trying to part them. Above the roar of jets I could hear the far off sound of thunder. I hailed a cab and directed it on a circuitous route to a small hotel I used to frequent on the outskirts of London. Paranoia never falls from fashion.

The rooms were small, though the furnishings were plush: all hardwood and lace curtains, with a small tiled bathroom containing a tub big enough to fit two in comfort. It had a fine little restaurant, with a well-stocked bar on the premises and an expansive lobby with elegant chairs that invited you to sit and read for a while. Overall, the place had the proud stature of a fine old racehorse after a lifelong career of winner's circles, now beyond stud, grazing in the sun amidst whispered tales of glories past.

The rat-trap two-seater Cessna flight from Paris to London in the gray hours before dawn had been harrowing. The buffeting winds and fickle thermals had played havoc with the legacy from Marceau's men, especially my ribs. With every twist of the fuselage it felt as if javelins were being thrust into my side. Compared with that, the train ride from Toulouse was a walk in the park.

While trying to doze with the rhythmic click-clacking of the wheels beneath me, I remembered that my mother would hop freights when I was a boy, when we had no money and had to get out of town fast. Once, on a trip from Minnesota to Idaho, flush with some new-found riches, we had ridden in a real rail car where there were upholstered seats instead of bales of hay and the passengers didn't wear ragged, food-stained clothes and smell like moldy laundry and stale whiskey. It has been a long time since I'd ridden a train like that and, with my hatred of flying, I wondered why I didn't ride them more often. I guess you just get used to the immediacy planes provide. That was the problem with the world. Time was moving too fast and we all had to hustle to stay abreast of it.

After stashing the small tartan suitcase and red leather valise Kaz had brought me into the closet, I headed downstairs to the small restaurant. The place was all dark leather and darker wood and smelled of yeasty beer, cigars and cooking oil. There was an old guy in a tatty suit and vest hunched over a Martini at one end of the short bar. He was toying with the olive at the end of a toothpick and mumbling to himself. Two old women dressed in identical gingham dresses with lace collars sat at one of the back tables drinking tea.

The bartender, black bow tie, polka dot vest over starched white shirt, was polishing glasses with a terry cloth towel. I ordered a cup of coffee. The guy's eyebrows curled in an arch when he saw my face but he said nothing, just filled a heavy mug with coffee and placed it in front of me. He slid a silver cream and sugar set in my direction, then returned to his polishing. I dropped two sugar cubes into the steaming liquid, stirred in a dollop of cream and sat sipping it, gazing at my reflection in the dusky mirror.

The cut from the goon's ring was a thin red welt crossing my cheek just below my eye. The swelling in my cheeks and nose had gone down but both sides of my face sported an assortment of colors; none of them appetizing. I had makeup in the valise which would cover all that, somewhat. The thing I worried most about were the ribs. My right side was still painful and I winced whenever I took a deep breath. If I ended up having to run anywhere, I was done for.

I finished the coffee and headed back to my room. Unwrapping a clean glass, I half filled it with water and went to sit by the window. It had started raining while I'd been in the bar. I parted the thin, yellow curtains, opened the window and watched the water fall to earth. There was a metallic, ozone smell to the rain.

My mind was free from antsy thoughts for the first time in days. The calm before the storm. We would all be meeting later in the day at the warehouse where Andreas had stashed the trucks. I took a last sip of the water, set the glass down on the sill, slipped off my shoes and crawled into bed, not bothering to remove my clothes.

The jangling of the phone woke me several hours later. It was Kaz. She asked if I was ready. I could hear the tension in her voice. I could feel it in mine when I replied I was. She said she'd meet me in front of the hotel in thirty minutes and to wear a jacket. I understood that last comment when I walked over to the window. A cool, moist breeze was blowing in. The rain had turned to a misty drizzle.

Kaz was true to her word, arriving thirty minutes later riding a dark blue moped. A line from a Sinead song flashed through my mind. Something about black boys riding mopeds but I couldn't tease out another line from my scattered thoughts. I wondered if Sinead was still recording. I had always rather liked her voice. There weren't a lot of English language radio stations on the island so I wasn't up on who was singing and who wasn't. I made a note to ask Kaz but knew as I did so that I would forget.

As I settled in the seat behind her, she gunned the engine and ran one hand up my leg. I wrapped my arms around her and she sped away from the curb. Her back was warm against my chest. I peered out over her shoulder and watched as she maneuvered through traffic. The rain splattering on the helmet's visor soon blurred my vision, turning the scene ahead into multicolored pinpoints of light.

My side began to ache, the pain pulsing to the rhythm of the machine. We drove for twenty minutes or so, then turned up a small alleyway that widened into a vast, concrete lot. Half the mercury vapor lights were out and the other half were flickering. Purplish shadows wavered and danced across the pools of water as we sped across the lot to a warehouse at the far end. As we approached, the front door began to rise. Kaz pulled in and I could hear the door reverse direction and close.

"Are you well?" Kaz asked when she removed her helmet. "The ride was not so rough on you?"

"I'm fine, Kaz," I said, though my voice sounded strained even to me. I heard a noise and looked up. Andreas was standing on a catwalk watching us. He turned away when he saw me notice him. Looking around I spotted the two trucks and the Range Rover parked off to one side. The carriage on the decoy truck was lower than the other. It was loaded and ready to roll.

"Who's driving the decoy truck," I asked Kaz.

"Kostas and Nikos," she said.

"Is that wise?" I asked. "Their English ..."

"Nikos is fluent enough," she answered. "It is Kostas who has trouble with reading signs. Nikos will drive the truck; deal with the shipyard authorities. Once the container is loaded, they will abandon the truck and fly to Athens. When we come within radio range of the city we will contact them. They will meet us on the highway and take over the driving. Their knowledge of the city streets is far greater than ours."

I nodded, smiling. "And they can read Greek. An important consideration for driving in Athens, believe me. OK. I can live with that. We'll be more than ready for relief drivers by then. So, everyone is here?" I asked.

"You are the last," she answered.

She turned and headed for the stairs. I followed. It was slow going up the steep, metal steps. My ribs ached from the ride over. I stumbled near the top and Kaz had to help me to the landing.

"Are you sure you can do this?" she asked.

"Do I have a choice?" I shook my head in an attempt to clear the pain. "I'm OK, Kaz. Really. I just have to take it kind of slow right now."

I took a deep breath, blew it out between pursed lips and walked into the room. There was a buzz of voices as I entered, which settled into silence as I hobbled to a table set out at the head of the room. A projection screen was set up just behind it. I heard Kaz shut the door and follow me. She set a leather briefcase on the table and opened it. Inside were several dozen transmitting devices, lapel mikes and earplugs. There were floor plans of the museum, descriptions and photos of the items we were interested in, together with a number of envelopes which I knew contained the payments for the hired help. There was also a brown folder, with all the papers the decoy crew would need to get the container loaded onto an America-bound freighter at Portsmouth. Beneath the folder was a cassette tape. I picked it up and examined it. There was no writing on the label. I looked over at Kaz.

"It's a recording of the night guard in the shack at the loading dock entrance. I took it the other night with a parabolic microphone. I thought you might need to hear what he sounds like, his accent, the way he speaks. Just in case."

Smiling, I nodded and looked around the room. Mac was sitting on an old easy chair, its leather arms split and the cottony stuffing oozing out, looking like mushrooms on the side of a fallen tree. The twins were sitting on a ragged love seat just behind Mac. Some thirty men and seven or eight women of varying nationalities were sitting around a long table. They looked as if they had all shopped at the same store for tonight's event. Blue shirts and trousers, knitted black caps, heavy boots. Half a dozen more men, dressed in uniforms identical to those used by the museum guards, sat along one wall. It took me a moment to spot Andreas standing in the shadows at the back of the room.

"You look like shit," Mac said, breaking the silence. Nervous titters ran through the room.

"Thanks," I answered. "Nice seeing you, too."

"Marceau's work?" he asked.

"Something like that."

"Rather a nice color scheme around the eyes."

"I'll relay your compliments the next time I see him."

I turned my attention to the rest of the room. I felt as if my insides were vibrating. I am rarely nervous while planning a job and never while on it but those hours just before, I find every noise too loud, every light too bright and the air too dense to breathe.

"OK," I said. "I assume none of you are here to join the Tuesday night bowling league. If you are, then you're in the wrong place. That meeting is two buildings over."

There was a moment of confused silence and then a scattering of awkward laughter, reminding me of why I'm a thief and not a comedian.

"You all know why you're here, more or less, but you don't know the specifics," I went on. "That's what you're about to find out. First, let me emphasize that this job will be dangerous, even foolish, perhaps. The chance of being caught is high, despite the precautions we've taken. You all know what you're being paid and must decide for yourselves if the money is worth the pain. If anyone has doubts, now is the time to leave."

I looked around the room. No one seemed interested in taking me up on my offer.

"Good. So, what are we going to do?" I looked around the room again, trying to catch each person's eye. "Well," I continued, "quite simply, we're going to steal the Parthenon Marbles from the British Museum."

Chapter 31

I leaned against the wrought-iron fence circling the British Museum listening to the rain hiss all around me. The air was thick with it, like a steam bath minus the soothing heat. Kaz had bound my ribs so tight, I could hardly breathe and, despite the wet suit I wore, I was shivering. The intermittent crackle in the earphone was irritating. I could hear Kaz's breath though she was too far behind me to make her out in the gloom. Peering through the bushes, I could make out the loading area with its subdued lighting. A red light shone over the huge metal door in the center of the loading dock. Above it would be the camera that swept the area.

Wiping the lenses of the night vision scope, I brought it to my eyes and scanned the yard. A van displaying the museum logo sat in one corner, the only vehicle in the area. I let my gaze follow the dock. A couple of empty crates, a dumpster and a piece of machinery covered in a tarp was all I could see.

Shifting my position against the fence, I pointed the scope in the direction of the guard shack. I could just make out the person inside. He, or she, seemed to be dozing. But it wasn't the guard in the shack I was worried about. It was the one viewing the cameras that concerned me. I had no way of knowing if my inside man was far enough inside.

Short of being in the control room, there was no way to know the sequence the cameras went through, how long they stayed on any one view or how diligent the night guard was in watching them. It was too much of a risk to make a dash for the guard shack and hope for the best. Instead, I was going to rely on the intense light of a laser beam to burn out the image-taking ability of the camera. I had used this technique before but never on a manned camera. Seeing the camera flare and go dead on a video tape long after the theft was one thing. Having it manned was another. How long would it take for the guard to respond? Would he respond at all or sound an alarm? The latter seemed far fetched, electronics being as finicky as they tend to be. I was betting he would send someone to investigate first.

"You set?" I whispered into the lapel mike.

"Almost," whispered Kaz. "Are you sure this is going to work?"

"It always has in the past," I answered.

"How will I know the camera is dead?"

"Do you see the tiny red light over the lens?"

"Yes."

"It should go out when the circuitry fries."

"Should?"

"What can I say? Thievery is an inexact science. And if it doesn't work, you'll know soon enough. All hell will break loose the moment I start crossing that loading yard. If that happens, run."

"Do not worry. Just remember to do the same." There was a moment of silence, then she said, "OK. I'm set."

"Andreas? Mac?" A grunt and a 'yeah' whispered in my ear. I heard the dull sound of the truck starting and then the Range Rover. I looked at my watch. Twenty-five minutes had passed since Kaz and I had scaled the fence. We had calculated fifteen. The rain was slowing us down. We had to get moving.

"Hit it on the next pass," I whispered to Kaz.

"Right," came her reply.

I held my breath, counting off the seconds in my head.

"Now!" she said.

I sprang from the bushes and sprinted across the empty loading yard, wincing and groaning the whole way. Jerking open the guardroom door, I brought up the gun in my hand and shot a dart into the guard's leg before he had time to wake up and forget what he was dreaming about. The effect was amazing. His eyes and mouth opened wide, closed just as precipitately and he began to collapse in on himself. I had to reach in fast to keep him from banging his head on the counter as his body began to roll off the stool he was sitting on.

"I'm at the door," Kaz said.

"Clear here," I grunted back, my ribs screaming in pain.

I managed to get my hands under the guard's arms and lower him down to the floor, tucking him into as comfortable a position as I could in the cramped guardroom. The radio in the room began squawking. Someone was trying to raise the guard. I ignored it as I used a plastic tie to bind the guard's hands. Fastening half a dozen of the plastic ties together, I wrapped them around his waist like a belt and secured his bound hands to it. Lastly, I gagged him with a cotton handkerchief. I had a moment of sympathy for the poor guy. He was going to be one sore puppy in the morning.

Ducking my head out the window, I could just make out Kaz standing by the entrance door to the loading area. I ducked back in just as the door opened and a guard appeared. He stood there a moment looking puzzled. When he raised his arm I thought he was going for the radio on his belt but instead he lifted his hat and combed his hair with his fingers. Replacing his hat, he stepped out further onto the dock. He was halfway to the edge when he turned and then crumpled headlong to the floor. Kaz stepped out of the shadow and waved.

Before I could wave back, the radio began squawking again.

"Philby? Where the hell are you? You better not be sleeping."

I grabbed a piece of cellophane from my pouch and picked up the radio. Crinkling the cellophane, I thumbed the switch and answered in my best British accent, thankful now for the recording Kaz had made.

"What's all that racket?" I said. "I can't make out a word."

"What?" came the reply. "It's the damned rain ... bloody radios are useless when it rains. And the damned camera's gone on the blink. Is everything all right out there?"

"Everything's fine. Quiet as a tomb."

"I've sent Thomas out. He there yet? I can't raise him on the radio. Hold on. Someone at the door." There was a moment of silence and then he was back. "It's Blake, here with my tea. So what about Thomas? He there yet?"

I hesitated a moment and then answered back.

"Yeah, he's here. Standing on the dock, waving his radio at me."

"Good. I'll make a note to have the repair crew look at that camera. You tell Thomas to get back up here and get another radio. And next time I call, Philby, you answer first thing or I might think you're sleeping on the job again."

"Sure, mate, sure," I answered and clicked off.

Putting down the radio, I slipped out of the guardroom and sprinted across the loading yard. I could have opened the gate from the guardroom but I reasoned there would be some indicator of that in the

189

main control room and didn't want to alert the guard there.

By the time I made it to the dock, Kaz had stripped Thomas of his jacket and hat and was wrapping the plastic strips around his waist. I cuffed his hands while she wrapped a handkerchief about his mouth. Together we lifted him and carried him to a secluded part of the dock.

"There is one camera high on the wall, to the center of the room," Kaz whispered to me. "It will not sweep as this one does. Wide angle, so staying to the edges of the room will make you a small target. With the jacket and hat, the man in the control room will think you are the person he sent."

"Right," I answered, slipping the jacket over the shoulders of my wet suit. It was a tight fit. The hat was worse, sliding off with the slightest turn of my head. She reached up, adjusted the cap and then kissed me on the cheek.

"Much luck," she said. "Shouldn't you wear your mask as well?'

"Can't," I answered. "Not until we take over the control room. I'll have to risk it without one."

Taking as deep a breath as I could, I looked once around the loading yard, then opened the door and stepped into the museum.

Chapter 32

The room was cavernous and the lighting dim. I spotted several electric lift trucks and a dozen or more small electric carts lined up along one wall. They all appeared to be connected to a gigantic electrical panel, red lights from the panel like the eyes of night creatures staring across the room at me. I closed the door and, remembering Kaz's words, made my way to the edge of the room, keeping my head as far down as I could without losing the hat.

I spotted a line of light at floor level: the exit door from the loading area. I tried to recall Wu's security diagrams but couldn't remember if that corridor had a camera. If it did, I was in trouble. It was one thing to pass as the guard in a huge, dark room. I'd never be able to pull it off in a lighted hallway. The guy's head had to be the size of a baseball to wear a hat this small.

"Kaz," I whispered. "I'm coming to the hallway that leads into the museum. It's lit up like a nighttime soccer game. Is there a camera in there?"

"No," came the whispered reply. "They had little money. Cameras only cover the exhibit rooms. Not the hallways."

"Right. I remember that. Thank Nicholas for tight budgets."

Kaz laughed, hearing me invoke Saint Nicholas, the patron saint of thieves. She had been amazed when I told her there was a patron saint of thieves and that he and Santa Claus were one and the same man.

"But he induced his thieves to return their plunder," she said, the laughter still in her voice.

"Well, we can't all be perfect," I answered.

I moved toward the door with less caution. Though I knew not having cameras covering the hallways was to our advantage now, soon it would turn to a disadvantage. With the cameras covering only the exhibit rooms, we would have no way of knowing where the guards were if they were to leave those rooms.

The bright light dazzled my eyes when I opened the door. It took a moment for my vision to adjust after the gloom of the loading area. Finding the switch, I hit it and cast the hallway into darkness. I had memorized the floor plans and could visualize the route I needed to take. Moving forward, I counted off doors until I came to the one I wanted. Opening it a crack, I peered out into a vast, dim corridor. Figures loomed along the far wall. Statues or pedestals, I couldn't make out which. In the far distance I could see the red glow of an exit sign. My target was just beyond that sign.

"Going in," I whispered. I could almost hear Kaz nod.

I stepped through the door and closed it behind me. Pulling the dart gun from the holster at my hip, I checked to make sure it was loaded, then began to make my way down toward the exit sign, the gun held low along my leg. This was a dangerous expanse of hallway. At any given time one of four or five guards would use this hallway to move from one part of the museum to another. There was also a time factor. Would my inside man be able to subdue the control room guard? And, if not, how long would the guard wait for Thomas before he called Philby again or, worse yet, sounded an alarm?

Midway to the exit sign, I heard soft footsteps to my left moving in my direction. A moment later a guard turned into the corridor and headed in my direction. He nearly jumped out of his shoes when he spotted me.

"Bloody hell," he said. "Nearly stopped me heart, you did. First those damn hellions downstairs and now this. That you, Thomas?"

I couldn't keep my head down forever, so I looked up at him.

"Actually, no," I said. Before he could react I shot him in the leg with a dart. He stood there for the longest time, his mouth forming a perfect 'O'. Slowly he began to spiral to the floor. I caught him before his head bounced off the tiles and unfolded his arms and legs until he was stretched out like a corpse. As I pulled plastic ties from the pouch around my waist I asked Kaz how far into the exhibit rooms I could venture without being picked up on the camera. I didn't want to leave the guard in the corridor and didn't want to waste time dragging him back to the hallway.

"A meter, no more. Why?" she asked.

"I ran into a guard. Had to dart him. I don't want to leave him here in case someone else walks by. I figured I could stash him in an exhibit room."

As I was cinching the last tie around the guard's wrists, I heard a noise and looked up in time to see another guard turn the corner. He came to an abrupt stop when he saw me kneeling on the floor and we stared at each other in silence for a long moment. I scrambled for the dart gun where I had left it on the floor. He let out a yelp, turned and ran. I shot off a dart at his retreating back but he stumbled trying to retrieve his radio and the dart flew by his shoulder as he disappeared around the corner.

Rising awkwardly to my feet, my ribs screaming in protest, I gave chase, trying to load another dart as I ran. Turning the same corner, I spotted him several feet away. He had the radio loose and was bringing it to his mouth to call for help. I plowed into him, knocking the radio free and we went down hard. Pain exploded in my side as if I'd been hit by a sledgehammer. The guard flailed at me with his arms, his blows glancing off my shoulders. Clubbing him in the face with my elbow, I wrestled him over onto his stomach and pinned him to the floor with my knee.

The dart gun had been knocked loose when we collided but I still had the dart in my hand so I plunged it into his buttocks with enough impact to break the seal. He yelped again, struggling hard, nearly throwing me off him before the drug took effect.

Nauseous from pain, I slid off the guard and over to the wall, trying hard to catch my breath and praying to St. Nicolas a third guard wouldn't appear. It was then I heard Kaz's voice in my ear.

"Danny! What's happening? Where are you?"

"I'm alright, Kaz," I gasped. "Ran into another guard, had a little problem. Give me a minute to catch my breath."

I put my head down between my knees until the nausea passed. I had to get moving, get these guards out of sight. I rose to my feet, leaning against the wall as a wave of dizziness overcame me. When it passed, I dragged the guard to where I had left the first one, cinched his hands together and dragged both guards into the exhibit room. By the time I was finished I was so short of breath I felt as if I was drowning. The pain was beyond words and I cursed every moment of Marceau's life to get through it. The only consolation to the whole affair was now I had two hats to choose from, both of which fit better than Thomas's had.

I stumbled back into the hallway and had just about reached the exit sign when I heard voices. Groaning, I hugged the wall and tried to discern from which direction they were coming and where they might be going. As the voices grew louder, I slunk back along the corridor until I came to one of the pedestals lining it. I folded myself up behind it, making myself as small as I could. The voices reached a peak and then began to diminish. I never saw their makers. I waited, holding my breath, until all was silent again.

Exhaling, I felt another wave of dizziness and nausea pass over me. I was tired and way overheated. I swallowed four more Ibuprofen, longing to shed the guard's wool jacket and the stifling wetsuit, knowing that would have to wait.

Once I was sure I was in the clear, I emerged from behind the pedestal and made my way to the door that would lead to the control room. Key card in hand, I looked around for the slot and found instead an old-fashioned key lock. Shaking my head at the skewed logic of minuscule security budgets, I reached into my pouch, pulled out a set of picks and had the door open in less than a minute.

A gloomy, carpeted stairway faced me. The runner was worn and threadbare in places with dark wood showing through. Piles of books were stacked up along one wall of the stairway reminding me of a loft apartment I'd had many years before. It had been a tiny, cramped place and only just accommodated what little furniture I had back then. My many books ended up stacked on the stairs that led to the sleeping area.

I stepped into the stairwell. Alert and wary, I made my way up and noticed a thick, Plexiglass window in the door at the top of the stairs. The greenish glow coming from within the room gave the window an iridescent look. Reaching the top, I pulled the hat down to my eyes and banged on the door. A blurred face appeared in the window. I heard a mumbled curse and fiddling with the lock and then the door opened. The man was shorter and thinner than I remembered him, the wig and phony mustache almost farcical. We stood facing each other for a heartbeat and then his eyes widened.

"About bloody time you got here," he said. His wrinkled face broke into a smile.

"Malcolm," I said. "It's been a long while."

I grabbed his extended hand and he pulled me into a crushing embrace. Malcolm Bastable had been one of my mentors and friends in the early days of my thieving life. He had opened the doors to Europe and beyond. A thief once himself, he had moved into the dubious position of broker and fence by the time I met him. He was a resourceful man who had never in his career come under the scrutiny of any law enforcement agency.

"William Blake?" I asked.

"Well, you wouldn't expect me to use my own bleedin' name now, would you?"

"I'm not sure I'd have made the phone call if you had," I answered.

His smile faded. "I was sorry to hear of Demetri's death," he said, surprising me with a bolt from the past.

"He was a good man, Malcolm," I said. "I'm glad you were able to make it to the funeral."

"Ah, yes. I wish you could have been there, lad. He loved you like a son, you know."

"Daniel?" Kaz's voice was a tense whisper in my ear.

"It's okay up here, Kaz," I said.

"I'm on my way," she said.

"Tell her to be wary of the cameras," Malcolm said. "We're coming up on a burst transmission and it wouldn't be good if she was in it."

"Understood," Kaz whispered.

I stepped past Malcolm and into the small room. There was a low, buzzing sound like air leaking from a tire and the faint, vinegary smell of functioning electronics left a taste of metal on my tongue.

"What happened to the guy who's supposed to be here?" I asked.

Malcolm inclined his head toward a dark corner of the room. "Nap time," he said.

I looked in the direction he'd indicated and could just make out a body in repose. "What did you do?" I asked. "Slip him a mickey?"

"Something like that."

"How long will he be out?"

"Sometime tomorrow, I imagine. He's a young pup, healthy as an ox so the potion shouldn't hurt him none."

"Gonna blow your cover, though."

"I'm bloody bored with this place anyway. I only took the job because I thought I could boost something now and then, you know? For all the money that's passed through my hands over the years, I haven't much to show for it. But I could never bring myself to bloody do it. I'm too old for this life."

"Well, Malcolm. I was serious in my offer. Though you can pretty much kiss England good-bye after this. Not to mention that terrible wig."

He sighed, chuckled, and pulled the rug from his head. "There's not much left for me here anyway," he said.

I turned to the console, looking over the dials and toggle switches. "Any idea of what any of this does?" I asked.

"Not a bloody clue, really," Malcolm answered. "Just what I managed to get out of Martin there since your phone call. I know it records everything and transmits it somewhere every thirty minutes. Beyond that, it's pretty much a bloody mystery."

"Were you able to get the recordings?" I asked.

"What recordings would those be?"

We both turned. Kaz was standing in the doorway. She stepped inside the room, eyed Malcolm then turned her gaze on me. There was more amusement in her eyes than anger.

"This is the one you were staring at," she said. "Back in the apartment. The inside man you spoke of."

"Malcolm, Kaz. Kaz, meet Malcolm Bastable. We go back a long way."

"Nice to meet you," she said. "Though it might have been nicer to know more of you, sooner." That was directed at me and I flinched until I noticed the smile tugging at the corners of her mouth.

"Not his fault," Malcolm said. "I wasn't sure myself if I could pull this off. Wouldn't have been good for him – or any of you – to rely on an old man like me."

"Old is often better," she said, winking at Malcolm. He blushed and smiled. "More experience, less risk-taking."

She glanced at me, still smiling, then brushed past me to examine the console. Reaching out her hand, she flipped a toggle switch and at the same time whispered into her lapel mike. "We're in," she said.

"On our way," Mac said. I could hear him gunning the engine of the Range Rover.

"Right behind," came Andreas's reply.

I watched Kaz as she examined the layout of the security room. In a moment she was seated at the console and her hands were racing across the keyboard. She was in her element now. I turned and stared at the monitors. Two of them were blank. The vertical hold on another was going, the picture rolling to the top of the screen every few seconds. The rest of the monitors flicked between scenes at two-minute intervals, showing various rooms throughout the museum.

"These recordings," she said, her hands never leaving the keyboard, "they wouldn't be from previous nights now, would they?"

"As a matter of fact," Malcolm said. He turned, grabbed a small leather bag and began rummaging through it. "Here," he said, handing Kaz several CDs. "I hope it's what you need. I had a hard enough time getting them. Old Martin there was beginning to think something was up with all my questions."

Kaz pulled her laptop from her bag and booted it up. Popping one of the CDs in, she began examining it. After a moment, she turned to Malcolm, a smile on her face. "These are perfect," she said. She slid from her chair and turned to a metal cabinet at the back of the room. Opening it, she began fiddling around with something I couldn't see.

"Inside my bag," she said. "There is a large, gray box with wires coming off the back."

I reached into her bag, found what she was asking for and handed it to her. "USB CD," she said and disappeared back into the bowels of the cabinet.

I looked at Malcolm. He shrugged, mirroring my confusion. Kaz emerged from the cabinet again. She caught our look and laughed. "Luddites," she said. "And don't just stand there. There is another bag at the bottom of the stairs and a camera to replace. And don't forget your masks."

"Right." I said. "And you might want to remind Mac and Andreas as well."

Chapter 33

Kaz was hunched over the console when I returned, whispering into the microphone, her fingers tapping keys on the keyboard.

"We have a problem," she said as I stepped up beside her.

"What now?" I asked.

"The replacement cameras," she said. "There must have been a leak of some sort in the area where they were stored. The first two we tried didn't work at all. Andreas is installing the last one now."

"Great," I said. "Not two hours into the job and we're already running into more problems than we anticipated."

"Stay calm, my thief, we will overcome this."

"OK," came Andreas's strained voice from my earphone. "I think I've got it hooked up. You getting anything?"

I was looking over Kaz's shoulder at the bank of monitors along the top of the control panel. Two men rolling a heavily-laden cart disappeared from one. I knew they would reappear in several moments in another. Kaz's fingers skimmed over the keyboard. She was humming softly. One of the monitors that had been blank flashed and settled into a flurry of waving lines, edged with electronic snow. We held our breath as it took a moment to clear and as it did, Andreas's masked face appeared, mugging for the camera.

"Got it," Kaz said and Andreas stepped away.

The image shuddered for a moment, resolved, shuddered again and then nothing. The screen showed a grainy, blurred image of the loading dock area.

"What's the matter with it?" I asked.

"The autofocus is not working."

"Can we fix it? Install another camera?"

"That was the last replacement. Andreas, see if you can turn the lens."

Blurry finger shapes appeared on the monitor, wrapping themselves about the lens.

"Won't budge," he said.

Kaz turned to me. "We'll have to use it as is," she said.

"What sort of problem is that going to cause us?"

"We will be unable to see the gate clearly, or anyone entering or leaving the loading dock area."

I gave it some thought. We could call it quits and leave but there would never be another chance to steal the Marbles if we did.

"Okay, we'll just have to deal with it. How's the party coming along?"

Kaz hit several keys and two of the monitors changed view to show the gathering on the second floor of the museum. It seemed pretty sedate. A tall woman with her hair in an elegant chignon was using a laser pointer to direct attention to a cluster of statues. Most of the occupants of the room, the hellions as the guard had referred to them, were gathered about her, though there were several who had wandered off onto their own private tour of the room.

It didn't look to me as if this smaller group, all young, buffed-up boys, were all that interested in Roman sculpture. I glanced at the monitor we had on the entrance to the room. Malcolm was leaning against the wall, cleaning his nails. The other guard, not one of ours, was standing near the teacher, trying overly hard not to stare at her. That he was smitten was obvious. Several times both of them had been called upon to usher escaping children back into the room.

"How many guards have we taken out?" I asked.

"Eight, now," Kaz answered. "Nine with the gate guard."

I looked at the monitor covering the room the Marbles were in. Mac and another man were working on one of the metopes. Two other men were lifting one of the frieze panels onto an electric cart already laden with several other panels. We had been in the museum for close to two hours and were barely a quarter of the way finished.

"This is taking longer than Mac figured," I said.

"There will be time," Kaz said. "You worry too much, *kléphtēs mou.*"

"Worry is what I do," I said. "It's why I'm still a thief and not a convict. And besides, it's about all I have to do on this job. I'm beginning to feel a bit useless."

"Nonsense," she said. "Without you, there would be no job to feel useless about." She laughed, a little uneasily I thought, touched my hand, then turned back to the console. I looked back at the room with the party. Malcolm was herding three of the aforementioned boys back into the room.

"Antsy lot, those kids," I said.

"It is the nature of children to be such," Kaz answered. "Why don't you go down and speak with Mac. See about his progress for yourself."

"Trying to get rid of me?" I asked, only half joking.

"If you must be told the truth, my thief, then yes, I am trying to rid myself of you. And not," she said, holding up her hand to stop my response, "because you are useless. I simply do not like to be watched as I work. Now go."

She was right of course. There was no point in feeling useless and at loose ends and also no point in my standing around doing nothing in the control room, which just served to exacerbate those feelings. If I was worried things weren't going as planned then I should go to the source, ask Mac how he felt about our timing. Despite my injured ribs I could do something. Wheel a cart, they were electric after all. How hard could it be? I checked the guard on the way out. He was sleeping. Snoring, but peaceful. I checked the warmth of his fingers to make sure his circulation wasn't cut off by the plastic ties and that gave me an idea for something I could do. With the exception of this one, who was too much of a burden to carry down the stairs, we had gathered all the guards we'd darted into a single room near the loading dock. One of the men Andreas had hired was there keeping an eye on them. I didn't expect them to wake up anytime soon but the plastic ties bothered me. They could cinch too tightly with just a little movement. The last thing I wanted was any permanent harm to come to anyone involved in this caper.

Once out in the corridor, I headed toward the loading dock. Halfway there, Mac fell in beside me. "Where you off to?" he asked.

"Check on the guards," I said. "How are we doing in there?"

"Slow. Maybe too slow. The panels are lifting out easily enough. The metopes are burdensome and heavy as hell; the little lift we found has made that job a bit easier. They're mounted much more securely than I had anticipated, though. It's taking a while to get them loose."

"We going to make it?"

"I think so. I'm a bit concerned about the pedimental statues. If they're as secure as the metopes ..." His voice trailed off. The silence didn't do my nerves any good.

"How's the party going downstairs?" he asked, changing the subject.

"As well as can be expected with a room full of hyperactive teenagers on an all-night expedition. Malcolm and the other guard are having a hard time keeping them in tow."

"Perhaps we could send someone else up."

"I don't think so. We need everyone we have down here loading. We're running behind schedule." We came to the doorway that led to the loading dock and turned in.

"You heading to the dock for a reason?" I asked.

"Yeah," he answered. "I want to check on the loading. We managed to damage one of the metopes ..."

"Damage!"

"A chip from the base, nothing more," he assured me. "One stack toppled against another and there wasn't enough excelsior in the carton to cushion the blow. Certainly what we have done is nowhere near the damage the British caused them in trying to clean them. That was a sickening thing to see. Barbarous!"

"So I'd heard," I said. "Mid-thirties it was discovered, wasn't it?"

"Late. 1938 or '39. They kept it hidden from the public until just recently. The stupid bastards used carborundum on them. That stuff is nearly as hard as diamonds. They use it to grind metal tools and smooth granite."

He stopped, leaned against a wall, pinching the bridge of his nose.

"Half the sculptures, nearly all the frieze panels and all the metopes were overcleaned to the point of ruin. I've been to the Acropolis museum several times, seen

205

the remaining Marbles they house there. Up close, I might add. Within touching distance. Did you know that the Elgin collection is the only one in the British Museum cordoned off from the public? And lit in such a way as hides the damage done to them. Seeing it up close, as I have tonight, it's appalling. They are a dull white or grey – the fine, honey brown patina gone, the shiny surfaces dulled."

He sighed a deep sigh, pushed himself away from the wall and we continued our stroll.

"Two thousand years those stones faced weather, war, half a dozen conquering nations and managed to survive reasonably intact," he said. "In little more than a hundred, the Brits all but destroyed them by trying to make them fit some ideal they had of Greek art. Preposterous."

"Kind of blows their argument for keeping them," I said.

"Yes. Which explains the extraordinary lengths they've taken to cover it up all these years," he said. "All things considered, they'd have been better off left in Greek hands."

"Well, if we succeed, the Greeks will get their chance to prove themselves better caretakers."

"Amen to that," he said.

We came to the door that led off to where we had the guards stashed. I turned in while Mac headed for the loading dock. The guy guarding the guards was an Albanian, a relative of Andreas's, who spoke little English. I nodded and he nodded back. The guards were laid out along the back of the room on sleeping bags, their heads resting on their rolled up jackets. I checked their respiration, the tightness of their bonds and the gags around their mouths. Satisfied that they were still in good health and secure, I left the room and headed to where the Marbles were. I was halfway there when Kaz's voice whispered in my ear.

Chapter 34

"We have a problem," she said.

"What?"

"I just picked up a police call. Someone must have spotted activity in the loading area and called the police. They are sending a car around."

"And we won't be able to see them clearly?"

"No."

"Andreas? Mac? Did you get that."

"Yes," came Andreas's voice. "I am clearing the dock now."

"Radio the guardroom," I said to Kaz. "Let him know trouble is coming."

"Is he going to be able to handle that?" Mac asked.

"He'll have to," I answered. "Please tell me we put a Brit in the guardroom."

"Dock's clear," Andreas said.

"I'm closing down the door," Kaz said. "And yes, the guard is British. I'm calling him now."

"Can you monitor him there?" I asked.

"I will tell him to keep his radio on transmit," Kaz answered.

"Good. See if you can raise Malcolm. I want him out there, just in case."

"I'm contacting him now."

I heard her whisper his name, heard his reply, saying he was on his way.

"Anything on the monitors yet?" I asked.

"Nothing so far ... ah, wait. There is something. It looks like a spotlight shining over the gate and into the dock area. I can't see anything more."

"They've driven past without stopping," came Andreas's voice. "They've seen the truck. They'll be back."

Standing in the empty corridor, chewing my lower lip, I tried to think it through. If someone had called them, even if we managed to convince them all was well, there was a good chance they would make another drive-by before the night was over. And the likelihood was that we wouldn't get a warning on that one. Taking them out wasn't an option. They would be in constant contact with headquarters and if they disappeared all hell would break loose.

I glanced at my watch. It was a quarter past twelve. We had four, maybe four and a half hours left before we had to be out the door, finished or not. I had one option open, one I hadn't wanted to use unless it was imperative.

"They're back," came Andreas's voice over the earphone. "And they're stopping this time. Malcolm is on his way out."

"Can you tell how many?" I asked.

"It looks to be only one." He was silent for a moment and then, "No, there's the other. He's stepped out as well, standing on the other side of the car, looking across the top."

"Covering his partner," I said.

"It would appear so."

"What's the other one doing?"

"He's shining a light about the yard. Now he's walking over to the guardroom. Hold on. Malcolm's reached the gate."

There was a crackle of static and then Malcolm's voice came through the earpiece.

"Morning officer, and a sodding bad one at that, eh? What can I do for you boys?"

"We got a call, came down to check it out. Mind if I ask who you are?"

"Blake, William, like the poet. I'm senior guard on the nightmare shift."

"Nightmare shift?"

"A little joke, son. Not much to keep one amused this time of night."

"We noticed that truck in the loading bay."

"Yeah. Pain in the arse, that one. Came in this afternoon, delivering some statues out for restoration. Broke down. Been a bloody time working around it. Owner's supposed to have it out of here tomorrow."

"Mind if we come in and take a look around?"

"Not at all. I'll have to get the key from the control room. Gate's on the blink again. Shouldn't be but a couple of minutes."

"Andreas," I said. "The loading doors to the truck …"

"Only one," he interrupted. "There wasn't time to close both."

I chewed on my lip, trying to decide what to do. No way could we let the cops in the loading area. It would appear the imperative moment had come.

"Kaz. You remember that little diversion plan we discussed?"

"The bomb scare? Yes. I remember it."

"I think it's time to put it into action."

"I will do it now."

I could hear her fingers flying over the keyboard as she made the preparations to have a bomb scare phoned into the central police headquarters.

"Bomb scare?" came Mac's voice.

"It was a last minute thing I came up with. Kaz rigged it. A modem, an electronically created voice file and a dozen cut-outs, so the line can't be traced back.

Once she activates it, it will call in several bomb threats on buildings all over London."

"All a good deal distant from here, I presume," said Andreas.

"You got it," I said.

"It is done," came Kaz's voice over the wire.

"Let's hope it works," said Mac.

"What's happening?" I asked.

"The remaining guard and the cop are discussing the latest soccer scores."

"Well, I suppose that's better than ..."

"Hold on," said Andreas. "The cop by the door is waving his hand. The other one is running back to the car. Looks like your plan is working. They're speeding off."

"How long do you think it will keep them occupied?" asked Mac.

"Hard to say. Six bomb threats in six very large buildings. That should take them well into the morning to sort it all out. By that time we'll be long gone."

"Amen," said Andreas.

"Going to make for a hell of a traffic jam," Mac said.

"I anticipated that," I said. "The locations are all in the southwest portion of the city, far from the roads we'll need to take to get to the Chunnel."

"Then I guess we should all get back to work," Mac said.

"And amen again," Andreas said.

Chapter 35

Time took on a surreal quality seeming to both slow down and speed up. By 0135 we had forty of the panels from the frieze loaded. The other sixteen were waiting to be boxed. Of the fifteen metopes, we'd only managed nine so far. The seventeen pedimental statues were strewn from Room 18 all the way to the dock. Only four were boxed and on the truck. Worry had become like breathing and everyone was growing weary and irritable. Especially Andreas, a fact which bothered me. I had never known him to walk away from any job in his life and yet that was what he was insisting we do.

"It is taking too long," Andreas said. "The men are tired, they grow clumsy. We should crate what we have in the loading area and leave ... before we are discovered and it's too late."

"He may have a point there, Daniel," Mac said. "The men are growing weary and we haven't much time left."

"We have two and a half hours," I said. "Three if we stretch it. You said yourself the statues were coming down faster than you expected."

"Yes," answered Mac. "That's true but the packing time is taking longer than I thought. They are more delicate than either the friezes or the metopes. And I don't know yet how we will get the column or if we even can with the time we have left."

"What about the Lady?"

"She will be a problem. Dismounting her will be easy enough but she is heavy and awkward and the men are tired."

I paced the floor, gnawing on an already over-gnawed knuckle. Somewhere along the line I had caught Gerasimos's passion for the Caryatid. Uniting her with her sisters had become my central focus in the last few hours.

"I could live without the column, if I had to," I said. "But the Lady has to go. I can't leave her behind."

"Fools!" Andreas shouted. "You are all bloody fools. Sacrificing everything for a bloody pile of rocks."

"What the hell is wrong with you, Andreas?" I shouted back. Andreas turned on me, glaring, his fists clenched. Mac hurriedly stepped between us.

"Fisticuffs are not going to solve anything and you both know it," he said.

I took a step back and Andreas did the same. "I am sorry," he said, bowing his head and staring at the floor. "It is the tension of the evening. Forgive me. You are right. We should finish what we have started."

My mind screamed that something more than fatigue and tension was bothering Andreas but it didn't offer up a clue as to what that something might be.

"What about getting more men?" Malcolm asked.

"Too risky," I said, turning away from Andreas. "We'd either have to go get them or risk telling them to come here. No, I don't see that happening. We'll have to make do with who's here."

"What about some of those playing guards?" Mac asked.

"Kaz," I said. "What's happening with the party?"

"It's quiet up there. Most are sleeping."

There were now two of our people in the room with the party. We'd also had to take out several guards who roamed the further reaches of the museum. In all we had seven of our men doing little more than walk about in darkened rooms.

"Leave one of ours in the party room and call everyone back here."

"Is that wise?" she asked.

"No. But it's the best I can do at the moment. Mac, Andreas, will that help?"

Andreas turned and started walking away.

"I suppose it will have to," said Mac. He gave me a worried look and hurried to catch up to Andreas. They hadn't gone halfway down the hall when a resounding crash followed by a piercing scream echoed from the loading area, freezing the four of us in place for a moment.

"This can't be good," I said as our mutual paralysis vanished and we began running toward the sound.

"Danny! Something has happened in the loading area."

"I know, Kaz. We're on our way."

As I passed through the loading area door, I spotted several men lifting an overturned electric cart off the leg of another man squirming in agony on the floor. Mac was kneeling beside the man, talking to him in Turkish, trying to calm him down. Andreas glared at me and began sliding several large pieces of a pedimental statue away from the man's pinned leg.

"What happened?" I asked.

"Looks like the wheel on the cart broke," Malcolm said.

"How is he?" I asked, kneeling next to Mac.

"Between curses he claims he will be fine with a brief rest."

"Hold him," Andreas said. "I must look at his injury."

214

Mac and Malcolm grasped the man's shoulder, pinning him to the floor.

"What's his name?" I asked.

"Arslan," replied Mac. "Arslan Demir, my best antiquities man, an archeologist like myself."

A grunt from Andreas turned our attention to him. He had a grave expression on his face and one look at Arslan's leg told me why.

"I doubt a few moments over tea and biscuits is going to do him much good," I said. "It's a compound fracture. He's going to need a hospital."

"Great!" said Andreas. "More delays. I warned you. The men are tired. Accidents happen with fatigue."

"How are we going to get him to a hospital?" Mac asked. "It's not like we can phone in an emergency, call for an ambulance."

"I may have a solution to that," said Kaz, surprising all of us.

"I'm all ears, Kaz," I said.

"I considered something like this might happen or that your injuries might worsen because of the strain so I made arrangements."

"Arrangements?" I asked.

"Yes. A Serbian doctor. He is not licensed to practice in the UK but he does anyway, amongst his own people and he is always in need of funds for supplies. He has made himself available to us should the need arise."

"He can't come here," I said.

"No," she answered. "Nor does he know what we are about, only that his services may be needed. On a discreet basis, of course."

"What do you think?" I asked Mac.

"We haven't much choice," he answered. "But how do we get him there?"

"My car is nearby," said Malcolm.

"That'll work," I said. "We'll have to send another man along. Malcolm can't handle him by himself."

"Arslan's brother is about. I'll find him."

"Good. I'll get their payoff. Malcolm, you come with me." I looked around. "Where's Andreas?"

Mac scanned the room. "I have no idea. Perhaps he is off sulking in a corner somewhere. I didn't see him leave."

"What is it with him lately?" I asked.

"I have no idea but I find it worrisome."

"As do I," I said. "Malcolm, let's get rolling."

Back in the control room I handed Malcolm an envelope containing the payoff for Arslan and his brother.

"Well, old friend," I said. His eyes were shiny and he had removed the mustache and wig, replaced his guard's uniform with street clothes. I walked up to him and, as I shook his hand, I slipped an envelope into his pocket. He looked at it and then at me.

"What's this?" he asked. "You've already paid me."

"Call it a bonus," I said.

"I won't be taking charity, now," he said, reaching for the envelope. I stopped his hand.

"Not charity," I said. "You earned it. Without those recordings, Kaz may not have figured out a way to bypass the transmissions burst. Not without a lot of work and a lot of time lost. And driving Arslan to this doctor is going to be risky. I'd say you more than deserve it."

"Thank you," he said, his voice a whisper. "This means ..." His voice trailed off.

"You gonna be okay?" I asked. "You have a way out of England?"

"Made a call," he said. "I'll be in Portugal in time for tea. Still have a few good connections left." He laughed but it was a sad, lonely sound.

"You know where I live, Malcolm. You're welcome there anytime."

"I appreciate that," he said. "I may bloody well take you up on the offer."

Chapter 36

An hour after Malcolm left, I was walking past the exhibit room when from out of the shadows, Andreas fell in step beside me. We walked in silence down the long hallway and were nearly to the loading area before he spoke.

"You are in pain," he said.

"Some," I answered. "Pretty useless at lifting anything. I thought I'd give packing a try."

"Wise decision."

"You want to tell me what's going on?"

"It's fatigue," he started, "and wor ..." drawing out the half-spoken word, emotion crossing his face like storm clouds in a winter night sky.

"And complications. Family problems, nothing more," he finished, though I swore he'd wanted to say something else.

I started to question him more when a gasp came over the earpiece, followed by the calamitous sound of a commotion.

"Danny," shouted Kaz, so loud that it hurt my ear.

"What? What happened?" I could hear Mac shouting, the sound of running feet, voices I didn't recognize. "What the hell is going on?"

We turned and ran back up the hallway and out into the corridor. The commotion became stereophonic as the sound came from both the earphone and further up the corridor.

"Kaz?"

"Danny! Hurry!"

I raced up the corridor, Andreas pulling ahead of me as I did my best not to double over from the pain in my ribs. I turned a corner in time to see three teenage boys run past, Mac and Andreas tight on their heels. I merged with them, realizing what had happened. We had been discovered. From the corner of my eye I saw Mac raise his dart gun.

"No," I screamed and flung my arm at him to dislodge his aim. The gun went off but the dart glanced off the wall and fell to the floor.

"What the hell did you do that for?" he screamed at me.

"They're kids," I shouted, slowing to a limping walk, unable to bear the pain of running. Mac matched my pace and through clenched teeth I said, "Ketamine's a powerful drug. I have no idea what it might do to the developing brain of a child, teenager or otherwise, and I'd rather not chance it."

He nodded his understanding. "Are you all right?" he asked. I waved him on. At that moment, Andreas caught up with the one boy lagging behind the rest. Reaching out, he grabbed the boy's collar and jerked him off his feet. The boy landed with a thud and a terrible howl that echoed up and down the corridors like a banshee's wail just as Mac and I caught up to them.

"Go," I said to the two of them. "Round them up. But no ..." I waved the dart gun in the air where the kid on the ground couldn't see. Mac caught my drift and nodded. I grabbed the collar of my shirt where the lapel mike was pinned. "And no names," I said. Both of them nodded this time, then turned and disappeared down the hall.

I knelt beside the boy. My breath was coming in gasps, my ribs a wreath of angry fire. The kid maybe fifteen or sixteen, his face stricken with a mixture of pain and fear. He was trying hard not to allow the tears rimming his eyes to fall to his cheeks.

One did anyway, splashing off his nose and rolling into the corner of his mouth.

"Chill out, kid," I said, with little sympathy for his plight. "No one's going to hurt you. What's your name?" I was talking through gritted teeth, the pain a grimace in my face. I think the look scared him more than my words.

"T-T-Tony," he finally managed to croak. The accent threw me for a moment. It wasn't British or anything else European. It screamed Cape Cod, Massachusetts, the whole New England seaboard. It screamed Boston.

I stood up and reached out my hand to help him to his feet. He was a big boy, well packed and the effort made me wince with pain. Taking a step back, I lifted the dart gun from its holster and let it dangle at my side. The kid stared at it a moment and then looked up at me. His face was a mask of fear. He had no idea I wouldn't use the gun.

"So, T-T-Tony," I said, mocking him so as to keep the edge between us defined. "What's a Boston punk doing in jolly old England?" His eyes widened. I had guessed right and the knowledge scared him.

"I ... we ... school ..." he said. I waved the gun in my hand, pointing in the direction the others had run. He took the hint and began walking. I stepped in behind him.

"K?" I whispered. If the kid heard me, he made no sign of it, just kept shuffling along.

"Danny? Mac and Andreas have closed their transmitters. What is going on? Where are the kids?"

"I have one here with me," I said. "Anything on the monitors?"

"Nothing. I am switching through them now but if they are in a hallway, I will see nothing. They are not on the dock or in the Marble room or back at the party."

"What happened?" I asked.

"I am not sure. All I know is three children appeared in the Marble room and then everyone began running like crazy people."

"What's happening in the party room?"

"It is still quiet. I do not think they realize anyone is missing."

"Radio the guard there. Tell him to stay alert. Somehow those kids got past him. I've got one. M and A are after the other two. Call the other guards. Have them come to the corridor outside the party room. I'll wait for them there."

A crackling sound came over the earphone and then Mac's voice. "I've got him," he said. "Little bastard nearly broke my jaw." I heard a faint 'fuck you,' and then a thump and a yelp. With a small wave of the dart gun, I signaled the boy I was leading to stop.

"Don't kill him," I said, a smile tugging at my lips. Mac was as gentle as they come but he could put on a mean act when it suited him. "Where are you?"

"Hell if I know," came his reply.

"Do you think you can find your way back to the party room?"

"Sure. I can do that," he said.

"Any thoughts on our mutual friend?" I asked.

"We split up when the kids did. I don't know where he is now?'

There was another crackle on the line and then Andreas's voice. "I am here. I have the boy. And there are two more guards for someone to gather up."

"Jesus. If this keeps up, we'll have the whole damn place bedded down for the night," I said.

221

"Probably should have done that anyway," Mac added.

"Is the kid okay?" I asked.

"But for the piss that stains his pants and his pride, the child is fine," Andreas said. I could hear the mirth in his voice, despite the fact that we all had known the embarrassment of pissing ourselves in fear at one time or another.

"Do you know where you are?" I asked.

"I always know where I am." Andreas said. "Unlike some amongst us."

"Fuck you, you Albanian bloodhound," Mac muttered.

"Boys," Kaz admonished.

"I think we're all a little tired," I said. "A? Head back to the party room. I've got our guards heading there. We need to contain this before it gets out of control. K? What's happening in the Marble room?"

"Those left behind are continuing to remove the Marbles. It is the same on the dock."

"Okay," I said, nudging the boy to get moving. "Let's finish this up."

Chapter 37

"Y-You gonna kill us?" the kid asked as we reached the top of the stairs.

"Not likely, kid," I said.

We had been talking on the way, mostly a one-sided conversation as the kid was still quite frightened. I went back to something he had said earlier and asked him about it.

"Football, you said. What position you play?"

"C-Center," he answered.

"And all of you play on the same team?"

"Yeah. We're over here on some dumb school thing."

"Pretty strong, are ya?" I asked, the first seeds of an oddball idea beginning to sprout.

"Strong enough, yeah," he said. I noticed that his fear seemed to recede the more we talked in areas where he could relate.

"Have to work out a lot, I imagine," I said. "Run? Lift weights, that sort of thing?"

"Yeah. Coach makes us run laps all the time in full gear. Sometimes we have to carry those little ten-pound dumbbells with us. Do curls. He can be a son of a bitch sometimes."

"You do any bench pressing, that sort of thing?"

"Yeah. Two, three times a week we have to spend an hour in the gym, working out on the weight machines."

The idea was fully formed now. I knew it was crazy but in a strange sort of way it just might work. Our guards were waiting down the hall from the party room. Mac arrived at the room just as I did. He had cuffed the kid he'd chased and gagged him as well. Andreas and his catch joined the crowd a moment later.

"Was that really necessary?" I asked Mac.

"Probably not," Mac said, sheepish, his anger long ago dissipated. "Bit of a royal pain in the ass he was, though." He rubbed his jaw, pulled a pair of wire cutters from his pocket and made to remove the plastic cuffs. I waved him off and stepped up to the kid. He had a surly look on his face with just a hint of fear in his eyes. He tried staring me down but couldn't hold it.

"You must be the quarterback," I said. His eyes widened at my knowledge and the fear spread to the rest of his face. "I'm going to uncuff you but make no mistake, I will take you down if you try to run again." I poked his stomach with the barrel of the gun to emphasize my point. "They're only darts but trust me kid, you would not enjoy the feeling when you woke up. Are we straight on this?" He nodded, shaken, obedient and unwilling to call my bluff about the darts. It was hard not to laugh. I stepped back, nodding at Mac who clipped the cuffs and untied the kid's gag.

I had our guards enter the room first. I monitored them through Kaz and when they had the teacher secured and the kids, most of them rubbing sleep from their eyes, gathered at one end of the long room, we walked in. I gave the quarterback a shove in their direction and he and the other two boys joined the group. Some were talking excitedly amongst themselves. A small group of them huddled around the teacher. A dozen of the boys stood off to one side by themselves, more or less flanking their leader, the quarterback. This was the football team.

Walking to the edge of where the main group stood, I started looking them over. There were thirty or more in all, equally divided between boys and girls. I tapped one boy on the shoulder and directed him to move over to where the football team was standing. He went with obvious reluctance. I tapped another boy and then another, trying to pick out the biggest amongst them. I came to two girls, identical in appearance.

"Sisters?" I said.

"Twins," they answered.

"You pretty strong?" I asked one of them.

"Strong enough," they said. Neither backed down from my stare. I smiled. I liked their attitude and there wasn't a hint of fear in their eyes. I nodded toward the group of boys and they moved over, with neither question nor hesitation. I kept moving amongst the class of students until I had them divided into two groups.

"What the hell are you doing?" Mac asked in a whisper when I rejoined him and Andreas. I could hear Kaz laughing in the earphone. She had figured it out.

"You wanted warm, fresh blood," I said, smiling. "Well, meet your new crew." And I turned and swept my arm out to encompass the two groups of kids. "You've got loaders and you've got packers. And best of all, they won't cost us a single dime."

Chapter 38

Mac and Andreas led the football group from the room. This was the larger and bolder of the two groups and they were taking to this idea like puppies to a colorful toy. Most of them had been bored out of their minds with the museum and the chance to work off all that pent-up teenage energy came as a welcome relief. I stayed behind with the smaller group, sensing their reluctance, their fear.

As I was gathering them together, the teacher, who had remained silent up to this point, finally spoke. "I … I can't allow this," she said.

As her words echoed through the room, the children stopped. Several of them broke away from the group and headed back to her. I turned to face her.

"I'm not sure you have a choice," I said, resting my hand on the butt of the dart gun. Her gaze traveled from my face to the gun and back.

"I don't believe you would use that thing on me," she said.

She had me there and she knew it. I sighed, half turned and turned back.

"Look," I said. "It wasn't my idea to involve you in this. But now that you are involved, I have to make a choice. I don't have enough people to guard you. And you're right, I won't use these things on you or the kids. And, to be honest, I could use the help."

"To steal from the museum," she said.

"Indeed," I said. "Stealing is what I do. And in this case, I am stealing what once was stolen."

"They weren't stolen," she replied. "The Greeks were under Ottoman rule at the time. It was the Ottomans who legally gave the Marbles to Lord Elgin.

226

The Turks were grinding them up to make lime for mortar. The British saved them from sure destruction."

I looked at her with incredulity. "You're a teacher and you believe that? Sorry to disappoint you but it's pretty well established the mortar story is a myth, spread to justify the theft of the Marbles. By the time Elgin came on the scene, most Greek houses were made of clay because of the extreme seismic activity. As for the legality, that's bogus as well. There were two firmans issued by the Sultan, authorizing Elgin to take drawings and make molds of the sculptures. There was nothing in them about shipping the Marbles to England. Elgin took that upon himself, hoping to gain favor and financial reward once he was back home."

"And that makes it right?" she asked.

"I'm not concerned with right," I answered. "Or wrong, for that matter. If you don't feel you can go along with this, then I will have to find some place to lock you up. I can pretty much guarantee that it won't be pleasant or comfortable."

"And if I opt for that," she said. "What of the other children? What will happen when, after you are gone, they have to deal with the consequences of what they've done? And what of the authorities? The children could get into a lot of trouble for this."

"I doubt they'll experience much grief from the authorities," I said. "Especially if the authorities believe they were threatened into helping."

"But you said you wouldn't use the darts."

"True," I said. "You know that. The kids know that. But the authorities don't. Unless you tell them."

"That still doesn't answer the question of conscience," she said.

"No," I said. "It doesn't. And I'm afraid I don't have an answer to that."

We stood there staring at one another for a long moment, her gaze intent as though she were trying to penetrate the mask I wore and read the expression on my face.

She broke the stand-off and asked "Why are you doing this? Is money so important that you would deprive the world of the beauty of the Marbles?"

I considered her question. It was a fair one and I felt she deserved some sort of explanation. I just wasn't sure how much to tell her.

"As for the why, all I can say is read your history. I've given you a taste of it. There's a lot more. And, I can only ask that you believe me on this, the world will not be denied the Marbles. Money has nothing to do with it. So, what do you plan to do?"

The silence in the room lengthened. The kids were restless, the shuffling of their feet throwing hissing echoes about the room. With a deep breath, the teacher gathered the children together and marched them toward the door. I followed behind, her question of conscience forcing me to wonder for the first time if I had made the right decision.

Chapter 39

By the time we made it to the Marble room, the place was in a frenzy of activity. The quarterback, once defiant, now directed his team to the task, as if it were a championship game. The twin sisters were a dynamo of strength and action, working harder than most of the men we were paying to do the job. I couldn't help but think that the larcenous nature of what we were doing gave some of them a buzz.

"That was the last statue," Andreas said, a hint of disbelief in his voice.

I looked at my watch. It was 0345. "Where's M?" I asked.

"In the other room, bringing down the Caryatid," he answered.

"He's got the girls with him?"

"The twins, yes. Gorgeous creatures, those two: brains, brawn and beauty."

"And attitude," I added.

"Yes," he agreed. "That as well. I wouldn't mind meeting up with them in ten years' time."

"Both of them?"

"Of course," he laughed. "A lover such as I am could handle two such as they."

"You're old enough to be their father," I said, laughing myself. "And if you utter a single cliché about older men being better I'll smack you."

Andreas shrugged his shoulders. "Truth is truth. Ask any young woman who has known the pleasure of an older man." He winked, laughed and walked away.

At that moment, the Caryatid emerged from the other room. This would have been the ideal moment for the opening notes of 'Thus Spake Zarathustra' to begin echoing from the loudspeakers.

The twins, holding up one end of the Lady, several of the boys from the football team spread out along her length, Mac taking up the rear position. Humankind's triumph over ... over what? Lord Elgin? The British Museum? Jesus, I was tired. Still, it gave me gooseflesh all over my arms as I watched them gently ease the Lady down onto two electric carts and step away.

"A regular Richard Strauss moment, don't you think?" I said to Mac as I walked over to him. He was wiping sweat from his brow with the corner of his shirt; breathing in short gasps.

"What?" he said.

"Nothing," I answered. "I'm just feeling a little punchy."

"Aren't we all," he replied. "And these woolen masks of yours are driving me crazy. You couldn't find silk?"

"Tight budget," I said. "So, I see you got her down."

"Indeed, though I have to admit the kids did all the work." He looked at his watch. "It's nearly four," he said. "We're not going to have time for the column, I'm afraid."

"I had a feeling it might come to that." I rubbed my chin, looking about the now depleted room. "OK. I can live with that. We'll let it go. Get the Lady packed and let's hit the road."

"What are we going to do with the children?"

"K?" I said.

"The loading dock is the ideal place," came her reply. "It's about the only place big enough where we could lock them in. If we bring up their sleeping bags and food, they should be comfortable enough until the morning guards arrive."

"Sounds good to me," Mac said. "I'll go and supervise the packing of the Lady."

"Good. I'll have a couple of the men get the kids' stuff from the party room," I said. "We'll meet on the dock."

"Right." Mac said and hurried off.

By 0430 we had the class rounded up in the loading dock and the crew paid off and gone. Andreas had the truck running. Mac was waiting in the Range Rover. Lights from a passing car washed over us and we all froze for a moment but it turned out to be nothing more than just an early morning commuter on his way to work.

Kaz had hung back with me and we turned and stood at the loading dock door, looking back over the weary faces of the class.

"You'll be safe in here," I said. "I want to thank you. I doubt there will be any trouble with the authorities. We did, after all, have guns and such and forced you to help us, right?" Some of the kids nodded. Most just smiled. The teacher looked stricken.

"Right. So. The morning guards should show up around seven so that will make your stay here just a little over two hours. Not as exciting as the museum itself, perhaps ... but then, who knows?"

I took one last look around the room. The twins and perhaps the quarterback looked as though they wanted to go with us. I smiled, saluted them, turned and almost ran into Kaz who was still waiting in the doorway.

"Ready to head for the shipyard?" I said in a somewhat louder voice than was really necessary.

"The shipyard?" she answered, startled.

"Of course," I replied. "We have a ship to catch." I stepped past her bewildered look and out of the museum. I heard her close and lock the door behind me.

She caught up with me as I was swinging into the truck alongside Andreas.

"What was that about?" she asked.

I looked at my watch and then back at the loading dock door.

"They'll be discovered within the next two hours. We'll barely have time to make it to the Chunnel in those two hours. It will be a madhouse here for the first thirty minutes or so, but you know that sooner or later, the authorities will interrogate them all. I'm sure a couple of those kids heard me and I'm counting on at least one of them, if not the teacher, to tell the authorities. If we can direct the search toward the shipyards, it will give us the time we need to get out of England. We were going to drop a dime on the decoy anyway, and we still will once we get to France. It's just that they will likely be closer than we had planned so the phone call will just confirm what they got from the class and put them closer to the goal we want them to reach. You better call the twins and let them know what's happened. They'll need to get a move on."

"You are brilliant, my thief," she said stretching on her toes to kiss me. I swung into the truck and she ran to the waiting Range Rover, the cell phone already in her hand.

"Now comes the difficult part," Andreas said, shifting the truck into low gear and pulling away from the dock.

"Amen, to that," I said.

Chapter 40

London traffic was a stop-and-go nightmare despite the early hour. From what we could gather from the early morning radio broadcasts, it was much worse in the western part of the city. Though the announcers weren't specific about the cause of the massive traffic jam that gripped west London, I knew the reason had to be the bomb threats we had called in earlier.

Kaz kept up a running commentary as we inched along through traffic on our way out of the city, her voice coming across the two-way linkup as though she were in the cab with us. Whereas we were tuned to the media broadcasts, she was deep into the police band, gleaning any information that came across the airwaves about the theft. She was also in touch with the twins who, at last report, were eating donuts and drinking too much coffee while waiting for their container to be loaded aboard a ship bound for New York.

As we came upon a mismatch between an American SUV and a Mini Cooper that had traffic merging into the breakdown lane, Kaz broke a twenty minute silence.

"They are on their way to the museum," she said.

I looked over at Andreas who just shrugged. "It had to happen sooner or later," he said.

"I would have preferred later," I replied. "We're only just out of London because of this traffic." Depressing the transmit button I said, "What have you got, Kaz?"

"They must have had a call. A car was dispatched. Your theory on the embarrassment factor may come to fruition. The code they used in the dispatch was a 'disturbance' call, not a break-in or theft."

"How long before the car arrives?" I asked.

"It should be there at any moment," she said. "The local station is not that far away."

I turned to Andreas. "You changed the plates on the truck, right?"

He gave me a curious look. "Plates?" he said. "What plates?"

"Smartass," I said. "Is there another route we can take? Bypass this traffic?"

"Several. But none that will allow trucks this size. We are better off where we are."

We crawled for another ten minutes, seeming no closer to the accident when Kaz's voice once again echoed through the cab. "I believe they have arrived," she said. "They have changed frequencies to one more secure. Hold on."

The silence from the speaker stretched into a minute; two. I caught myself holding my breath.

"Several more cars have been dispatched but not from the local precinct," came her voice at last. "These are coming from Special Branch."

"Any specifics?" I asked.

"Not before the switch of frequencies but now, with the change, they are feeling more secure and are talking more openly." There was another long moment of silence and then, "They have gathered up the class. Someone has called the American Embassy. Oh, and an ambulance for the guards."

"Do you think they are on to the decoy yet?" I asked.

"No. I believe not. There is no indication of this. I do not believe they are fully aware of what has happened."

"How are our boys over there?" I asked.

There was another long moment of silence.

"The container has been loaded," she said at last. "There is no sign yet of police activity at the dockyards. The twins are preparing to abandon the truck as instructed and head to the airport. They will be in Athens and out of harm's way soon."

"We're past the accident," Andreas interrupted. "Open road ahead."

"Good. The sooner we get away from the city, the better I'll like it." To Kaz I said, "Keep on monitoring. If things start to go sour, we'll have to make the call early."

"The farther out to sea the ship is, the better."

"I agree but it's a moot point if our true destination is discovered."

"Yes, you are correct. I will inform you if anything disturbing happens."

Andreas shifted up through the gears and soon we were moving along at a brisk pace. As he swung out to pass another lorry, I listened to the wind whistling around the air seals in the window. The tires thumping against the expansion joints in the road echoed the beat of my heart.

Several miles passed in silence when I noticed Andreas glancing anxiously out the side-view mirror.

"Problem?" I asked.

"I'm not sure."

"Danny?" came Kaz's voice over the speakers.

"Damn," said Andreas.

"What's going on."

"There is a police car following you," said Kaz.

"Is he going to stop us?" I asked Andreas.

Before he could answer, I saw flashing lights reflected in his side-view mirror.

"I'd say that's a yes," he said.

As Andreas slowed, preparing to pull over, I pressed the transmit button.

"Kaz," I said. "You and Mac keep going and swing back as soon as you can. Don't attract his attention."

"Will do," she said.

"The paperwork is in order," said Andreas as he brought the truck to a stop. "The truck is new, so there should be no problem there unless he insists on examining our cargo."

"So I should take the dart gun with me?"

"No," he said. "You should stay in the truck. No point in making him and his partner nervous."

"He has a partner?"

"Unlike predators in the wild, the domesticated cop in England always hunts in pairs."

"Here he comes," I said, spotting him in the mirror. I could see the patrol car but the sun's glare on the window prevented me from seeing the partner.

"Is there a problem, officer?" Andreas said, leaning out his window.

A cherubic face appeared in the window, looking not a little like the British comic Rowan Atkinson in his Mr. Bean role. The first words out of his mouth and the tone that conveyed them burst that illusory bubble.

"Step out of the truck, sir," he said, stepping down and away from the door.

Andreas glanced in my direction, grabbed a folder from behind the sun visor, opened it and slipped several sheets of paper from inside. He peered at them quickly, slid one back inside and stepped from the cab, leaving the other sheets behind. I looked them over. Half a dozen manifests, all for different towns.

"Moving a bit fast weren't you, sir?" said the cop, as he thumbed through the papers Andreas handed him. "And you look a bit heavy as well." He looked up, studying Andreas's face. "French, eh? You don't look French to me."

"Bosnian," Andreas lied. "Born in France."

"That explains it," the cop said. "Years of driving on the wrong side of the road and then you people come over here and get confused having to drive on the proper side. Hard for some to adjust."

I winced at the 'you people' remark and saw Andreas do the same, trying hard to keep a scowl from his face. I depressed the transmit button on the microphone.

"Kaz," I said.

"Here," she answered. "We circled around and are fifty meters behind your position."

"We've got trouble," I said. "This cop's a nasty one. He's going to want to inspect our cargo. Can you get him called off? Fake an emergency somewhere nearby?"

"I'm already on it," she said.

I glanced in Andreas's side mirror but the two were out of sight. No sign of them in my mirror either so they had to be at the rear of the truck.

"Hold on," she said. "I've got something. There. I've sent out an alert. It will show up in their patrol car any moment.

Andreas and the cop appeared in my line of sight. They both looked angry, the cop stabbing his finger in the air in the direction of Andreas's face. A sharp blast of the siren made both of them jump. The cop turned, listened to something out of my earshot, made one last stabbing gesture at Andreas with his finger and hurried to the patrol car. A second later I saw it pull away in a cloud of smoke, the tires leaving two serpentine trails on the highway as it sped off. A second after that, Andreas was climbing back into the cab.

"I don't know what you did," he said. "But I'm glad it was fast. He was insisting on inspecting the load, despite the seal on the door."

"Not me," I said. "Kaz and her keyboard magic. What now? What did you say to him to get him so angry?"

He started the truck and began maneuvering back onto the highway. "Now we get the hell out of here and avoid the motorway."

"Why avoid it?" I asked, activating the microphone so Kaz and Mac could tune in to what was going on.

"CCTV cameras," he answered. "All the motorways are monitored. Our destination is listed as Merstham so they'll be expecting us on the M25. It will look suspicious if we turn up on the M20 outside of Farmingham so we'll stay on the A20 instead. It parallels the M20 all the way to Folkestone. It will cost us some time but that's unavoidable. And just to be safe, we'll need to make another change of plates. The cops will likely radio those on the M25 to be on the lookout for us."

"Won't they become suspicious if they don't see us on the M25?" Kaz asked.

"Perhaps. But if they do, and if they decide to search, it will be in an area of the country where we are not and, with new plates, we will no longer be the truck we were."

As he shifted up through the gears, I asked him my second question again.

"Nothing," he replied. "He was an asshole."

"And you lost your temper."

"Yes. No. It doesn't matter. He's gone now."

"Thanks to Kaz's quick thinking," I said, anger straining my words. "And it could have mattered. It could have had us cuffed and sitting in a jail cell. What the hell is wrong with you, Andreas?"

"It's nothing. I'm tired. I told you before this would be my last job. Now, get off my back and let me drive."

I hesitated, wanting to probe him further, knowing it would do little good. I would get nothing from Andreas he didn't wish to give.

"How long before we arrive in Folkestone?" I asked.

"Several hours," he answered. "Perhaps more."

"Watch your speed."

He glared at me but said nothing.

Chapter 41

As we rolled into Folkestone, I set the mike down on its bracket on the dash and looked around. Road signs flashed by, directing us to the Chunnel's entrance. Andreas turned into a huge parking lot, swinging the truck about and bringing it in behind a short line of similar trucks. During the ride, Andreas had remained sullen and quiet, exacerbating my worry.

Soon after we arrived, I spotted the Range Rover turn into the lot and pull up behind a line of passenger cars. Kaz stepped out and disappeared, presumably in search of the WC. Scanning the parking area, I had several anxious moments when I spotted patrolling police. One of those moments turned terrifying when a patrol car pulled up alongside the Range Rover. I watched with a mixture of fear and fascination as the two cops chatted with Mac. I've known Mac for many years. He's diamond hard and as flexible as a willow branch, with an engaging sense of humor that could make an executioner crack a smile. Sure enough, when the patrol car pulled away, both cops were laughing.

I lost sight of the Range Rover when a lorry blocked my line of sight. Shortly after that, we were loaded on the train. I felt a weight lift off my shoulders as it began to move. We had made it. The next crucial moment would come when disembarking in France.

Andreas and I made our way to the Range Rover.

"Have a pleasant chat with the police?" I asked Mac.

"Quite," he answered. "Nice fellows. Bored out of their minds and wishing they could get up to London where all the excitement is."

"Oh? Did they mention what the excitement was about?"

"No, though they dropped enough hints to give one the gist of it. Something hush-hush, that affected several tall buildings, had traffic snarled up something awful and the authorities talking in code. I can't imagine what that might be."

"They must have found your response amusing. I noticed them laughing as they drove off."

"Oh, that. Nothing, really. They asked where I was headed and I told them I was on my way to steal a painting from the Louvre."

"And they found that amusing?"

"Indeed. Wished me luck, too."

We settled back for the long ride and listened to various news stations and the reports coming over the police radio. There was nothing on the news about the theft and a dearth of fresh information we could glean from the police broadcasts. We were midway to France when the London police turned their attention to the dockyards. By the time we unloaded at Sangatte, they were all over the Southampton docks, stopping all container trucks coming and going. They had not yet found the ship with our decoy container.

Mac and Andreas were standing alongside the Range Rover, the ever-present cigarette hanging from Andreas's mouth, when I returned with a tray of hot coffee and a brown bag filled with pastries. Kaz was hunched over the radio, writing furiously in a small notebook.

"What's happening," I asked.

"They are still at the docks," Kaz said. "That's the last I've heard." Andreas nodded, spitting the cigarette from between his lips and reaching into the bag I held and withdrawing one of the pastries. He stared at it for a moment and dropped it back in the bag.

"We are in France where pastries are an art form matching that of Cezanne, Monet, Edgar Degas and you purchase this shite?" he said, a look of consternation on his face. "I'm ashamed of you, Daniel."

"Well, excuse me. It was all they had."

I leaned into the Rover. "What about our ship?" I asked. "It should have set sail ten minutes ago."

"It has," Kaz said. "The police are trying to shut the harbor down but they are facing opposition. They won't reveal the why and the dock authorities are giving them a hard time. There is a power struggle of sorts going on there."

"Still no news of the theft?"

"Nothing. The police presence in that part of town is drawing a lot of media attention but no one is explaining why. It is causing a lot of confusion."

I stepped back and turned. Mac was alone now, Andreas being nowhere in sight.

"Where'd ...?"

"Beats me," Mac said. "I was listening to you and Kaz. When I turned back, he was gone."

I looked out across the vast parking lot, chewing the inside of my cheek. Trucks and cars came and went in a steady stream of traffic. Several people were heading toward the loading area. I couldn't see Andreas anywhere.

"Is it just me," Mac said, interrupting my thoughts, "or does our Albanian friend seem a bit preoccupied?"

"Not to mention hair-triggered," I said. "He damn near got us busted back there."

"Busted? How?"

"First, he was speeding, which got us pulled over in the first place. Then, he got into it with the cop. If Kaz hadn't come through with that alert ... well, I'd rather not think about that."

"Hmmm. Distracted, temperamental … and this silence. Not like the cool-under-pressure-with-a-fanatical-attention-to-detail Andreas we all know and love, is it? And this tight-lipped composure he's adopted? It used to be you had to hit him with a hammer to shut him up. Now, if you get half a dozen words out of him, it seems like a flood of conversation."

"I've noticed changes, too," said Kaz, stepping out from the Range Rover. Her hair was disheveled, blowing about her face in the breeze. I looked over at Mac. His face was drawn, dark circles shadowing his eyes, his clothes rumpled and soiled. I could well imagine I looked the same. We all needed a hot shower and a change of clothes. "He has been very distant, very quiet to me as well," Kaz continued. "Do you think he is ill?"

"I don't know," I said, rubbing my face with my hand. A shave would come in handy as well. "He's been acting odd since he arrived in Bize. I had a talk with him before he left. Claimed he was burned out, that this would be his last job. Started talking all weird about family and friends and the sacrifices we make for the life we lead. I wish I knew what was going on with him."

"And he isn't drinking," said Mac. "Did you notice that? Leastwise not as much as I'm used to seeing him drink."

"Yeah," I said, nodding in agreement. "Back in Bize he left a nearly full bottle of Marc on the table. I've never known Andreas to walk away from a bottle that wasn't bone dry."

At that moment Andreas rounded the corner of a building midway across the lot. When he looked up and saw us staring at him, he hesitated then continued toward us.

"WC," he said to our unasked question. "We should get moving. There are many miles ahead of us."

He continued past us and swung himself up into the cab of the truck. The three of us shrugged in unison. I turned and hurried to the truck while Kaz and Mac got in the Range Rover.

Pulling myself up into the cab, I asked Andreas, "How far to our first stop?"

"Several hours," he said, without looking at me. He eased the clutch out none too lightly and the truck leaped forward, throwing me against the seat.

"Hey," I said. "Take it easy. There's precious cargo back there."

"I am aware of how precious the cargo is," he said, shifting the truck into second gear. "Very aware."

I stared at him for a long moment, a hundred questions vying for attention in my mind. He refused to meet my gaze and I knew that asking any of those questions would only get me a blank stare and no real answers. Exhausted beyond words, I gave it up, bunched up a pillow against the door frame and rested my head. It had been a long night and we had many a kilometer to travel before we slept.

Chapter 42

At Dunkirk we turned our backs to the sea and began heading southeast along the crooked Franco-Belgian border. At one point the truck began to buck and falter like a skittish colt but it soon smoothed out. Andreas muttered something about fuel injectors under his breath, mixed with a few choice curses, but said nothing more on the matter. The problem didn't recur and I soon forgot about it.

Andreas wove through the twists and turns as though he knew the roads as well as the lines on his hand. I had no doubt he did, better perhaps. From time to time I could see Kaz and Mac in the Range Rover following behind us. There was silence from the radio. I knew Kaz would announce anything she thought important.

I dozed somewhere in there, waking when the truck turned onto a narrow, bumpy farm road. "What's up?" I said, sleep making my jaw feel heavy and not my own.

"We are almost at our first stop," Andreas said.

I sat up and looked around, rubbing sleep from my eyes, the Range Rover in sight in the wing mirror. My watch told me it was just past eleven, London time. We were making our way down a narrow, rutted lane, a dense border of thick-leaved trees on either side. The remnants of an old wooden fence wove in and out of the trunks. The ground on the other side of the windbreak had been farmland once but was now fallow and overgrown. Craning my head out the window, as much to get the wind on my face as to see the sights, I could see patches of blue sky through the dense branches. Rays of sun burst through like miniature spotlights, illuminating the ground before us.

After about a kilometer, the road widened and several rundown buildings came into view. The wood was dark and stained, the patchwork colors of drying cement. The house was little more than a shell, the windows broken, the chimney crumbled in a heap of stone at its base, long planks warped and twisted or gone altogether so that you could see inside. Though the front roof was intact, the rear had to have caved in, as the inside of the old house shone with sunlight. Two other buildings looked to be in much the same shape. One had all but collapsed in a heap on the ground. A large barn stood off to one side. Though as aged as the house, it looked to be in decent shape.

Half a dozen men in work clothes and heavy boots emerged from the barn. Andreas turned the truck toward them.

"The recrating crew," he said to my unspoken question. He pulled the truck to a stop and we both got out. The Range Rover circled the house once and pulled up alongside. I walked over to join Mac and Kaz as Andreas began oiling the hinges on the huge barn doors. A moment later he had them open and a moment after that the truck was hidden inside. The recrating crew followed him in and swung the doors closed behind them.

Several moments later, Andreas joined us at the Range Rover.

"The men will recrate the Marbles and be gone by nightfall," he said. "As for us, it would be unwise to return to the highway before dark. I stopped here on my way to London," he continued. "There is a working well on the property with a large reservoir on the roof of one of the outbuildings. I filled it. The sun should have warmed it enough so the water won't freeze everyone. I suggest we all use it. It may be awhile before we get another chance."

We were all touched by his thoughtfulness, but he walked away before any of us could thank him. By unspoken consent, Kaz went first, followed by Mac, then me and Andreas last. The water wasn't as warm as the aches and pains in my body would have liked but it felt good to be clean again. When I stepped from the shower, I saw that Kaz had laid out a clean set of clothes on the wooden bench for me. I dressed and returned to the barn, passing Andreas as I did.

"That was thoughtful," I said. "Thanks." He grunted an acknowledgment but said nothing. I watched him as he moved off to the small outbuilding that contained the makeshift shower. His head was hung low, his shoulders stooped as if he were carrying a burden he could barely sustain. Kaz was curled up asleep when I arrived at the barn. Mac was lying on his back in a pile of hay, staring up at the dusky rafters.

"Our friend's disposition seems unchanged," he said when I walked over to him.

"Yeah, I noticed," I said. "I thought he'd lighten up a bit once we got on the road. Or at least once we were through the Chunnel and into France. Doesn't seem to be the case."

"The shower was a nice touch, though."

"Typical Andreas," I said. "Tough, gruff, hard drinking and loud but with a heart of gold."

"Sounds like a noir detective," Mac said. "Except lately, he's been anything but tough, gruff, hard drinking or loud."

"But still the heart of gold," I added.

"I wonder what's wrong with him?" Mac asked. "I wonder if we should be worrying more?"

"I'm not sure there's anything more we can do besides worry. This is really Andreas's part of the gig, the main reason I wanted him along. Do you think any of us could have found this place? It's not on the Michelin map. I know. I checked. And that little farm road we took getting here? It's not there either."

"You two should stop grumbling and get some sleep," Kaz said. "Or at least be quiet so I can get some sleep."

"She's right," I said. I got up and walked over to where Kaz was lying. She moved the light blanket and I crawled in beside her. In moments I was out cold.

I dreamed I was standing in a luxurious marble shower stall, the water hot, steam enveloping me as the heat drew the weariness from my bones. As I lifted my face to the spray, the water turned bitterly cold and the marble walls of the stall became dull, gray iron bars. The water streaming from the nozzle transformed into pellets of ice which stung and broke my skin, my blood running in small rivulets into the drain at my feet. Looking out between the bars I could see Mac and Kaz in similar cages, their mouths open in screams I couldn't hear above my own. I woke, choking on that scream, my face soaked with sweat.

The light in the barn had grown dim. I tried to recall my dream, shivering in the chill I felt. It slipped away like wisps of dark smoke. Within moments I could remember not one detail of it.

Kaz knelt down beside me and stroked my shoulder. I sat up, brushing hay from my hair. "What time is it," I said.

"Just past seven," she answered. "The London police have expanded the search."

"Any news in the media?" I asked.

"Nothing. I believe it's time we made the call."

"Do we know if they've contacted the French authorities?

"Interpol? There is no indication of that. Though they would not through the channels I am connected to."

"Make the call," I said.

Kaz removed a cell phone from her pocket, turned it on and speed dialed a number in London. "It is time," she said, disconnected and turned the phone off again. Someone in London had just earned five thousand euros for a quick and anonymous call to the police directing them to a ship bound for America. The political ramifications of stopping, boarding and inspecting a foreign vessel should tie up the authorities for hours.

Or so I hoped.

I stood up, tried to stretch the weariness from my muscles, gave up and went searching for Mac and Andreas. I noticed the hood of the truck was open, a cloth apron over one fender with a line of tools stretched along it. I remembered the problem we'd had earlier and realized that Andreas must have been working on it while we slept.

I found Andreas in the back seat of the Range Rover and Mac curled up in the pile of hay where I had left him earlier. By the time I had them awake and together, Kaz had the Coleman stove lit and coffee brewing.

"Is the problem with the truck serious?" I asked Andreas, once we were all gathered together and the coffee was poured. Kaz and Mac turned their attention to him. His face seemed to cloud, his eyes cast down, away from our gaze.

"It is a minor problem," he said. "I am nearly finished. We will be ready by nightfall."

We finished our coffee in silence. Andreas returned to working on the truck. Kaz settled herself in the Range Rover to monitor the news. Mac produced a deck of cards and he and I settled into a quiet game of poker using the Marbles as chips. In the end, he ended up with them all. You would think a thief would make a good gambler but that had never been the case with me. I just couldn't get the hang of it.

Just as we were gathering up the cards for another round, Andreas stepped into the barn. Through the open door I noticed the sun had set. "The recrating is finished," he said. "The men have gone and it is time we departed as well." He turned away without another word and walked to the truck.

We made our way along the farm road, Kaz and the Range Rover in the lead. It was slow going as we traveled down the narrow, bumpy lane with no headlights on. Andreas had us stop fifty meters from the main road, got out of the truck and disappeared into the gloom, presumably to check the road for traffic. A few moments later he was back and we were on our way again.

At the junction with the main road, Kaz pulled over to the side and let the truck take the lead, falling in behind once we made the turn. Kaz lost contact with the London police reports shortly after. What news reports we could get were scattered and gave little information.

Andreas was hunched over the wheel, the muscles of his arms tight, his brow furrowed. He didn't look as if he'd slept at all. I tried to engage him in conversation several times and earned little more than a slow nod and a few grunts for my efforts. After awhile I gave up and stared out the window at the shadowed wayside as it passed.

Chapter 43

It's some twenty-five hundred kilometers from London to Athens as the crow flies. Our crow, however, was forced to zigzag its way across the country so that distance would be doubled, or even tripled, before we arrived at our destination.

We were traveling over tiny, poorly maintained, roads. Often when we approached small towns and villages, Andreas would abruptly turn off onto unmarked, rutted dirt roads and we would find ourselves wending our way through a vast expanse of vineyard or winding through thick, treacherous forest, the branches of the trees so low they scraped across the top of the truck like fingers across a blackboard.

Just past the village of Manbeuge, we passed into Belgium and the countryside began to get hilly. Our progress slowed even more than through the relatively flat expanse of France.

It was nearing dawn when we passed thorough a narrow portion of France that juts into Belgium. Soon after entering Belgium again, Andreas turned off onto what was little more than a set of overgrown paths. How he had even seen the turnoff I couldn't guess but he'd made the turn as if he'd been doing it all his life.

After a kilometer we came to what had once been a clearing but was now overrun with trees. The old farm house that had once stood here was a pile of rubble on the ground. The barn wasn't much better. Two sides had collapsed and the roof was tilting at an alarming angle. Andreas circled the barn, then pulled in from the rear. Kaz pulled the Range Rover alongside the decrepit structure. It didn't appear that our second stopover would be anywhere near as fine as the first.

The day passed without mercy. None of us was adventurous enough to want to stay beneath the dubious shelter of the barn so we spent our time wandering about the property, playing cards, trying to find a radio station, anything to pass the time. We were keyed up, lost in our own thoughts, with sleep proving elusive. I managed to doze late in the afternoon. I was just beginning to dream when Kaz shook me awake. It was time to go.

The drive was the same slow grind the previous night had been. I daydreamed. I dozed. I stared out the window seeing nothing. We were just about through Luxembourg before I even realized we were in it. A broken-down bakery truck on the side of the road had an address in the town of Bettembourg painted on its side. I had stayed there once, long ago, and knew it was situated south of the city of Luxembourg, very near the French border and mere kilometers from Germany. I looked up at the sky overhead. It was devoid of clouds, the stars like crystals of ice, glittering in a black void.

Very soon after we rolled into Germany, Andreas did a bizarre thing. I was expecting us to continue southeast toward Austria. Instead, he turned northeast toward Frankfurt. I questioned him about it but he explained my concern away by telling me these roads were less traveled and, despite the slight diversion, would stand us in good stead. I returned to my daydreaming.

I was shaken awake when the truck once again began balking whenever Andreas tried to accelerate. Very soon it became apparent that we would have to stop. Finding an area alongside the road big enough to accommodate both the truck and the Range Rover ate up several jerky kilometers. Finally Andreas found what he was looking for and pulled over. There wasn't enough room for the Range Rover so Mac, who had taken over from Kaz, pulled up alongside the truck. Kaz got out and walked over to where I was standing.

Andreas lifted the hood of the truck and began fiddling with something I could neither see, nor would have understood if I could. He was cursing under his breath, wiping sweat from his forehead with the sleeve of his jacket.

"What's up?" I asked.

"Injectors," he mumbled, offering no other explanation. I looked over at Kaz. She shrugged her shoulders.

"Can you fix it?" I asked. He gave me a sour look and turned his attention back to the engine.

"I guess he can fix it," I said to Kaz. We walked over to where Mac was sitting in the Range Rover, leaving Andreas to his work.

"Sorry," I said. "Parking lot's filled up."

"What is happening?" Mac asked.

"Something about an injector," I answered. "Could be a while."

"I saw a spot back over the rise where I can park this," he said. "I'll be back in a few minutes."

Kaz turned and looked up the small hill toward a copse of trees not far off. "I believe I will take this opportunity to commune with nature," she said.

"You have to pee," I said.

"You are so indelicate, my thief," she said, smiling.

I watched her cross the road and disappear into the woods and, giving a shake of my head to Mac as he drove off, I walked back to the truck. Mac joined me several minutes later.

The accumulated weight of my worry settled on my shoulders as I paced, anxious and worried as a long-tailed cat in a room full of rocking chairs. The situation wasn't all that bad, I tried to tell myself. We were several hours from dawn and Andreas had said he could fix the problem. But my gut was screaming that something was wrong. I just couldn't grasp what.

The answer came with a roar of engines, the sweep of powerful halogen beams that illuminated the road fore and aft of where the truck was parked. Much too late, all the pieces fell into place. Andreas's quiescence, his disappearance at Sangatte, his strange behavior since arriving at Bize. I turned to him. He had stepped down from his perch over the engine and was holding a Walther PPK pointed straight at me.

"Why?" I asked.

"Do you remember our talk in Bize," he replied.

The look on his face was that of a tortured man and his words came back to me with a jolt. 'Which would you give up, Daniel? Your family for your friends? Or would the friends be those betrayed for family?' He saw comprehension dawn on my face.

"They have my brother," he said, anger gripping his voice like a vise. "I am sorry."

Armed men surrounded us. Mac turned to run but was knocked to the ground and dragged across the road to where we stood. He brushed at the sleeves of his jacket and gave the men around us a contemptuous look. I longed to glance up into the woods where Kaz had gone but I forced myself not to. If they didn't already know of her presence then I didn't want to give it away. I feared that Andreas might say something but he kept his words to himself. I noticed a figure was making its way through the group of men but the bright lights made identification impossible.

"Well, old chap," came the familiar voice. "We were beginning to think you wouldn't show."

"Kellerman," I said, somehow not surprised. I started to lower my arms but he stiffened and brought the gun he was holding to bear on my chest.

"Easy there, friend," he said, stepping close enough for me to see him now. "Not that I think you'd be foolish enough to try anything but let's just pat you down first, eh?"

He nodded his head and one of his men began to frisk me. When he found nothing he stepped away.

"Much better," Kellerman said. "Now we can all relax."

"You're working for Marceau," I said, lowering my hands.

"Working for?" he said. "I wouldn't go that far. Let's just say that we've chosen to join forces toward a mutual goal."

"And that goal would be?" I asked, knowing the answer but not expecting to get one from him. I wasn't disappointed.

"That's unimportant," he replied. "Your role in this is nearing an end." He walked over to the truck and began running his hand along the side. "So, what do we have here?"

"Chocolate chip cookies," I answered. He laughed and turned to face me.

"You still owe me four hundred euros," he said, a cold smile on his face, the gun leveled at my chest.

"I don't suppose you'd take a check?" I said. I glared back at him, a smile of my own pasted to my face. We stared at each other for a moment and then he began to laugh.

"You have managed to raise the ire of a very dangerous man," he said when the laughter subsided. "Marceau is quite determined to see you dead."

"What about you?" I asked. "Are you determined to see me dead as well?"

"That is not for me to decide," he replied. "Nor, in truth, do I care one way or another. However, Marceau cares and so it will be he who decides your fate."

Andreas stepped from behind me, the gun loose in his hand. "That was not the plan," he said. "Marceau assured me they would be freed."

"Alas, my Albanian friend, plans change."

"My brother," Andreas said, looking around. "Where is my brother?"

Kellerman made an exaggerated show of looking around. "No brother," he said. "How odd. It would appear it's not your day at all."

He gave a nod of his head and without warning Andreas staggered forward, the Walther falling from his hand and clattering to the pavement. He stumbled and fell hard. Hands grabbed me, wrestling me to the ground where plastic cuffs were tightened around my wrists. Mac was struggling but someone punched him in the stomach, bringing him to his knees. The entire fight, such as it was, was over in moments and the three of us were dragged to a van and thrown not so gently into the back.

The doors slammed shut and I could hear the men walking away, talking amongst themselves. Mac was cursing as he tried to regain the breath that had been knocked from him. Andreas was moaning, an anguished sound that seemed to reverberate about the confined space into which we'd been thrust.

I moved to the rear of the van and pressed my ear to the door. I could hear someone shuffling outside but beyond that it was all just faint noise. There didn't seem to be a pursuit going on and my hope grew that Kaz's presence was unknown. Very soon I heard the truck start and soon after that the van rocked as two men entered the front. A moment later we were moving. Though there were no windows and despite no sense of direction, I knew where we were going, which didn't make me feel all warm and fuzzy.

Chapter 44

A sharp turn and the sudden jostling of a bumpy road woke me from a dazed sleep. My arms were cramped, the muscles in my neck screaming, my fingers were numb and cold. The ache in my battered ribs was like a hot coal nestled against my lung. I tried to shift my position but found my legs were still asleep.

Retreating into myself, I sought some center, some place of calm and began sending thoughts to my legs, forcing them to move. When at last they did, the rush of blood made my skin feel as if thousands of ants were crawling and biting their way from deep within. The feeling passed and I shifted to as comfortable a position as I could find. Enough light was drifting around the doors at the side and rear for me to just make out the interior of my rolling cell.

Mac was on his side, across from the door. He was curled up in a fetal position with his arms stretched behind his back. He was snoring and I envied him his sleep.

On the far side of the van, against the wall that separated us from the driver's compartment, Andreas sat staring off at something I knew I wouldn't be able to see even if the van were ablaze with light. He was mumbling beneath his breath but I couldn't make out the words.

I sat there for a moment, trying to blame him for the fix we were in but I couldn't work up any anger. If anyone was to blame, it was me. I should have seen it. Andreas, in his own troubled and torn way, had all but told me what was going on. And, if I was going to be honest in this moment of introspection, I had to ask myself would I have done anything different had it been Kaz they held over my head?

The van's ride smoothed out and slowed to a stop. I heard a clanking, metallic sound I recognized. My suspicions as to our destination were confirmed. The van started up again and within moments the echo from the engine told me we were inside the large hangar that marked the entrance to Dieter's stronghold.

The van stopped, the rear door opened and the three of us were dragged out. As we were led across the room, I spotted several bodies laid out against a far wall. The cars I had seen on my last visit here were riddled with bullet holes. One of the men leading us opened a door, shoved us into a small storeroom and slammed the door. There was the sharp snap of a lock and we were alone again.

The hours crept by like mice on Qualudes. A thirst was building in me and I was in desperate need of a bathroom. When a guard brought in water several hours later, I told him so. There was a hushed conference outside the storeroom and, one by one, we were led off to do our business. I was taken first. The evidence of an intense gun battle was everywhere. I saw several more bodies, stacked up like cordwood, in a corner of the room. The helicopter that had been in the building the last time I was there, was now a charred ruin.

The two men escorted me to a dirty bathroom on the far side of the hangar. They removed my cuffs and one of them stood watch as I sat on the john. A pool of blood was congealing on the floor at my feet. Some poor soul had had the misfortune to be sitting on the pot when the end came for him. I shuddered. Hell of an ignoble way to go. I thought of Elvis and shuddered again.

When I finished, I was led back to the room and cuffed again, this time with my hands in front of me. I found myself thankful for the small favor. Mac was led out next. I looked around the room for Andreas but he was no longer there.

When Mac returned, we sat against one wall and made small talk until the words ran out. Neither of us discussed Andreas, or Kaz, or what fate might hold for us. The latter was too obvious. Andreas and Kaz were beyond our hope or control. Mac fell into a light doze and I followed suit.

I dreamed of gunfire and explosions. Someone – me, I realized with a shock – was shooting at the Marbles, blowing them to dust with a weapon that looked like something Arnold Schwarzenegger would carry in one of his Terminator movies. First the metopes, then the panels from the frieze and finally the pedimental statues. All now just chips of white marble strewn about the ground. I was taking aim at the Caryatid, ready to blow it to pieces, when I was shaken awake. I stared up into Kaz's eyes and felt sure I must still be dreaming. I started to speak and she pressed her fingers to my lips.

"Hush," she whispered. I became aware that the gunfire from my dream was still echoing here in wakefulness.

"What's going on?" I whispered back. "How did you get here?"

"I don't know to the first," she answered. "To the second I will explain later. We must hurry, now, if we are to escape. They are killing each other all over the compound."

She cut the cuffs off and then turned to Mac, wide awake now. After freeing him, she handed me the Beretta we'd stashed in the Range Rover. I turned it

260

over in my hands several times, then jacked a shell into the chamber. I looked up as Kaz handed Mac a semi-automatic. She had a similar weapon slung over her shoulder.

"You come well equipped," I said.

"There are many such weapons lying about," she said. "Hurry."

We scrambled across the room to the door. I opened it a crack and peeked out into the hangar. Several new bodies had joined the ones I'd seen earlier. They hadn't yet been gathered up into nice, neat piles and lay in various grotesque poses near the middle of the room. We slipped past the door, ran hunched over to a bullet-riddled Rolls and dropped to the ground alongside it.

"The Range Rover is outside," she said. "We may be able to escape while they are all killing each other."

Kaz and Mac moved toward the front entrance. I stayed behind.

"No," I said. "I'm not leaving the Marbles behind." Mac and Kaz turned and looked at me as though I was insane, which, I had to admit, was pretty much how I sounded. "And I'm not leaving Andreas to them," I added.

"But he betrayed us," Mac said.

"It doesn't matter," I said. "And which of us wouldn't have done the same in the circumstances? Or been torn apart over such a decision? No. I won't leave him or the Marbles. Marceau wants a confrontation, I'll give it to him. You two go on. This is no longer your battle."

Mac and Kaz looked at each other. No words passed between them but Mac shrugged and Kaz said, "I will not leave you."

"Nor I," added Mac.

"Then let's go find Marceau," I said.

I was several steps ahead of Mac and Kaz, the Beretta down at my side, when I moved toward the door that would lead us into Dieter's compound. I jumped when the door flew open and a figure staggered from the shadows. It was Kellerman. There was blood running down the side of his face, matting his hair and staining his shirt.

"You," he said. He fell back against the building, raising his weapon as he did. A burst of gunfire punctured the air to my right. I pulled the trigger on the Beretta and returned a single shot. It caught him high in the chest, slamming him back against the wall. The Mac 10 he'd fired at me slid from his hands and he sank to the ground.

I stared at him and then at the gun in my hand. "Jesus," I said, feeling shaky and off balance. "I've never shot anyone before."

Kaz and Mac materialized on either side of me. Kaz touched my arm and the shaking stopped.

"It was him or you, my thief," she said. "Keep that always in mind."

"And better him," Mac added. "We should probably go. Before more of his kind show up."

"My thief?" Kaz reached up and touched my cheek.

"Yeah," I said. "You're right. We need to hurry."

I made a wide circle around Kellerman's body and entered Dieter's compound, Kaz and Mac close on my heels. We found ourselves in the long corridor that led to the elevator. Several more bodies populated the floor in our path.

We reached the elevator. The door was open, the chrome walls speckled with blood. We stepped inside. I pushed the button for the lowest floor and the doors slid closed without a whisper. The descent was slow and charged with tension. We had no idea what might greet us when the elevator stopped. The doors opened and we each stepped to one side, Mac and Kaz raising their Mac 10's, me the Beretta.

We were met by a scene of utter carnage.

Bodies and blood were everywhere. A desk was overturned, its oak top splintered with bullet holes. I spotted the woman, Gisela, who had met mc at the elevator the last time I was here. She was slumped against a wall, two bodies beside her, another across her legs. Her white blouse was stained with blood. She still gripped the knife she'd used to kill the three men around her.

We crossed the room into the corridor that led to Dieter's inner sanctum. The forged paintings that had once covered the walls were now mostly torn up pieces of canvas. I wondered if Gail, the forger, would be saddened by their fate. The floor was strewn with broken glass. When we came to the end of the corridor, the vault door was closed and locked.

"How are we going to get past that," Mac asked. I tried to think of what to do and then it came to me. I hurried back up the corridor and returned carrying Gisela in my arms. Her body was still warm.

Resting her body near the door, I flattened her palm against the lock while Mac kept her body from falling. It took a moment before we heard a whir and then the click of the locks and the door swung open an inch. Laying her down gently, I pulled the door all the way open, standing behind it in case we were greeted with gunfire. Nothing happened and after a moment, the three of us stepped into what had once been Helga's lair.

This room, too, was in chaos. Helga's expansive chrome and glass desk was now little more than glittering shards and slivers. I looked around the room, half expecting to see Helga's body but there were no bodies in this room. No blood either. The window that looked into Dieter's gym was shattered. As the door to the gym was closed and I doubted that Gisela's hand would open it, the three of us made our way over the window sill, careful not to cut ourselves on the sharp shards of glass remaining in the frame.

Though the gym was dark, I spotted Dieter's body, or what was left of it, in a heap beside the Stairmaster on which he had climbed to the moon. It looked as if someone had emptied an entire clip from a Mac 10 into him and then, for good measure, emptied a second one. Kaz gasped when she spotted him, turning away. I heard Mac gag and felt the same feeling come over me. The stench in the room was horrendous.

Suddenly the room erupted in gunfire. As I turned to face it, a searing pain lanced through my right shoulder and the Beretta clattered to the floor. Kaz and Mac were crouched down, firing back the way we had come. Before I followed my gun to the floor, I saw several men fall from the blistering wall of fire being returned to them.

More shots came from somewhere in the gym. I heard Mac cry out and Kaz screamed. A booming voice cried out and then there was silence. The lights came on and from where I sat on the floor I watched Marceau enter the gym through the hidden door to Dieter's gallery. When he saw me, a smile broke across his face and his eyes shone like the glint off the wings of a carrion fly.

Kaz helped me struggle to my feet. Mac was on the ground beside me clutching his leg. I heard someone moan and noticed for the first time the huddled figure against the far wall of the gym. Recognition was like a blow to the solar plexus. It was Andreas. He was rocking on his heels, the battered and bloodied body of his brother in his arms. The sounds that came from his throat were like those of a caged animal, beaten and starved beyond hope. I turned and faced Marceau with a murderous rage in my heart.

"Is it worth all this death?" I screamed.

"This and much more," Marccau answered. "And my greatest joy of the day will be to see you amongst those who have fallen."

Marceau stepped further into the room, followed by two men carrying a single, crated painting.

"That's the last of them, sir," said one of the men.

"Good," replied Marceau. "Get it into the truck. We'll be leaving *toute de suite*."

If I thought I'd had all the shocks that were coming to me for the day I was wrong. The men carrying the painting had no sooner left the room when Helga walked through the door from Dieter's gallery.

"Herr Samsel," she said, her voice cold and sharp. "How I have longed for this opportunity to discuss certain paintings with you."

She stood alongside Marceau, towering over him. I looked from one to the other and then over at Dieter's body.

"He was a loathsome man," she said, all but spitting out the words. "Always with his little bimbos surrounding him; his eternal desire for youthful flesh."

"You?" I said, unable to keep the surprise from my voice.

"Indeed," she replied.

"He trusted you."

"He trusted no one! And now he is dead. I shall at last come into what is rightfully mine."

She started moving toward me, stopping several feet away. Kaz started to stand in front of me but I pushed her away and took a step toward Helga. I knew she could break me in half without raising a sweat but she wasn't going to get away without a scratch.

"Helga," Marceau said. Helga turned and faced him. The smile on her face faltered when she saw that he was pointing his gun at her.

"What is this?" she asked. "What are you doing?"

"You didn't honestly think, my dear, that I would share all this with the likes of you, did you?" he said. "Once a betrayer, always a betrayer."

Before she could make a move, he fired a bullet that shattered her skull. Like a giant Viking statue wrested from its pedestal, Helga fell to the floor and was still.

"I would love to stay and chat more," Marceau said, "but I fear it is time to go. Pity. I would have so enjoyed making your last moments as painful as possible, but ..."

He shrugged his shoulders and leveled the gun in my direction. Kaz screamed and began to move toward me. At the same time, there was a roar from across the room. Andreas had risen to his feet and was moving toward Marceau with astounding speed. Marceau, rattled by the scream, turned, the gun still pointing in my direction. Andreas plowed into him like a runaway freight train. The gun went off. Kaz hit me like a lineman going for the quarterback. The bullet burned the air centimeters from my skull. I felt my legs twist out from under me, felt pain lance from my ankle to my groin.

As I hit the ground I heard a muffled gunshot. Andreas had knocked Marceau backward, pushing his body up the wall until his feet left the floor. He had his hands about Marceau's neck. Marceau fired again and, though Andreas's body rocked from the explosion, he didn't let go. Marceau's eyes began to bulge and his face deepened in color. The gun he held clattered to the floor. His body began to jerk and quiver and his bladder voided, urine darkening the front of his pants and spilling out over his shoes.

Before long his body stopped moving but still Andreas held on, his fingers tightening until you could hear the small bones in Marccau's throat begin to crack. Finally Kaz ran to him and gripped his shoulder. He turned his head to look at her. Blood was dripping from the corners of his mouth. She whispered something I couldn't hear. I saw a smile touch his lips and then both he and the body of Marceau crumpled to the floor.

I struggled to a sitting position, the pain in my leg, my chest, all but unbearable. I stared across the room, watching as Kaz bent over Andreas. She looked up at me, tears in her eyes, shaking her head. The room was hot, the light so bright, that everything faded before my eyes. A stadium of confused noise engulfed me and I felt as if the earth were shifting beneath where I sat.

I don't remember falling.

Chapter 45

I awoke not knowing where I was or how I'd got there. We were inching down a dark road. I looked around and realized I was sitting in the backseat of the Range Rover. My right shoulder felt as if it were on fire. My left leg was stiff, the knee swollen to the point of immobility.

Andreas was sitting across the seat from me, wrapped in a blanket, his head down, twin trails of drying blood at the corners of his mouth. I mumbled something about needing a bathroom and Kaz found a spot to pull over.

Mac appeared alongside the Rover, hobbling on a makeshift cane. And, much to my surprise, Alix appeared a moment later. She and Kaz helped me from the backseat and Kaz led me a short way into the bushes. When we returned, I spotted the other truck. I looked first at Alix, who was stretched over the backseat of the Rover tending to Andreas, and then at Mac.

"Dieter's collection," was all Mac said. I nodded. So much had happened since I'd passed out in Dieter's gym.

"How long have I been out?" I asked Kaz.

"Twenty-four hours," she said. "Maybe longer."

"Where are we?"

"Bosnia," Mac said. "We think."

"Andreas was able to give us some directions at first," Kaz added. "But the last few hours we've been driving blind. I've just been following the compass southeast and avoiding any towns and villages."

She went on to explain how, while leaving Dieter's compound, they had found Alix hiding in a closet. She had dressed my wounds as well as those of Andreas and Mac. The gunshot to Mac's leg had been a through-and-through. I was not as lucky. There was a bullet lodged in my shoulder. When I looked to them for news of Andreas, Alix shook her head while Kaz's eyes filled with tears. Mac turned his head away and stared off into the trees.

"What about Andreas's brother?" I asked.

"Dead," Mac said. "We have his body wrapped up in the back of Dieter's truck. It's air-conditioned."

Kaz and Alix unpacked some loaves of bread and a jar of thick jam from the back of the Rover. Mac got the Coleman stove going and soon we were sipping coffee. Watching the way Mac and Alix behaved together I could tell they had taken a liking to each other. Funny how, from the dark loam of adversity, a bright flower can bloom.

It was a silent meal, each of us lost in our own thoughts, grieving for what had happened, what was yet to happen, each in our own way. We packed up in silence, Kaz and Alix doing most of the work. Kaz helped me into the backseat of the Rover while Mac went to the truck with the Marbles and Alix to the one with Dieter's collection.

Still within our own dark thoughts, we were once again on our way.

Chapter 46

Andreas died as we crossed the border into Albania.

"Family – and friends," he whispered, gripping my hand fiercely for a moment, his eyes blazing. Then the light in them faded and his fingers slipped from mine in a last, long expulsion of breath. I stared at his motionless form, wanting to shake him awake, to undo all that had happened. I felt an emptiness that defied words and though I searched for the tears I knew were there, I could not find them.

We made our way across the desolate country, turning up roads that too often petered out into nothing, forcing us to turn around. Only Kaz had ever been to Andreas's village and that had been years before. After a great deal of frustrated cursing on her part, we came to the village where Andreas had been born.

The houses were worn and weatherbeaten, the streets rutted and unpaved, yet there was warmth to the place, a sense of community. People gathered and watched us pass, a strange procession of vehicles rolling through their tiny village. After several false turns, we found his mother's house. The look on her face when she came to the door said she knew that our appearance did not bode well.

The wailing began when we showed her the body of her oldest child and then her youngest. Soon the anguished cry enveloped the entire village. Several men helped us carry the bodies to a small church. A tiny graveyard stretched out alongside the building, the gray markers shining dully in the morning sun. Backs were turned to us and soon we were alone beside our caravan. It was time for us to go and leave them to their grief.

The village receded, though for hours I thought I could hear the wails of the women. I was sitting in the front seat now, beside Kaz. She rested her hand on my knee. I could feel tears welling up inside me, seeking a way past whatever it was that blocked their passage to my eyes.

Andreas had saved my life at the cost of his own. Nothing in my experience allowed me to know how I should feel about that. What I should do. Or if I could go on with that dark and terrible knowledge. Kaz squeezed my knee as though reading my thoughts.

It was when the sun glared overhead, a colorless and empty hole in the sky that the tears came. It felt as though they would never stop.

Chapter 47

The smog hung heavy over Athens as we wended our way through the northernmost hills that surround the city. Kaz had made a phone call and we were expecting the twins to meet us at any moment. We passed a blinking marker and after that spotted an old brown Datsun sitting on the side of the road, its emergency lights flashing. It pulled out onto the road as we approached and we followed it into the city.

The streets of Athens were thick with traffic, despite the late hour. We were all beyond the point of complete exhaustion now and I was thankful Kaz had arranged for Kostas and Nikos to link up with us and lead the way. We would never have found it on our own.

It was well past midnight when we came to the warehouse I had rented in case we needed to stash the truck before delivering it to the Acropolis. As it turned out, it would be needed after all. We pulled the truck containing Dieter's treasure inside, leaving the truck with the Marbles out on the street. Mac and Alix declined an offer to come to the island, choosing instead to return to his home in Turkey. Nikos agreed to drive them to the airport. After a tearful farewell, they drove off into the night.

Kostas drove the truck while Kaz and I followed in the Range Rover. There was a fearful moment when Kostas broke through the chain barrier that blocked the service road leading up the hill to the base of the Acropolis, but no one seemed to notice the racket and soon we were far away from the dense traffic on the street. We parked the truck near the Rock of the Philosophers, wiped down the interior thoroughly and left the doors unlocked with the key hanging in the ignition.

I looked up at the lights that illuminated the great temple and smiled for the first time in days. Kaz came up to me and kissed me on the cheek. We stood there, hand-in-hand for a long time.

"We must go, *mein dieb*," she said at last.

I let go the breath I was holding, the prayer for Andreas and his brother drifting from somewhere deep inside me and out into the night air. Slipping my good arm around Kaz, she helped me hobble to where Kostas had the Range Rover waiting. With one last look, I slipped into the backseat, Kaz beside me, and we drove away.

Chapter 48

Fall is a beautiful time on Kefalonia. The weather cools, the tourists depart and the island settles in for winter. The oranges that bathed in the rich light of the summer sun hang fat and juicy on the trees.

I still wore the sling on my right arm, though I had been removing it for hours at a time, flexing my arm, getting the movement back. The crutches I'd had, had been replaced with a cane, making moving about a lot easier. The leg was still sore. I wore a brace on the knee and if I put too much weight on it, it felt as if a saber was being run up the left side of my body. But I was mending.

Mac had arrived several days earlier, looking fit and healthy. Alix was with him. I had never seen Mac looking so happy. They had just returned from Albania where they had visited Andreas's grave and given his share of the job money to his family.

The old café where all this had started had experienced an amazing transformation. The money the twins had earned on our little adventure had gone into expanding the place. There were new tables and chairs complete with umbrellas to ward off the sun. They had installed a whole new kitchen and indoor dining area and the menu had increased considerably. I have to admit I liked it the old way but the family seemed happy with the changes and I couldn't begrudge progress.

I had met with Eleni as soon as I'd felt able enough to move around. She refused to accept the return of what money I had left, saying Dino would have wanted me to have it. There were tears in her eyes when I introduced her to Kaz. The two of them hugged like long-lost mother and daughter. I had invited Eleni to this little affair but she had declined, saying she had to fly to Athens for the unveiling of the Marbles. She was being honored for her – unspecified – contribution to their return.

The tables within and without the taverna were filling up with our guests. Malcolm had made it, sporting a Vandyke beard and thin mustache, both real, and a new mop that fitted him better than the last one I'd seen him in. I had hoped that Wu could attend but he had begged off, sending a framed painting of the British Museum in his place. It was hanging now below the awning alongside the door to the taverna. It was a strange curiosity to most of those attending this party; those who were not privy to its true meaning. That was okay. Much of a thief's life is lived in secrecy, after all.

Kaz set a plate of goat chops on the table. As she sat down beside me, I saw Gerasimos walking across the square. His face split into a wide smile when he saw me and he hurried over and pulled up a chair at our table. I introduced him to Kaz, Mac, Alix and Malcolm.

"I'm surprised to see you here," I said. "I thought you'd be in Athens for the unveiling."

"I have a flight later in the afternoon," he said, reaching over and plucking one of the goat chops from my plate. "I'll be there in time for the reception. What of you? Why are you not attending? And what of your injuries? A skiing accident, wasn't it? I had no idea you skied."

"I'm healing well." I said. "It was my first time on the slopes. That's why I banged myself up so badly. As for the reception, why would I want to attend? The Marbles have nothing to do with me."

He stared at me for a long moment, then smiled, taking a bite from the chop. "Of course not," he said, chewing slowly. "How could their mysterious return have anything to do with you?"

"Mysterious return?" I asked, all innocence and surprise. "What do you mean 'their mysterious return'? I thought the Brits returned them as a goodwill gesture? That's what I heard, anyway. It's all over the news."

He continued to stare at me, searching my eyes for some truth he hoped to find. "Let's just say that's the official explanation, the one that went out to the press."

"And the real explanation is different?" I asked.

"To be sure," he said. "The most amazing thing of it is, just a few months ago, in this very place in fact, we were discussing what might happen if, say, the Marbles were to magically appear on the doorstep of the Acropolis. And *voilà*, they do. An extraordinary coincidence, wouldn't you say?"

"Well, stranger things have happened," I replied. "Though it is a mighty big coincidence. Are you saying that someone stole them and left them outside the Acropolis? What happened then? What did the British do?"

"It would appear that way," he said, finishing the chop and wiping his fingers. "It was rough going there for a while. The British were outraged, threatening us with sanctions, reprisals, all sorts of horrors, if we didn't return them. There were moments when I thought we might go to war. Then, suddenly, they just capitulated."

He shrugged his shoulders.

"What could they do, really? We had the Marbles. We weren't going to give them back. They couldn't, or wouldn't, reveal to the world what had happened. In the end they went for the PR value of 'giving' the Marbles back to Greece. What the world saw in all the publicity shots was the column from the Erechtheion, which the thieves left behind, and some replicas of the metopes the museum had stashed somewhere. Even the Louvre in Paris returned the one metope it had. All in all, I think it worked out well for everyone. I am glad, however, that Greece is part of the EU. I doubt we would ever have gained admission after what happened."

"Oh well," I said. "That wouldn't have been such a big loss. I do rather miss the drachma."

Gerasimos laughed, opened a beer and sat back in his chair. A smile was toying at his lips though he was trying hard to maintain an air of indifference.

"I understand," he said after a moment, "that they, the Brits I mean, received an anonymous gift. One which may well have led to their letting go of the Marbles."

"Really?" I said. "I hadn't heard that. What did they receive?"

"Well, much as the Marbles appeared here in Athens, it seems that six, very important, very expensive and very much believed-to-be-lost, paintings showed up on the doorstep of the British Museum. Isn't it odd the way great works of art find their way around these days?"

"Yes indeed," I said. "I wish something like that would happen to me. I could use the money."

Everyone at the table laughed. Katrina emerged from the kitchen along with several of her sons, all carrying trays overloaded with food and drink. They set them down on the tables and all the guests began digging in.

We spent several hours talking and eating and consuming huge quantities of beer and ouzo. Gerasimos bade us farewell toward the latter part of the afternoon. Before he left, he handed me a sealed envelope.

"Eleni asked me to give this to you," he said, and with that, he left.

I broke the wax seal and removed the note. It smelled of roses. I read the note, smiling as I did. Tears crept into the corners of my eyes but I wiped them away before anyone but Kaz could notice.

"What's it say?" asked Mac.

Kaz reached over and took my hand. I felt choked up for a moment, my throat constricting around the words.

"It's from Eleni," I said, my voice cracking. "She wanted me, us, to know that at the dedication tonight, the room the Ladies will be housed in will be officially named 'The Andreas Agani Room.' "

I folded up the letter and returned it to my shirt pocket. Kaz leaned over and gave me a kiss. Mac, Alix and Malcolm were silent, though I could see tears glistening in their eyes.

"So," Mac said, "Any blowback?"

"A friend let me know the coppers were all over my old flat," Malcolm said. "I was long gone of course, and I stripped it clean before I left so I doubt they found anything of value."

"Interpol showed up here as well," I said. "Several times. Eleni headed them off, provided an alibi. Spiros went with Kaz and me to the Alps, to explain the sling, and provide an alibi for the ruse."

"I'm surprised they didn't want to do a thorough medical exam," Mac said.

"Oh, they wanted to, believe me," I said. "Spiros had that covered as well, providing an emergency medical report from the ski lodge clinic in Switzerland and a follow-up report from a local doctor. They chafed, but in the end they went with it. What about you and Alix? You two catch any flak?"

"I had a visit from Israeli Intelligence," said Mac.

"The Mossad?"

"Strange, I know. I was expecting Interpol and got the Mossad instead. But it was about the Marbles, all right. They wanted to know my whereabouts at the time of the heist. I had all the documentation prepared proving Alix and I were in China the whole time. They looked it over, they went away, that was it. Have you heard anything concerning the events at Dieter's?"

"Nothing official. Interpol appears to have suppressed any news of the incident. You'd expect that, of course, when one of yours is dirty. Especially one as high up the food chain as Marceau."

"There were a few tidbits of rumor floating about Lisbon while I was there," Malcolm said. "Something about a quarrel amongst thieves that turned violent. Nothing about Interpol, though."

"Now, now, Malcolm," I said. "Let us not besmirch thieves. We tend to be a pacifistic lot, averse to violence. Dieter and his kind are criminals, not thieves. There is a world of difference between us."

As evening approached and the weather began to cool, people began to leave the taverna. Malcolm bid us goodnight, saying he needed his beauty sleep. At last, it was just Kaz and me, Mac and Alix left sitting at the outside tables.

"So, the Brits received some paintings," said Mac, sipping the last of his beer. "I wondered what you had planned for them."

"I was surprised you didn't want any part of them," I said.

"I've never had much love for paintings. Besides, it was your gig. You should enjoy the spoils."

"Yes," I answered. "Well, I tried to be judicious in what I sent them. It only seemed fair, after all. I've sent several others to the Louvre and spread some more around to other museums. It took a bit of work, but I even managed to find a way to fund the sports program and some afterschool programs at that Boston high school. I kept a few paintings in reserve, of course, though I did send the Washington back to the White House via a surreptitious route."

"But why?" Alix asked.

"Why, indeed?" echoed Mac.

Kaz turned to me and smiled, squeezing my hand. I lifted the shot glass of Brettos ouzo to my lips and sipped it down, setting the glass on the table.

"Well, partly because I'd heard the British were giving the Greeks a hard time and I just figured, you know, a little salve couldn't hurt. But mostly, I felt that works of art, such as those hidden for so long behind Dieter's door, should be shown to the world again, appreciated for their beauty by everyone with the price of admission."

I looked around the table. Kaz was trying hard not to laugh. Mac and Alix were looking at me like I had suddenly sprouted horns.

"And besides," I continued. "I have to have something worthwhile to steal."

Epilogue

It's been said that when Elgin removed the Caryatid from the Porch of the Maidens and transported it to England, those that remained wept. A month after she and the Marbles were returned and set in place in the new Acropolis Museum, a guard, making his rounds, thought he heard a noise in the part of the museum where the Ladies were kept.

Later, when he told friends what he'd heard, they accused him, in jest, of being drunk on the job, though they all knew he never drank anything stronger than Greek coffee. The guard didn't mind, he let them have their joke. He knew what he'd heard and the thought of it made his heart swell.

He had heard the ladies laughing.

Afterword

Stealing the Marbles is, of course, a work of fiction, Danny and company merely somewhat bothersome figments of this author's vivid imagination. The plight of the Parthenon Marbles is, however, quite real. At the turn of the nineteenth century, Lord Elgin did indeed dismantle and ship fifteen Metopes, fifty-six panels from the frieze, seventeen pedimental statues, a column from the Erechtheion and, saddest of all, one of the ladies from the Porch of the Maidens from their ancient home in Greece to his home in England.

One could, I suppose, debate whether these antiquities were given to him by the Ottoman Empire, whether the Ottoman Empire could rightfully give them away in the first place or whether Lord Elgin took it upon himself to take them. One could also argue that their removal saved them from further destruction but considering the damage done to them while in the care of the British Museum, I'd say that would be a hard argument to win. There is an abundant amount of research on the all these matters so I'll let you, the reader, decide for yourself what transpired. Might I suggest Lord Elgin & The Marbles by William St. Clair and The Elgin Marbles/Should They Be Returned to Greece by Christopher Hitchens as a good place to start.

Both of these books, along with a host of websites devoted to the Parthenon Marbles, were invaluable to this author's research.

What is not debatable by anyone is Greece's long held desire to regain their precious heritage. Since winning their independence from the Ottoman Empire in 1832, the Greeks have been calling for the return of the antiquities taken by Lord Elgin, a request steadfastly refused by the British government.

I believe this author's position as regards the Parthenon Marbles is obvious. If you have gotten this far and feel as I do that the Marbles should be reunited with their homeland, please visit www.stealingthemarbles.com and join me in my campaign to Send The Marbles Home.
Thank you.

E. J. Knapp
August, 2010

About the Author

E. J. Knapp was born during a thunderstorm in Detroit, Michigan, several years before the Motor City discovered fins.

Raised in a working-class, blue-collar neighborhood, he morphed into the stereotypical hoodlum a teenager, growing up on the west side of Detroit, was expected to be. Dropping out of high school at sixteen, he hit the road in his 1960 Chevy and has, in one way or another, been rolling down that road ever since.

He has published numerous short stories in various on-line magazines. He is also the author of a non-fiction work, *The Great Golden Gate Bridge Trivia Book* published by Chronicle Books in 1987.

He and his friend are temporarily nestled in the armpit of Florida, in the flood zone of the Suwannee River, hunkered down with his six cats and the inevitable strays that seem to gather wherever he settles.

He is currently working on his next novel and dreaming of the day he can get back to his beloved San Francisco.

Titles from Rebel e Publishers
http://www.rebelepublishers.com/

Shadows
by Joan De La Haye

Sarah is forced to the edge of sanity by the ghosts of her family's past. Suffering from violent and bloody hallucinations, she seeks the help of psychiatrist and friend, Michael Brink.

After being sent to an institution in a catatonic state covered in blood – from stabbing her unfaithful boyfriend – Sarah is forced to confront the truth about her father's death and the demon, Jack, who caused her father's suicide and who is now the reason for her horrific hallucinations. Unlike her father, Sarah refuses to kill herself. She bargains for her life and succeeds.

In Sarah's struggle to regain her life and her sanity, she discovers there is more to the world than she could ever have imagined, and it leaves her seeking the answer to the nagging question, "Who is really mad?"

'Author Joan De La Haye has crafted a darkly entertaining book with SHADOWS and I can't wait to see what she has in store for readers with her next book!' *Fatally Yours*

'This is a book that refuses to be put down … It was an intriguing book. Readers will find this a non-stop read.' *Horrorbound*

'This supernatural story is cleverly written and filled with many freakish twists … never even imagined. The author gives tidbits along the way … but lets the complete mystery go on until the very end. Her writing reminded me a bit of Steven King's – it keeps you gripped to the story and wanting more, while never revealing all of the details until they are ready for the reader to know.' *Pretty Scary*

Killerbyte
By Cat Connor

A killer with a gift for inventive and macabre deaths..... An FBI Agent with an equally unusual imagination and sense of humor....

With a new and exciting voice, **Cat Connor** introduces Ellie Conway, an FBI Agent who challenges the rules with her attitude, sense of the ridiculous and how she tackles a serial murderer with a difference: a murderer connected with Ellie's internet poetry chat room.

With a litter of bodies 'presented' in unexpected places, *Killerbyte* is a provocatively bizarre and entertaining dance. Ellie, with the aid of Mac Connelly, must track down a seemingly motiveless and ghost-like murderer, who defies detection. After her own mother is dispatched by this slaughterer, Ellie fears for the lives of everyone close: her lover Mac, her father, her boss Special Agent Caine Grafton, and chat room colleagues. Reluctantly she begins to suspect her boss, colleagues and, her brother Aidan.

A chance remark provides a connection between past hurts and present pain.

'In all, I found Killerbyte to be an excellent read. The tension created by the suspense is so heavy as to be almost tangible, the action is both exciting and gruesome, and the mystery is extremely well-executed. Add to this Ms. Connor's polished and enjoying writing style, and you have a book that is almost guaranteed to please.' *The Book Wenches*

'I highly recommend this book and am going to read anything else this author has written immediately. Buy this book! You WON'T be disappointed.' *Ebook Guru*

'Don't start this late at night, you will need to finish it once you start, no way you can sleep without knowing who dunnit.' *UnBound*

Terrorbyte
By Cat Connor

Ellie Conway is back: wisecracking, kicking ass and using her psycho-prophetic talents to grapple with a murderer with ulterior motives, secreted behind a series of grotesque crimes.

Now a Supervising Special Agent, Ellie is confronted with outlandish connections which include chlorine, bourbon, gold ribbons and missing children. She and her team race to find the link between these murders, the Pentagon, the Military, Eastern European terrorists and yet again, her poetry.

The most horrifying connection is that of The Butterfly Foundation, formed by Ellie and her husband Mac, to offer support and sanctuary to the children of mentally ill parents.

When Agent Sam Jackson is stabbed at a crime scene, a Russian FSB Agent, Mischa Praskovya, joins her team, much to her chagrin. His actions lead Ellie to believe that he knows more than he is prepared to admit about the perpetrators of the murders.

The case puts Ellie's life in jeopardy. It causes her to question whether she can protect those affiliated with the Foundation. The realization that the issue is global forces her to seek help from the highest level to close borders, airports, train stations, military bases, in an attempt to bring to justice those responsible.

The denouement leaves Ellie facing a shocking truth and a grievous loss.

'I love these books, they are the perfect literary answer to NCIS, Bones, Criminal Minds and so on.'
Un:Bound

'Terrorbyte drew me in immediately and kept me intrigued and fully involved throughout the entire novel. It made me think, alternately amused and saddened me, and impressed me with its intelligent and well-crafted narrative.' *BookWenches*

Land That I Love
by William Freedman

When two rival presidents in the distant future, foes since their youth, declare a galactic hyper-power war, a series of events ensue which transforms America's place in the world … and beyond!

With devilish delight William Freedman upends icons, sacred cows, role models and expectations with laugh-out-loud irreverence.

His characters defy tradition and stereotyping, revealing the mayhem and high jinks which – without doubt – exist within the hallowed halls of existing rival countries, let alone imaginary future nations and governments.

Outrageous slap-and-tickle combined with political prods and withering insight make Land that I Love a compelling lampoon. Add 'Blazing Saddles meets War of the Worlds' and you begin to appreciate the riotous read in store.

Move over Tom Sharpe, Christopher Brookmyre, Aldous Huxley, George Orwell, David Sedaris, Eoin Colfer, Ambrose Gwinett Bierce …

'Values roasting on an open fire… In a mad romp through the long corridors of extrapolation fiction, Freedman maps a universe where commercial interests have taken unabashed control. An unbroken line of folly and unrestrained force have fractured America and made the remnants a steamroller with a leader and his enemies no longer trying to sort who did what in their quest for opportunities to attack. A biting and chewing satire that shreds the eye of the needle. Frighteningly funny, terribly believable, and entirely readable.' *Ben Parris*, author of *Wade of Aquitaine* (Blueberry Lane Books).

'Irreverently over-the-top in places and chillingly right-on-the-mark in others but always funny, Land That I Love will make you laugh and cry from the beginning to the end. Especially the end.' *Leonid Korogodski*, author of the upcoming sci-fi novel '*Pink Noise*'.

'A hip, clever, and extremely funny SF satire on the entire first decade of the 21st century. With its purgative guffaws, LAND THAT I LOVE serves as a kind of necessary medicine for those of us who are still feeling ill from the outrageous cultural and geopolitical idiocies of the aughts'. *Matt Cardin*, author of *Dark Awakenings*.

The Gates of Hell
by Caroline Addenbrooke

From the courts of southern Europe, to the legendary lost civilization of Afar on the west coast of Africa, a cast of characters as diverse and fascinating as the two continents, embark on a dazzling and fearsome journey.

Catalina, to reveal the truth of her ancestry, find her brother, and return the Caliph to Portugal; her husband, Rui, to break with the past and seek the gold of Afar; Mbemba, unlawful King of the Kongo, and friend to Rui, driven to murder his father and siblings to claim the throne, and pursue his ambition to change the future of Africa; Dela Eden, gifted with the Sight, and a destiny determined by her calling and her grandmother, Ramla.

All are drawn into wars and terrors in pursuit of their dreams. All learn the power of retributive justice. All experience their individual Gates of Hell.

Caroline Addenbrooke writes in the tradition of 'For Whom the Bell Tolls', 'Gone with the Wind' and 'The Winds of War' with this richly-textured and multi-faceted tale of misdirected ambition, greed, needless war and ultimate resolution.

'At first glance, this book looks to be an historical adventure full of strange and exotic places with danger lurking in every page. However, once the reader begins their journey, they will start to see incredible details into a lost world. This story has elements of intrigue into old world politics and social standards with a dash of romance. I very much enjoyed this story and feel that

I will continue to find some new detail with additional readings.' *Ebook Guru*